A REFUGED BANNED

MICHAEL ALLEN GEORGE

MARUGE
PUBLISHING

A REFUGE BANNED

MICHAEL ALLEN GEORGE

**This book is for my parents
William and Laverne George**

They never missed a chance to sit
down and read a good book.
They also had the good sense to
never over censor their children.
Because of that and the availability
of books in their home,
they made avid readers of all their children.
They would hate the book banners
of today!

PROLOGUE

Seventy-five men of swat team Fahrenheit-now, dressed in all the gear required when faced with serious danger, were lined up to listen to the governor's pep talk before they mounted their various vehicles. It was, they were told, one of the single most important battles against serious crime they'd ever fought.

The governor's speech further reaffirmed that very message. The people they were going up against had committed crimes against God, nature, and the government.

The men were also told that of all the people they were about to do battle with, it was absolutely essential that none, not one of them, should be allowed to go free. No matter the circumstances or how many of them there were. Enough buses would be provided to haul each and every one of them to the county lockup.

There was a lot of room there now. The governor, a one Rod Dasadist, had insisted that most of the prisoners already locked up be set free. He wanted plenty of room for the major criminals who were about to be captured and locked up. So he wasn't concerned about the crimes of those people he set free. They were nothing compared to the crimes of those about to be arrested. They were, from governor Dasadist's point of view, among the worst kind of people anywhere. They were readers. They read books.

Once the swat members were all mounted, the team set out on their mission. Around half of the team members were calm about what they would be facing. The other half were understandably nervous. They were new to the team and had no real idea what they would be facing. This type of mixture of veterans and rookies was typical on these missions. Few new members ever made any more than one raid. Most quit the swat team shortly after the first raid they participated in. They simply weren't conservative enough to repeat what they'd been part of.

This was to be far and away the biggest raid they'd ever made. Most people in Wisconsin were now obeying the law, but this bunch just didn't seem to want to learn. So the governor had decided that they had to be raided, arrested, and jailed. Trials and prison terms would take some time though. He didn't as yet have enough judges under his control to ensure convictions on everyone, no matter who they were.

As soon as they arrived at their destination, they surrounded the campus, then stationed at least one man at each door on every building. They then pulled their bullet proof plastic masks down over their faces for safety. Each team going into one of the buildings had a man with a teargas gun along to help control the dangerous people inside, if the swat guys needed help.

The largest building was a series of classrooms. Inside were students in the tenth through the twelve grade. The first classroom the swat team forced their way into was a tenth grade english class. The team leader was delighted when he saw the book they were all reading. It was To Kill A Mockingbird. A book especially hated by the governor and all his close associates. None of the swat team would have been able to understand what a great American novel it was. As they were with almost everything they ever read, they didn't understand the novel. All they knew was that it was about some white guy trying to help some black guy. Something they all knew was a very bad thing to do. Governor Dasadist hated anyone with skin a different color than his white stuff.

The men of the swat team screamed to the treacherous students to stand and raise their hands over their heads. Because of the mortal danger they were in, two of the swat men handed their automatic AR15's to the man next to them. They then began to search the students for weapons. The search of the boys was minimal. With the girls it was a different story. A very thorough search was required. Extra care was taken when they got to the areas the swat guys were sure would be the hiding places. Around the girl's breasts, inside their bras, and between their legs. Never mind that they'd never found even one weapon on any student in all the raids they'd made in the past. The girls who resisted the searches were forced to remove their bras and panties, which were not returned. All of the girls were terrorized by the swat guys. To them, wearing all the gear they did, along with the helmets hiding their faces, made them look to the girls like something from outer space. When one of the girls would break down and cry, the swat guy's hid their laughter behind the mask their helmets provided.

The raid continued from classroom to classroom. The teachers were held away from the students. The males among them were often beaten. No reason was ever given for the beatings. They were just handed out. The causes of them could be for something as serious as questioning the right of the swat team to be there, to having the wrong look on their faces. Either way, there was little the victims could do about it.

It was different for the women. Any of them who showed much age were forced to strip and perform oral sex on any of the swat team who wanted it. All the rest were methodically raped. The younger, prettier girls were often left on the floor, bleeding and wondering if death wouldn't have been preferable to what they'd been forced to suffer through.

The children six and under were loaded onto a separate bus and taken to a special facility set aside just for them. It was a small building with one room. They were each given a light blanket, a plastic plate, a spoon, and a glass. They were told to hang on to them, because if they were lost, they would not be replaced.

Two of the girls who were especially attractive were taken aside by a dozen of the swat men and repeatedly raped. Sure that the rapes would continue, they tried to escape. They only got as far as edge of the campus. They were shot in the back several times each.

As soon as all the dangerous prisoners were loaded onto the provided buses, the torching began. Gasoline was poured on the floors of each of the buildings and on the wood siding outside. All the buildings were lit at the same time, so the flames rose high enough to be seen for miles. No fire departments were called to put out the blaze.

A brother and sister were in the basement of one of the burning buildings. He was six and she was five. He had taken her into the basement when the raid started. He was sure that they'd be safe down there. Their hiding place was safe from the marauding swat team, but not from the flames. They burned to death.

When the local fire department was called by a passing motorist, there wasn't much fire left to put out. They found the burned children. It was also obvious to them that all the fires were intentionally started. They filled out and filed all the necessary paper work, but only a few of them called anyone in the media. It was enough though, to start its own kind of firestorm.

The governor got involved as soon as the first report of the fire was on TV. He called a news conference, and reported that his own state swat team had raided a huge meth operation. It also said the the fires were caused by the meth labs exploding during the raid.

The complex of buildings, he said, were previous believed to be a private school. His team of crime hunters, he claimed, had through meticulous research and detective work, proven otherwise. For the most part, the media bought into that claim.

It only took two days for the story to pretty much disappear from the news cycle. There were only four kids killed in the whole escapade, so it was no big deal.

That left the governor extremely pleased with the raid. It managed to get rid of a fairly large group of people reading books that he knew no one should ever be allowed to read. The fires had also destroyed a large library. A place among those most hated by the governor. They were all full books filled with lies about minorities and sexual deviants. The worst books of all though, were books that said something negative about religion.

One of the more recent of those devil's handbooks was called Jasper's Story. It was a relatively small book, but it had several negative passages about God. It was banned now, but was still being produced. It was also selling somewhat better since it was banned. The governor knew that it was time to get after the publisher of the book. If they weren't willing to stop publishing the book, he would have to find a way to shut them down. He couldn't allow a book like that to continue to exist. All too often it was something like that book, however small it might be, that screwed up the plans of someone otherwise destined for power.

Power was exactly what Dasadist wanted. He was going to win in the primaries, and then the election itself. He was going to be president. And once he was there, he fully intended to stay there for the rest of his life.

CHAPTER 1

Shanty Lucas didn't know why she bought the book. It wasn't something she'd normally read. She did it secretly because she was somewhat embarrassed about it, but she usually loved a good romance novel. When you're the CEO of a multi-billion dollar corporation, reading romance novels would tend to make a person appear to be too feminine, and therefore vulnerable.

When she finished reading the book, titled Jasper's Story, she was disappointed that she finished it so quickly. From the first few pages, she felt as though some of the characters in it were old friends of hers, even though others were the kind of people she had learned to dislike and avoid. All the way through, the good people seemed very much like some people she knew. She wasn't sure she could call them good friends, but they were friends of a sort. Thinking of them, she decided to give them a call and see how they were doing. Mack Thomas answered his cell phone almost immediately.

"Hello, Shanty," he said when he answered. "What is it that's giving me the pleasure of talking to you today?"

Shanty laughed. It felt especially good to hear Mack say nice things to her. Like a lot of women, she had a not so secret crush on him. She loved the way, when she talked to him, that he made her feel that she was important in his life. Not because of the billions she was worth, but instead it was only because of who she was. Given her place in life, it was a rare feeling.

"I called because I was thinking about you. About all of you. I know this might sound a little strange, but I just finished a really good book about an old man, his life, and how he was forgotten in his old age. Anyway, some of the people in it reminded me of most of all you guys."

"I guess that could happen. What was the name of the book?"

"Jasper's Story. Have you read it?"

"I think you could say that. Actually, all of us here at Refuge Rescuers have read it."

"You're kidding. All of you? Did everyone like it?"

"I would have to say that they were, in the end, satisfied with it."

"Talk about strange. That's a strange way to describe what you think about book you've read."

"If you promise not to tell anyone, Shanty, I'll tell you a secret about the book?"

"If you ask not to say something, no matter what it is, I won't say anything. Not ever. But what could you know about a book like that, that I shouldn't talk about?"

"We wrote it."

"You what?"

"We wrote that book. I did most of the rough draft, but then everyone here at Refuge Rescuers contributed something. Especially Dad's wife, Theresa. She was a teacher at one time, and she had the most influence on the writing itself. As you know from the book, we only had contact with Jasper for a few hours, but he made a big impression on us."

Shanty laughed again. "You guys wrote that book? I have to tell you, Mack, I loved it. It was awful sad in some ways, but it was an inspiration too. And I loved the part where you criticized God for breaking up Jasper and his true love Matti."

"The truth is, we had to write about that. But writing about those things has gotten the book banned. Which is not all bad. The sales of it have picked up since it was."

"I didn't know that." She sighed. The sound that went with it made it obvious that she didn't approve of banning books. "It's going to continue to be published though, isn't it?"

"So far as I know." It was Mack's turn to sigh. "But there's been a lot of talk among the republicans about shutting down the publishers who continue to produce banned books."

"Those assholes," Shanty complained. "What the hell do they think they're proving, banning books?"

"They're trying everything they can to control people's minds. If most people knew the truth about what's going on, they'd never vote republican again. The problem is, they don't know. Or if they do, they are the morons who just don't care."

"You are damn sure right about that, Mack. Between religion, which is nothing but simple minded mythology, schools controlled by religious school boards, those conservative, so called news networks, full of paid liars like Fox News has so many of, and dozens of other distractions, it's no wonder so many people are so ignorant."

"Yeah. Sometimes it seems as though people are willing to believe damn near anything. Like the school that Dasadist had his team of goons attacked and burned. It was no meth lab. It was just a private school trying hard to teach kids real subjects, rather than the pure bullshit that's all too often being rammed down their throats."

"Yeah, that scumbag Dasadist has been getting away with a lot. It's too bad he even seems to have control over nearly all of law enforcement in that state of his. What they did to that school really should be investigated."

"I agree, Shanty. But there's not a hell of a lot we can do about what goes on in Wisconsin."

"It's too bad the FBI hasn't gotten involved. You'd think someone, somewhere, would be curious enough to get involved."

"Well, we're just putting the finishing touches on a book that's a sequel to Jasper's Storie. Maybe we could look into what happened at that school when it's ready to go to the publishers."

"What the hell, Mack. What was I thinking. Damn right you guys can look into it. I'm going to hire you to do it. And that way, it doesn't matter what resources you use, or what the costs are."

"Are you sure you want to get involved with something like that? You know what those bastards behind the school burning are like. It could actually get dangerous."

It was a day for Shanty to laugh, because she did it again. "I know all about that crap, Mack. But my home is a virtual fortress, the car that takes me to work, when I go, is bullet proof, and my bodyguards are well trained. Most important of all, other than kill me, there's not a damn thing anyone can do to me that hasn't already been done."

"I think we have a deal then. I'd like to find out what really happened to that school. But before we go any further with this, we do need to talk about the money part. How far do you want to go? What we do or don't make on this investigation isn't important, but the expenses could run up fairly high."

"Mack, given the amount of money I have, your expenses and the wages of everyone who works for and with you, will have no effect on me at all. So you can stop all your thoughts, worries, and ideas on that level. I flat out don't give even one little damn about it."

"It looks like we're good to go then. It'll be a few days before we get started, but I'll give you a call when we do."

"Good. Have your tech person, Sue, get with my tech person, so we can set up some kind of dedicated communication system between you and I. I want us to be able to contact each other no matter what else is going on."

"I will do that, Shanty. Is there anything else you want me to do before we get started on this?"

"Nothing right now. But all through this, Mack, I want you and everyone who works with you to be careful. I want that to be the priority. I don't think I'd like myself much if any of you guys were hurt while you were working for me. Finding the truth of what happened at that school is important, but not near as important as all of you guys staying safe."

"I'll make that my first and strongest instruction when we plan our investigation."

"Good. Now keep me informed on how it's going. I'll talk to you later."

Mack knew when he hung up the phone, that the conversation the next morning at the breakfast his father and his father's wife cooked every day, would be very interesting. He also knew that given the quality of every member of Refuge Rescuers, he would have a lot of volunteers for this investigation. The amount of danger involved wouldn't matter to any of them. Their only concern would be whether or not they could be part of it.

CHAPTER 2

Mack and his wife Lisa, talked a lot all through the evening about all the book banning, the attack on the school in Wisconsin, and the fact that they were hired by their billionaire friend Shanty Lucas. It lasted until they went to bed, so when they woke up they were anxious to talk to everyone gathered for breakfast in the morning.

Mack's Father, Ben, along with his wife Theresa, cooked the meal for everyone who was part of Refuge Rescuers every morning. It was their normal habit to be among the last to arrive for the meal, but this morning they were the second couple there. Mack's uncle Roy and his wife Wanda, were always the first. Because they were so early Roy didn't make his usual dry humor type comment about their perpetual newlywed behavior. A behavior that, considering how long they'd been married, was a bit of a surprise to everyone. Along with the surprise, it created some admiration and even some jealousy.

Mack and Lisa barely noticed how quiet Roy was. They were too anxious for everyone else to arrive for the breakfast, so they could talk about their next investigation, to pay attention to anything else.

As soon as everyone was there and settled in, Mack brought it up. He barely finished describing the basics of it before they all started talking about it. Larry Jameson, the most recently hired detective, asked the first question.

"Why did Shanty Lucas hire us for an investigation as large and difficult as this one is going to be? She could have afforded a lot bigger agency than what we are. Does she figure that we'll do the job cheaper or something."

Mack answered the question. "It damn sure wasn't because she was trying to save money. The expenses we are allowed are open ended. The why of us getting hired is because she trusts us. When she called me, it wasn't about anything to do with any kind of investigation." He explained the conversation he had with Shanty that started with talking about the book, Jasper's Story and how they ended up with her hiring

Refuge Rescuers to investigate the wide spread book banning and the domestic terrorism that was going along with it. In particular, the terrorism perpetrated on the private school in Wisconsin.

Lisa was the one who asked Larry the necessary question then. "Do you think, Larry, that it's a bad idea to take on this investigation? You sounded as if you don't trust Shanty."

"I'm not sure that I trust anyone with her kind of money. The rich tend to be way different from us ordinary folks. They pretty much always have an ulterior motive for everything they do."

"For the most part," Mack said, "I agree with you. The thing is, Shanty is different. The biggest difference is the simple truth about her and money. She truly doesn't much give a damn about it. As far as her hiring us, the investigation never occurred to her until I mentioned us looking into that school incident as soon as the next book is done."

Roy was the next to comment. "I think Mack is right about Shanty. That trust fund she setup, that we can use when we work for people who can't afford us, has sure come in handy. And what was done at that school does need investigating, Every bit as much as the book banning. I'm a reader, the same as the rest of you here, and it surely does piss me off when some useless, jackass republican politician tries to tell me what I can or cannot read."

The comments following Roy's were all positive about the investigation, and the only concern any of them had was what role they were going to be able to play in it.

Sue Sartor, who was the agency's number one technical person as well as Larry's live in partner, asked the most relevant question. "Where do you want me to start my research? The school. Or the book banning?"

"Start with the school," Mack told her. "If we can prove that governor is guilty of a serious crime, it not only will help get him voted out of office, it might help us get after more than a few of the book banners."

"I know," Ben, who was Mack's father, said, "That I'm not an official part of Refuge Rescuers. But it does seem to me that this investigation is as important as anything the agency has ever done. Banning books is one of the first things the despots of the world do. If it gets carried far enough, along with most of the rest of what the Republicans do, freedom is going to be a dead issue."

That was the last comment about whether they should or shouldn't take the case. Everyone was in favor of it. All of the discussion that followed was about the investigation itself.

Mack knew, without a doubt, that Sue would initially carry the heaviest burden. Being the technical expert, she would be spending many hours online, researching the book banning itself, the violent attack on the school, and as many people as they could identify who were involved in any of the corruption they were looking into. Mack especially wanted Sue to learn everything she possibly could about governor Rod Dasadist.

It didn't matter, as far as Mack was concerned, how many people involved were caught and convicted. If they didn't get Dasadist, the entire investigation would be less than successful. To give Sue more time to research him, he put Julie, who was Lisa's sister and in training to be a detective as well as Sue's assistant, to work full time with Sue. She was expert enough now to be a big asset to Sue.

She knew when Mack gave her the assignment that he was right in doing it. At the same time, she was somewhat disappointed. She, like nearly everyone connected to Refuge Rescuers, was hoping to work in the field on this case. The one exception was their receptionist, Donna. She started as a client. She'd been repeatedly raped by her husband and his friends, and after Rescuers managed to solve her problem she was on her own. When the job of receptionist opened up, she took it. That was as far as she had any desire to go. She was more than happy to leave any and all detective work to someone else.

The other assignments were postponed until Sue completed the initial research on the school attack. It didn't take Sue long to find a long list of names of the people who were inside the school buildings when they were attacked. It was long enough, so they decided for each of them should work alone at the start, so they could interview as many of those people as was possible.

That procedure delighted Larry. Since he was as new as he was, and still in training, this would be the first chance to work alone on a case as important as this one. For Mack, Lisa, Roy, and his wife, Wanda, this part of the investigation would be relatively routine. For them, they knew that the danger and difficulties would begin when they started going after the swat team members and the book banners themselves. Dasadist in particular.

They already knew enough about him to know that he was always surrounded by several thugs, acting as body guards. The only time he was away from them is when he was in bed with his mistress, representative Margie Baylor Blue.

She was his mistress, but was often shared with another book banning coconspirator, senator Ted Crustiest. There were at least another hundred republican representatives who were, to one degree or another, involved in book banning. About twenty-five republican senators were involved with it. But given the latest news, the first three politicians they talked about were the most likely people behind the violence perpetrated on the students and teachers at the school.

As Sue found the names and other information on the victims, Mack handed them out. Roy got the first list, followed by Wanda, then Lisa, and finally, Larry. Mack took the list after that. From then on, each detective would get a new list as soon as they finished one.

All the interviews of the people from the school would be recorded, but each one would be written down too. The written copies were then put together in an organized method. Donna and Julie did it in between their other assignments, which meant there were always a lot of interviews which were not yet organized.

At the end of the first day interviewing, everyone from Refuge Rescuers was feeling the weight that the knowledge of a terrible evil will do to a person. They had a short meeting to discuss what they'd learned from talking to the victims of the school raid. The consensus among them was, the so-called swat team was not a trained part of a police department. It was far more like Hitlers SS troops during WWII. Evil men who enjoyed inflicting pain on as many people as they possibly could.

Of the people willing to be interviewed, there were few who didn't talk about how bad all the females were treated, regardless of age. Most of the women from ages as young as fourteen to as old as seventy-five, claimed to have been raped.

The problem the Rescuers had, was the fact that so many of the people who were in the school were afraid of talking to anyone. The few who'd gone to the local police to report the fact that they'd been raped, were turned away. Governor Dasadist had warned all of the local police in Wisconsin that doing anything with anyone from the school would make them co-defendants at the drug trials.

Even with all that, a large percentage of the people interviewed, including some of those who were raped, thought Dasadist was a good governor. It was the Trump syndrome all over again. People who considered themselves conservative and listened to Fox News and their various so-called reporters tell lies, just didn't seem to be able to learn, or want to know anything worth knowing.

So it was with a lot less enthusiasm that the Refuge Rescuer's detectives went out to do their interviews. Lisa was the first of them to run into trouble. She was hoping to interview a tenth grade student. A man answered the door when Lisa knocked.

She explained who she was and showed him her ID. He gave her a friendly smile and invited her inside the house. She got as far as the middle of the living room when the man grabbed her from behind and wrapped his arm around her neck in a choke hold.

"Okay, Lady," he said to her, "the kid ain't here." Another man walked into the room. "So since you decided to come around here sticking your nose into things and places where it don't belong, you are going to have to pay the price for doing it. That price is my brother and me having some fun with you."

Lisa, who was a trained fighter with skills neither of the two man could have ever imagined, knew they wouldn't listen to anything she said. She told them anyway, just to be fair, "You don't want to push this any further," she explained. "Because if you do, I will be forced to retaliate. If I do, I have to tell you, I don't always know when to stop. I think that today is one of those days. So if you don't let go of me right now, I hope your hospitalization insurance is in good standing. A few weeks in the hospital for two men can get expensive."

As she expected they would, they had a hardy laugh at her words. She let them get to the peak of it, then went into action. Having practiced the move a few hundreds of times, she reached behind her and jammed her fingers into his eyes. He screamed in pain and reached for his now blinded eyes, she slammed the palm of her hand into his nose, breaking it and sending torrents of blood running down his face.

With him rendered harmless, she turned to the brother. "Are you ready?" she asked.

"For what? What are you talking about?"

"Your brother, standing there bleeding and trying so hard to see, said you two were going to have some fun with me. Are you ready for your fun?"

"I don't want nothing from you, Lady. So back the hell off of me."

"But you got a big laugh when I told you two to not try anything with me. Now I think you should try to do what you thought you could do to me. That way, when I kick your ass, it will be more legitimate."

"I told you, I don't want anything to do with you."

All the time they'd been talking, the man was backing toward the door. Lisa knew what he was doing, but let him do it. She didn't have any real desire to hurt him. Having scared him so much that he wet his pants was enough punishment for him. As soon as he reached the door, he opened it and ran. Lisa took a hard look at the man she'd injured. His eyes were beginning to clear and his nose bleed had also let up, so she left the house. She knew she wasn't in any trouble. Not even in Wisconsin. Big macho men like the one she'd injured couldn't call the police and complain. If either man did, they'd have to admit they were beaten by a woman less than half their size.

Mack was the next one to get into trouble. It wasn't until his third interview of the day that it started for him. He was hoping to talk to one of the teachers. The man was in his late thirties and taught history. One of the subjects most hated by the book banners. A woman answered the door when he rang the bell. He guessed her age to be in the late thirties, but she still looked as good as she would have in her twenties. Mack showed her his ID and explained why he was there.

"Well, come on in then. My husband has been ill ever since the school was raided, so I don't know if he'll be able to talk to you or not. Can I get you anything to drink while you wait for me to try to get him out of bed?"

"No, I'm fine."

Mack's wait was close to fifteen minutes. When the woman came back to the living room where Mack was sitting, she apologized for making him wait so long. "My husband won't be talking to you either. He said he just doesn't feel up to talking about it today. What happened at the school scared him something awful. He hasn't, for the most part, been able to talk about it much. But maybe I can help you. He and I have talked about it a little, so I think I can answer some of the questions you might have."

Mack looked at the woman. There was something about her that seemed different from the way she looked when he first got there. It took him a few more minutes to figure out the difference. It was a simple thing. She'd taken her bra off.

While he was looking at her, she was watching him closely. When she was sure he'd noticed what she did, her smile broadened and she said, "I really am sure I can help you out if you let me," she promised him. She moved from the chair she was sitting in to the couch next to him. She rested her hand on his leg, just above the knee. "Now what kind of questions do you have for me?" she asked, sliding her hand a few inches higher on his leg.

At this point Mack knew he was in trouble. He had to get out of this house, but he wanted to do it without upsetting this woman. He also knew that he wouldn't be able to do it by telling her some bullshit line most men might try to hand her. She looked and sounded too intelligent for that. So he decided to tell her the truth.

"I don't want you to take this the wrong way," he explained. "What I'm going to tell you is the truth. I find you incredibly attractive. The trouble is, as much as I'd like to take you up on what I think you're offering, I can't do it. I'm very much in love with my wife, and I've promised her that I would never stray. So I hope my walking away won't upset you in any way. If it weren't for my sense of duty about doing the right thing, I would surely more than love to stay. Like I said, you are a beautiful woman, and I would consider being with you an honor I don't deserve."

Her smile was gone now, and she had a hard time meeting Mack's eyes. "I should have known better," she said, "but it has been a very long time. And not because I haven't had any chances. I've turned them all down. Until you walked into our house I had no intention of cheating on my husband. But he's totally unable to do anything in bed other than cry and sleep. There's something about you Mister Mack Thomas that changed my mind about what I was willing to do, that made me want to do something I didn't think I'd ever do. It's okay though. You can go now. I won't be upset with you. Just remember me if you ever change your mind."

"I will do that," Mack told her. "But I'd better get moving. There's a lot of people I still need to talk to."

She walked Mack to the door. He normally didn't do it with people he'd been talking to, but for her he held out his hand to shake hers. She took his hand, then pulled him close to her and kissed him. It lasted long enough to put wide smiles on both their faces.

Just before he went out the door he said, "Just so you know, you made me wish I could stay."

Tears washed over her smile as she closed the door.

CHAPTER 3

Governor Rod Dasadist was angry, which was nothing unusual for him. Anything that happened that didn't go along with what he wanted pissed him off. Especially things like the reports he'd been receiving from several of his informants, who were being paid for the information they reported to him with Wisconsin tax dollars, had several times mentioned the fact that some obscure private detective agency was snooping into the school raid.

"What the hell do you propose we do about them?" he asked Ted Crustiest and his mistress, Margie Baylor Blue.

"If they were a Wisconsin business," Crustiest claimed, "there are a number of things we could do. A drug raid would be the most obvious thing. Hit them near the end of their day when they're tired. Kill most, if not all, of them. Plant the drugs, then get the local authorities involved. But they're from Minnesota, and you know how those goddamn liberals that live there are. They will get real pissed if we raided and killed a bunch of them. Hell, their goddamn governor hasn't even banned any books."

Blue thought otherwise about them. "I think we should send a team of our guys over there anyway. It won't take much to catch them off guard. It'll be mostly just a simple matter of killing all of them as quick as we can. We damn sure have the fire power. Hell, I'll be more than glad to be part of the killing guys if you want. Nothing could be more fun than shooting a bunch of liberals. They're private detectives, so it won't be like we shot a bunch of cops."

"Given your position in the government," Dasadist said. "I think it'd be best if you stay out of the live action. It's one thing to help plan it. It's something entirely different to take part in that kind of effort. No matter how important to our cause it might be."

"I suppose you're right, but I sure would like the chance to use at least one of those automatic weapons that you've been stockpiling on a live target."

"Again, it's not a good idea right now." Dasadist paused while his eyes rolled up into his head and he dreamed of the life he fully expected to see in the not too distant future. "I can promise you one thing though. When I win the next election and take the oath of office as president, I will fix it so you get a lot of chances to go after your live targets."

"That will be great," she answered, "but in the meantime we have to deal with those detectives sticking their noses into the school raid. I think the first thing we need to do is get most of our guys out hunting. We know who everyone is that was at the school when we raided it, so we should have our guys roam the city where they live. When they spot one of those detectives, our guys should kill them."

"That's a good idea," Crustiest agreed. "But I think it would be a good idea for them to work in pairs, just in case any of them detectives know how to shoot. I think it'll improve the chances of a solid kill when they catch up to any of them."

"I won't argue with that idea," Blue said. "It's a good one."

"I fully agree with the both of you," Dasadist said. "So let's get to work on it. Blue, I'd like it if you would make the copies of the pictures of those detectives, then have someone distribute them to everyone of the swat team members. While you do that, you can instruct them on what to do when they are found. Make sure to tell them that the method of killing doesn't matter. All that matters is the end result. The bastards end up dead."

"What do you want me to do?" Crustiest asked.

"I want you to put together a team of sorts to go to Minnesota and check out the headquarters of that Refuge Rescuers bunch. I think we'll give the swat guys a week or so to take out as many of the detectives here as they can. Then we'll hit them in Minnesota with double the fire power we think we need."

"What are you going to be doing?" Blue wanted to know.

"I'm going to have some meetings with a few billionaires. We need to go beyond just the Wisconsin treasury for the money we'll be needing to finance our war on those private detectives. And I'll be talking to a new one this time. I've invited Shanty Lucas and she's agreed to meet with me. She's one of the wealthiest people on the planet, so I'm expecting a damn good contribution from her."

What he didn't know was what Shanty hoped to gain from their meeting. His expectations were all about getting a large contribution from her. He believed that with luck, he might talk her out of as much as ten million. What he could never have figured out, with or without a calculator, was that ten million to her was small change. His abilities in all levels of math were too limited. Almost as limited as his ability to judge the character of someone in her position.

He was sure she would be all for his policies of banning not only books, but also sex on any level other than for procreation between married people, all religions from Catholicism to atheism, with the exception of evangelical, and all laws against guns and hunting of all kinds. He hated jews the most. More than that, he wanted to rid the United States of all non-white people. Overriding all of his vast hatreds, was his dream of eliminating any and all forms of freedom. People, he was sure, needed to be tightly controlled, and he was the perfect man to do it.

Totally unknown to Dasadist, Shanty was very much the opposite of him. She learned at a very young age, that despots like him were useless, as far as ever doing any kind of good in the world. They were simply pure evil. Her father taught her well on that score. He started raping her at a very young age, and didn't stop until the day he was shot to death. Her now dead husband hadn't been any better. He'd beaten her so bad that even after a dozen plastic surgeries on her face, some of the scars he gave her were still visible.

Given the endless differences between the two of them, it would have seemed natural for her to have turned him down. Instead, she excepted his invitation with enthusiasm. She did, however, insist that they meet in her office at her corporate headquarters where she was the CEO. It was a multi billion dollar company called Life's Protection Corporation. Its main product was high quality guns. When she took over the company, she immediately phased out the manufacture of all assault rifles and cheap hand guns. The facilities that made those guns now manufactured top of the line hand tools.

She wanted the meeting to take place in her office, because she fully intended to record it, both audio and video. She also planned to contribute enough money too Dasadist, to make him believe they could be partners in his efforts to ban nearly everything that made life worthwhile for the average person.

With her in that position, she could stay informed of his plans. She could keep Refuge Rescuers alerted to them too. It would make it much easier for them to interfere with a large portion of Dasadist's plans.

After she told him what she was willing to donate during their first meeting, Dasadist did tell her about many of his plans. He failed, however, to tell her of his planned assassination of the entire staff of Refuge Rescuers. That was something Mack and the rest of the agency would need to learn the hard way.

CHAPTER 4

Mack and Lisa were about ten minutes late arriving at the trailhead. As they frequently did on Saturday mornings, they forgot they weren't newlyweds when they woke up. By the time they remembered what they were supposed to be doing, it was a rush to shower and get ready for the weekly hike in the wildlife refuge.

Mack hiked it from the time he was still a child, but still looked forward to it every chance he managed one. His favorite hikes were with Lisa, or with the wife of his best friend, Sheriff Dale Magee. Kathy was a famous singer and almost as beautiful as Lisa. She had nearly everything a person could want, but her favorite times were when she and Mack alone spent a day in the refuge.

On this Saturday she wasn't going to enjoy it quite as much as her days with only Mack. Four couples were making the hike. Along with Mack and Lisa and Dale and Kathy, were Roy and Wanda and Larry and Sue. One of the traditions when they took hikes in this group was the fact that each of the couples split up and walked with someone else's partner. It was started by Kathy, after Mack showed her a kindness she desperately needed, that went beyond what anyone else was willing to do at the time she needed it. The one constant in the way they did the group hikes was Mack and Kathy. She always took his hand even before the hike started. His was the only hand she ever held on one of their refuge hikes.

On this day, Dale and Wanda walked together. Lisa was paired with Larry, and Roy with Sue. With the exception of Mack and Kathy, it was entirely a friendship thing. Even so, the only two who didn't have some kind of past connection were Lisa and Larry.

Holding hands as they walked occurred more often than not, and it was something Larry was somewhat uncomfortable with. He was by far the newest member of the hiking group, and it seemed a strange thing that it didn't bother any of them to watch someone else hold their partners hand.

The saving grace in the whole thing was the fact that he was beginning to understand. One way or the other, he couldn't miss seeing the strong bonds between all of them. Bonds that carried over and through the entire detective agency.

Along with the show of friendship during the hike, another element of it, which was every bit as strong, was frequent stops along the way. Mack and Kathy were always in the lead, and he was the one who picked those places. He could get their attention and have the bunch of them kneeling down and watching a small lizard, or even an unusual bug of some kind. The stop could also be to watch a fox too far in the distance for any of them but Mack to see, until he pointed it out.

The refuge had burned a few years prior to this hike, and it had been predicted by many conservatives of all types that it would take as long as a hundred years for it to recover. So Mack delighted in mentioning that, and then pointing out the remarkable recovery the refuge was making.

Another remarkable thing was the fact that only Larry questioned it when Kathy kissed Mack every time they stopped, no matter what the reason. It drove him even crazier when Sue would occasionally do the same to Roy, even though her's weren't nearly as ardent as Kathy's. In truth, it wasn't uncommon for any of them to hold hands and share an occasional kiss. For them, it was just a way of saying I'm glad to have you as a friend. Lisa especially enjoyed kissing Larry. He always tried to act shocked by it, but she knew he'd become rather fond of her gesture. Fond enough, so that he'd actually kissed her once. Only on the cheek, but that was a big step for him.

Lisa was about to do it to him again, when what was supposed to be their quiet, relaxing day in the refuge was interrupted by gun shots.

Mack reacted first. "Probably poachers. We'd best check it out."

"I'm coming with you," Lisa said. The tone of her voice wasn't a request. It was a demand.

"I wouldn't expect anything else," Mack answered. "I know all of you want to come along too, but I think you, Larry, and Roy, should stay here with Sue and Kathy. They aren't armed."

"Okay," Roy agreed. "But if you find you need us, fire three shots as fast as you can and we'll come running."

More than anyone, even Dale who was a sheriff, Mack was glad to have Wanda along. If it came to some kind of shooting, she was the best shot.

As soon as they started up the slight rise to the west of them, where the gunshots came from, they heard another round of them. Mack broke into a run, and the rest followed his lead.

He knew they had to be careful as they approached whoever it was dong the shooting. They were firing rifles, and all Mack and those with him were carrying was hand guns, which at a distance didn't stand a chance against rifles.

As they topped the rise, not too far in the distance they saw four people standing over a fallen deer. Three men and a woman. One of the men was holding a skinning knife, but was only standing there staring at the dead animal, as if he wasn't sure what to do with it. The woman, who was obviously a female even from a distance, appeared to be trying to tell the man with the knife what to do next. None of the four noticed Mack's group until they were within about a hundred feet.

Their expressions were universal shock when they saw four guns pointed at them.

"You can carefully lay those rifles and the knife on the ground," Mack told them. "You are all under arrest."

"What the hell for?" The woman, who didn't look much older than eighteen, asked. "We haven't done anything wrong."

"I have to tell you, Young Lady," Dale explained, "that you have broken more than one law. Number one, you're poaching. You've been firing guns in this refuge. Guns aren't allowed here, not to mention firing them. You're off the trail system, so you're trespassing. And I'm sure you're guilty of other violations too."

"Even if we are guilty of all that stuff," she asked, "who the hell are you to do anything about it?"

Dale took out his badge. "I'm the sheriff of Clayborne County. That's all you need to know."

"I don't think you have any authority in here. This is a private wildlife refuge. I'm pretty sure that whoever owns it has to be the one to do something about what we're doing. If, in fact, it really is against the law."

Dale gave her a big smile and pointed to Mack. "Meet Mack Thomas," he told her. "He's chairman of the board that manages this refuge. He also is one of the major owners of the place. So you are under arrest."

None of the three men had as yet said anything, but they were all casting dirty looks at the woman. "You said you knew what the rules were, Darlene," one of them complained. "It looks like you don't know nothing."

"Well, it's supposed to be okay."

"What ever made you think that poaching was okay?" Mack asked.

"That governor over in Wisconsin said it was okay. He said that when he was giving a speech a couple of days ago. He said hunting rules were unconstitutional, and that hunters should go ahead and hunt whenever they wanted to. Nobody had the right to stop us from doing it."

"Dasadist lied," Mack said. "He should never have said that. He's only the governor of Wisconsin. Not dictator of the United States. He has nothing to do with the gun or hunting laws in Minnesota."

"I still don't think you can arrest us," Darlene complained, while Dale used his cell phone to call for a couple of cars to come and pick up the poachers.

When they all got to the sheriff's office, it turned out that all four of the arrested individuals were eighteen, and still living with their parents. Parents who were all republicans. Parents who were super irate about their precious children being arrested for something as feeble as killing a deer. Animals who should be shot regardless. They did, after all, occasionally eat expensive, imported, ornamental plants in peoples yards. And any damn fool should know that in doing that, it made them pests. Pests that should be shot or in some way be eliminated.

The father of Darlene, who was part of management in a division of the Life's Protection Corporation, spoke up for all of the poacher's parents. "I don't know who you people think you are," he threatened, "but you were purely out of line when you arrested our kids the way you did. I just hope you're smart enough to realize the size of the law suite you will be facing if you don't release all four of them now. And I mean right now."

Mack stepped up for his group. "You can try that bullshit if you want to. We both know it won't work though, don't we. Those kids, if you want to call them that, are old enough to know the law. So they will pay for their crimes."

"But that's not fair," the father whined. "All they did is shoot a deer. One lousy deer. What the hell's the difference? That refuge is full of them. They're nothing more than pests anyway."

This time it was Lisa, whose patience with people like this father was near nonexistent, answered him, "That's just your opinion. The opinion of a moron. If nothing else, that deer cared one hell of a lot about what those kids did. They took a purely innocent life and destroyed it. They did it only for the fun of doing it. They pretty much couldn't have even eaten it. The carcass was so full of bullet holes it was too damaged to eat. That means their murdering that poor deer served absolutely no purpose at all. It was nothing more than malicious cruelty."

"Now you're saying our kids are just cruel?"

"I damn sure am."

"Again, you just aren't being fair." The man continued to keep the whine in his voice. "They're just kids. I don't think they intended, even for one minute, to be cruel."

Rather than elicit any sympathy from Lisa, it only further pissed her off. "Everyone of those brats," she snarled at him, "is over eighteen. If they don't know now how cruel what they did was, all that proves is that you and the rest of you parents, don't have much in the way of parenting skills."

This time her comments got to him, so he decided to try to threaten her. "I want you to know," he said, "that the company I work for, in a high management position, is now negotiating to buy out Lands Magnificent. It we don't, it's entirely possible that their resort here, in your county, will close. You keep it up with what you're doing, and I will strongly recommend to our CEO that the resort be closed even if we do complete the buyout of Lands Magnificent."

Lisa came close to laughing at him. "So you really think Shanty will listen to you when you tell her to shut it down. I certainly hope she does. There's nothing any of us here would like better than to have the damn resort shut down completely. Then it could be bulldozed down and the land could be returned to the wildlife refuge it once was. And still should be."

His face was filled with shock now. He was a resident of Clayborne County, and was sure that the Lands Magnificent Resort was an essential part of the county's economy. His threats to have it shut down were only that. Threats. Now these people holding his daughter and her friends want it gone. Something here just didn't balance with his way of thinking. He knew then, that his usual bullying tactics weren't going to work. Especially since they somehow knew his CEO, Shanty Lucas.

His tone of voice was changed when he asked, "Okay, what do you want me to do now?"

Dale answered him. "Pay all the fines for your kids and take them home. Explain to them that what they hear on Fox News, which should be called Fox Lies, is all lies. And forget about taking their guns with you, as they are as of now confiscated, as is the vehicle they drove, illegally, into the refuge. And make sure to tell them that if they are ever caught poaching or in any way harming anything in that refuge again, it will be jail time."

He didn't argue with Dale at all. Instead, he told the rest of the parents what they had no choice in doing, and they lined up to pay their fines. Only their children cried about losing their guns. And Darlene cried about losing her BMW convertible.

Mack and everyone who was with him in the refuge earlier were all more than happy to see the poachers and their misguided parents leave. But they were sorely disappointed to have lost so much of their day in the refuge with Mack.

To make up for it, Roy convinced his brother Ben, Mack's father, to grill up the steaks he took out of his freezer. All of the rest of the people who were part of Refuge Rescuers, who lived on the four hundred acres owned by Mack and his family, were invited.

As they all settled down to enjoy each other's company for the late afternoon and evening, no one was surprised when Kathy sat down in Mack's lap, and obviously had no intention of moving. Her walking the refuge with Mack day was taken away too soon, so she had every intention of making up for it now.

The best thing about it was the fact that everyone understood why she felt the way she did, and none of them were upset about it. Least of all, Dale or Lisa.

CHAPTER 5

After both Mack and Lisa ran into situations that could have turned into something far more serious than they did, he decided that for the rest of the time interviewing witnesses of the travesty perpetrated on the Wisconsin school by governor Dasadist's goon squad, called the Swat Team Fahrenheit-now, should be done in pairs.

Because there were other cases to be dealt with, and since Larry didn't have a detective partner, Mack put him to work on those. Roy and Wanda partnered up on the school interviewing, as did Mack and Lisa. What he didn't know was that they were being watched closely by several of the governor's men. Men who would have liked nothing better than to have the chance of beating Mack senseless and repeatedly raping Lisa. They had the same attitudes toward Roy and Wanda.

When Dasadist decided that Mack and Lisa, along with Roy and Wanda, had pushed their investigation too far, he sent some of his toughest goon squad members out to put a stop to what they were doing. But rather than do them any immediate physical harm, his intention was to have them brought to him personally. That way he could straighten them out about what they were doing. He was sure that by the strength of his dynamic personality, it would be no problem to intimidate them. He knew he was better and more powerful than even Donald Trump. So how could they not be intimidated.

He had no real idea of who, or what kind of people, that Mack and Lisa were. He also didn't know that they were already aware that the governor had something planned for them. He had hinted about it in a conversation with Shanty, and she, of course, informed them of his plans. She didn't know enough to be sure what he was going to do, but knew enough to carefully watch for anything unusual going on around them. So they were prepared when a large, black SUV with windows tinted black started to follow them.

Lisa called Wanda and gave her their location and destination. That was all Wanda and Roy needed to know to move quickly to be a backup for Mack and Lisa.

Mack knew the town well enough by then to pick a spot to stop and confront whoever it was who was following them, without the chance of any bystanders getting hurt. As soon as they stopped and got out of Mack's pickup, four large, muscle bound men got out of the SUV. All of them were so focused on Mack and Lisa that they didn't even notice Roy and Wanda park and get out of Roy's pickup. Their main thoughts at that moment were about Lisa, and what they wanted to do to her. All they needed was the chance and an excuse they could give the governor for doing it.

One man stepped in front of the other three. He was sure that his build alone would intimidate Mack enough to immediately do what he was told. Lisa was no kind of a problem. She was only a tiny and harmless little woman who couldn't possible do anything other than what she was told to do. He obviously didn't know anything about her.

"You two," the man said, his voice as gruff as he could make it, "will be coming with us now. The governor wants to have a little talk with you. You've poked you noses into business that's none of yours too damn much already." He took Lisa's arm, thinking he could lead her to the SUV and push her inside. She didn't agree with his idea and pulled her arm loose from him.

"If you put your hands on me again," she growled at him, "it will be the last thing you do today."

At the same time, two of the men tried to do the same thing to Mack. He too broke free. As he did, Roy and Wanda moved up close to Mack and Lisa. Mack held up his hands and told the four men, "We have no intention of going anywhere with you assholes. You can tell your pissant governor that if he wants to talk to me, he'll have to make an appointment. He'll also have to agree to meet at some neutral place, in Minnesota, not Wisconsin."

"It's like this," the muscle man who could talk said, "you are going to come with us, whether you want to or not."

"I don't think so," Mack said, his voice calm but firm. "So it would be a real good idea for you to back off and go tell that book banning bastard Dasadist what the only conditions are that I will ever meet with him."

"That's it," the talking man said, "it's time for you and this little lady to come along before we are forced to hurt you." He tried to grab Lisa.

His move on her didn't work at all. Lisa was a true fighter, and wasn't about to give this man any quarter at all. He was more than twice her size and three times her weight. He was a fair amount taller than her, but not quite enough to save him. She went into a sudden spin and as she came around her right leg was high in the air. Her foot, covered by a western style boot, made a perfect landing in his mouth. It was led by her boot's high heel and took out all of his front teeth, leaving nothing but jagged edges. As her right foot touched the ground, her left foot went up and connected hard between his legs. He doubled over and down he went.

Mack was his usual self and didn't attempt anything fancy. He slammed a left hand into his man's gut, then a right hand under his chin knocked him out. Roy did much the same to the man in front of him. Wanda wasn't so kind. She broke her man's nose bad enough to cause a rather copious flow of blood. She then threw several punches into his gut, and ended her destruction of him with a straight on, extremely hard kick between his legs. Instead of falling on his face, he sat down hard, with a completely bewildered look on his face.

Mack grabbed the hair of the talker man and lifted his head. He was obviously beaten, and bleeding profusely from his mangled mouth, but still conscious. "You tell your governor that if he pulls a stunt like this again, it will surely piss off all of us. And tell him what I said about a meeting. Neutral ground in Minnesota. And added to that, you four are the only bodyguards he is allowed to have with him for the meeting." Mack dropped his head.

They left the men where they were. If they needed medical care, Mack figured it was their responsibility to get it, not his. They on the other hand, were afraid to seek it. They knew that Dasadist would be decidedly unhappy with them if they involved anyone who might bring in any kind of higher authority into what went down at the school. The one thing he didn't want was the FBI involved. They still had the power to investigate what he was doing, and he still didn't quite have enough control to stop them. He considered it imperative that all of his activities be kept within the Wisconsin legal system, which he was now close to completely controlling. He also knew it wouldn't be hard to continue to fool so many of the average residents of Wisconsin. It was the damn liberals in other states who would cause him problems.

His reaction when his four men made their limping return to his office was one of utter disbelief. How was it possible that four of his men could be bested so totally by two ordinary men and the two women with them? Could there be more to them then just a cheap little detective agency? If there was, how could his skilled research people have missed the fact?

It never occurred to him that the fact that he didn't like modern technology, and therefore didn't understand it, might have something to do with it. Because of that, the equipment he provided for his online research team was inferior to start with, and now outdated. For many of the team, their training was seriously flawed. It was the kind of thing that never entered the far less than brilliant mind of Rod Dasadist.

His solution to the problem was simple. He walked through the huge office where his research team was located, frequently stopping to slap or pound on one or another of the many dozen antiquated machines. Each time he did, he screamed at the people there, all of them struggling with the fear of losing their jobs. Up to this point, working in this office was a gravy train. They all knew that all of the equipment was inadequate. Just as they knew their research was always inferior and incomplete. But because they also knew Dasadist well enough to be aware of the kind of person he was, they were from the highest to the lowest ranking among them, afraid to tell him what the problem was. That left them in a difficult place. They either needed to find the courage to tell him about the equipment problem, or continue providing him with inadequate research.

Finally, one woman from middle management of the department decided she was tired of living in fear and spoke up. She found that talking to Dasadist was very little different from trying to walk in midair. There simply was no solid substance to him. For him, it was up to the people working for him to get the job done no matter what the circumstances. From his point of view, writing with a manual typewriter wasn't all that different from writing with a word processor. Given that, he would find it impossible to believe there could be a difference between word processors. And they were simple computer applications compared to the multitude of them available to do the work they were having little success in doing.

Instead of getting through to Dasadist about the real problem, the woman accomplished nothing more than getting herself terminated. Her firing was followed by a lecture to the entire staff of researchers, about them not putting full effort into fulfilling their responsibilities. "They simply weren't," he complained, "using their God given intelligence in everything they did. I always did," he claimed, "and that's why I didn't make the kind of mistakes they did." When he left them, he left them wondering as they often did, "How could people as stupid as he was, think they were so smart."

Given the vast numbers of people who were very much like Dasadist, it would seem to be an answer easy to find. Unfortunately, it wasn't. It would take generations of studying the human gene pool to find any answers. Even then, they would be sketchy.

CHAPTER 5

The custom made fifty foot RV that parked near Mack and Lisa's house was a welcome sight to everyone who was part of Refuge Rescuers. It was Friday night, and Shanty Lucas and three of her most trusted bodyguards had come for a visit. She was there for the weekend.

Mack was the first to greet her as she exited the RV. His first reaction to her was shock. The last time he'd seen her, she was still recovering from a severe beating her husband had given her. Her face then was a mass of scar tissue that left her a long way from being pretty.

Years had gone by since then, and Shanty had gone through multiple plastic surgeries. Only a few visible scars remained. Her transformation from not at all pretty to the beautiful woman she was before the beating, was beyond anything Mack had ever thought was possible.

As she approached him to give him a hello hug and kiss, all he could do was say, "Wow!"

She smiled at his reaction, and instead of a kiss on the cheek to go along with her hug, she gave him a genuine kiss on the lips. "Wow to you too," she said when they broke it. "If it wasn't for my high regard for Lisa, I think I'd like to continue that for the entire weekend I'm here."

She then turned away from Mack, and starting with Lisa, she took the time to greet each and every one of them. But none of them got the kiss Mack did. Something that Lisa did take note of. She wasn't upset about it, but she did add Shanty to a long list of females who had, in the past, reacted exactly that way with Mack.

While their reactions to him could, at times, be somewhat disconcerting, it also gave her a sense of pride in the fact that he was always true and loyal to her. At least, that is, within the boundaries she'd set for him.

After Shanty finished greeting everyone, Mack asked her, "Are you hungry now, or would you rather relax for a while before we eat?"

"I wouldn't mind relaxing for a bit first. I'm sure Ben and Theresa are doing the cooking, and I want my stomach ready for the feast when we eat." When she visited them the first time, she had been amazed at the quality and quantity of the food. She was even more amazed when she learned that they'd produced most of it themselves. What she didn't know, was that she was in for an additional treat this time. Larry, who did't eat meat, was roasting vegetables, something he could do like no other.

Initially, Shanty's bodyguards stood back, out of everyone's way. That didn't last. Mack, being who he was, wouldn't allow it. While it was necessary for at least one of them be alert and watching the surroundings at all times, Mack gave each of them a soft drink and insisted that two of them join the group. They gratefully did, and each hour switched the awareness duty.

The entire evening was kept as a social visit, so there was no talk of her true reason for the visit. That was left for the next day, when Lisa and Mack would sit down for a serious discussion with her first. After that, when some decisions had been made and plans laid out, they would go over them with the ones who would be directly involved in them.

For this late afternoon and evening, they did their best to set the cares and worries of the world aside. After they ate their fantastic meal, Kathy brought out her guitar and and started to sing. Her first song was a slow one, and Mack took Shanty out on the portable dance floor they had setup. They held each other rather tight while they danced, and it was obvious to all who watched them that she thoroughly enjoyed holding him the way she did.

Mack stayed with her for the first three songs, then turned her over to Dale. After that, she was out on the dance floor as much as she could have possibly wanted to be. Even each of the three bodyguards managed one dance with her. Something they delighted in doing.

After Kathy took a break, then went back to singing, she motioned to Mack to join her on the stage. It was now a kind of tradition for her, when they were in the audience, to sing a love song to Mack, then to Dale. She always made a point of directing the song to them, and leaving no doubt that she loved the man she was singing to.

After Mack left the stage, Shanty captured him for another dance. "Now that, Mack, was something that wasn't there last time I was here. That was something I never expected to see, given who you and Lisa are. What really surprised me was her reaction. I was watching her part of the time. She didn't seem at all upset by what Kathy was doing. Neither did Dale."

Mack was at a loss as how to answer her. She'd been through so much in her own life, that he was afraid the story behind what Kathy did might upset her. So he hesitated to answer her.

She put a hand on his shoulder. "It's okay, Mack," she said, her calm voice telling him that whatever it was that was going on between the four of them was okay with her.

He sighed then, looked her in the eye, and said, "I will tell you all about it before you leave Sunday. But I'd rather not do it tonight. It's a very long story, and I think Lisa should be there when I tell it."

Shanty chuckled some, then said, "Just so you know, I won't lay any judgements on any of you, no matter what the story is. I suspect that there's going to be as much fun in it as anything else anyway."

"The one thing I have to tell you, Shanty, is that none of us are having what could be called some kind of sordid affair. It did, admittedly, start as somewhat of a tragedy. Then, over the time we've had to resolve the issues we all started with, it has evolved into something very special."

"With you involved, Mack Thomas, how could it be anything else."

Later in the evening, after the music stopped and everyone was gathered into smaller groups talking, Lisa and Kathy approached Shanty. She seemed to be enjoying herself, yet carried the look of someone who was just plain lonely. As they reached her, they each leaned close to her and kissed her on the cheek. They then each took one of her hands and pulled her up on her feet. They led her to Mack, who was talking to Sue and Larry. They positioned Shanty just right, then Kathy said, "Sit."

She did, and for the rest of the evening, instead of Kathy or Lisa sitting on Mack's lap, it was Shanty. She took full advantage of it, and frequently she took the liberty of planting a generous kiss on him. He, of course, did his best to fight her off, but found it difficult to do. Lisa and Kathy stayed close by, and giggled at his feeble protests.

For Shanty, the last part of the evening was a lesson in what real, honest friendship was. So much of her life was nothing more than some kind of horror story that no amount of money could have helped. But here, she could feel as if she were surrounded by real friends. By honest love. And knowing she was really wanted and cared about while she was in the arms of the most decent man she'd ever known. The only thing wrong was the fact that when she left his lap, she couldn't take him with her. With that knowledge, she did her best to enjoy what she had while she had it. She was somewhat surprised though, that what she loved the most about snuggling in Mack's lap was his touch. Just the mere touch of his hand on her back sent shock coursing through her. It was a feeling she'd never gotten from any other person in her life. Especially not any man.

When the night was finally over and everyone was saying goodnight, Shanty felt the first real happiness of true friendship she'd ever known, when all four of them walked her to her RV. And then starting with Lisa, who was followed by Dale and Kathy, with Mack the last one, she was kissed goodnight. Three on the cheek, the last where in counted most.

Sleep came easy to her that night. It lasted until shortly after dawn. As the sleep left her and she remembered where she was, she left her bed with a smile. Anxious to get outside, she quickly did a minimum of her morning rituals, slipped a bathrobe over her nightgown, and left her RV. She said good morning to the guard stationed at the door and walked toward Mack and Lisa's house. She didn't really expect to find anyone up and outside yet, but walked around to the back of the house where the deck was anyway.

"Good morning," Mack told her as soon as she was around the house. "You're certainly up early."

"Good morning to you too, Mack." She unconsciously pulled her robe a little tighter around her. "And yes, I am up earlier than I normally would be. But after the great time I had last night, I slept better than I have for a very long time, so I woke up early. I decided the thing I wanted to do most was to go outside. With the air you have here, breathing is so much better that it is at home."

"I'm glad that you're enjoying it. Can I get you a cup of coffee? I just made a fresh pot."

"I'd love one. Just black would be fine."

Mack brought her a cup. They sat quietly in a couple of chairs for a while, sipping their coffee and watching the meadow in front of them come alive. Shanty saw, and enjoyed watching, most of the critters now doing whatever they normally did each day. But now and then, she was delighted when Mack pointed out a shy fox or even a coyote who blended in with its background well enough to be difficult to see.

She seemed to be enjoying the watching enough to make Mack want to take her out in the meadow so she could get closer to all the life out there, and see even more. He stood and held out his hand for her. "Let's take a short walk," he said, "so you can get an even better feel for what life in our meadow is all about."

"But I'm not dressed yet," she argued.

"That's okay, Shanty. None of the critters out there will care. And I certainly don't."

"I won't either," Lisa said, surprising them as she came out the back door to join them. "So go ahead and let Mack take you out there. There's a lot more to see than you know. It's our private little refuge. He doesn't share it with just anybody."

Mack took her hand and they started walking around the edges where the grass met the trees surrounding it. Butterflies flitted and fluttered around them constantly. Grasshoppers and other insects moved through the grass ahead of them. Twice they stopped to let a bull snake cross the path in front of them. Shanty squeezed his hand when she saw them, but didn't show any other signs of being afraid of them.

She was startled though, when a small herd of five deer, four of them does, bolted away when they got close to them. They were at the farthest distance possible from Lisa and the deck she was on, when Shanty got a rare treat. It started with the rustling of leaves and branches, some distance back in the wooded area. Even Mack wasn't sure what was causing the noise as it grew closer. She nearly fainted when the large brown bear walked out of the trees about twenty feet in front of them. It was a female, who fortunately for Mack and Shanty, didn't have any cubs with her.

This time Mack squeezed Shanty's hand. "Just stay calm," he instructed her, "and don't do anything either fast or loud. I'm not totally positive, but I think she's been here before. If it's her, she seemed to be harmless when we saw her last time."

Shanty was still somewhat scared of the large, possibly dangerous animal. At the same time, she was excited about seeing it. It was her first time ever of being closeup to any kind of large predator animal. She'd never even been to a zoo. The only thing she knew about bears was that they sometimes attacked people when they met them out in wild places. So she naturally wondered if this bear was going to attack them. The one thing that curbed her fear was the fact she was sure Mack would shoot it if it did. What she didn't know was that Mack wasn't armed.

It was a standoff for a while. The bear stood in the path, watching them and occasionally lightly shaking her head. She didn't growl or roar or make any kind of aggressive move. For five full minutes they stared each other down. Then the bear yawned, mostly to show them how important she thought they were. She lifted herself up a few feet, dropped back down, turned, and ever so slowly walked away.

"I'm fairly sure," he explained to Shanty, "that she was the same bear we've seen here before. She acted almost as if she knew us, and didn't consider us to be a problem."

"Well, she managed to scare the hell out of me," Shanty said. "But at the same time, I was sure you would protect me if I needed protecting."

Mack couldn't help himself. He chuckled at he comment. "The only trouble is, Shanty, I'm not armed. I don't always wear my gun out on the deck, this early in the morning."

"But you weren't scared of that bear. Why weren't you?"

"I didn't see any reason to be. For the most part, they don't go around attacking people just for the hell of it. Unlike all too many humans, they know that any kind of confrontation can get them hurt. So they only get aggressive when they are hungry and hunting for food. Even then, they'd prefer not to attack something that could hurt them. Any other times they're aggressive, it's to defend themselves."

"You know, Mack, when you talk about things like that bear, and tell me about the refuge or any part of the world that's still even partly wild, you seem to glow while you're doing it. You should, you know, be working somewhere in some kind of wildlife management position. Why aren't you?"

"To start with, my lack of formal education. I don't have the pieces of paper to prove that I know what I know. Since I've been in a position where I could go back to school and get those pieces of paper, I've been awful busy being a cop of one kind or another. And now, if I ran off and did it, I'd be letting too many people down. I have to include myself in that group too. I'm pretty sure that doing what I'm doing, and staying right here trying to take care of the refuge that's left, I'm doing more to help the environment than I could the other way."

"What would you like to have if you could have it?"

"To get back the refuge that was stolen for the damn Lands Magnificent Resort. But it's too late for that. It is possible though, to push it north. Some people wouldn't like it, but it would be a good thing to do."

"We have a lot of things to do right now, Mack. With the school burnings and book banning, we all are going to have our hands full. But when we get those issues at least partially settled, I think you and I need to sit down and talk about the environmental stuff. Everything from expanding the refuge to doing something about that resort."

"Now that is something I will be more than happy to do."

"Good. But now take me back to my RV. People will be getting up soon, and I am not really dressed for mixed company."

"But you're here with me right now."

"Yes, Mack, I am. But for you, I think I'd make an exception for just about anything."

She kissed him for the first time that day, then took his hand and walked with him back to her RV. Even though there was an armed guard at the door to it, he waited until she closed the door behind her before he turned and walked back to the deck and Lisa.

"I watched you," she said as soon as he got there, "with the bear. It seemed to me that it might have been better for you and Shanty to back away from it, rather than just stand there the way you did."

Mack could tell from her serious expression that she was unhappy with the way he reacted to the bear. "It was the same bear you and I have come in contact with before. So I wasn't worried about what she might do."

"Maybe not, Mack. But next time you think I've pushed something too far, I want you to remember that bear before you open your mouth to me about it."

"Okay, I get the point. But at the same time, seeing that critter up close the way we did, gave Shanty something to remember when she goes back home."

"I'm sure. I'm also sure that's not the only thing she'll remember."

"I can tell by the tone of you voice, Lisa, that you are unhappy about something. What else, besides the bear, did I do wrong?"

"It's not, exactly, like you did something wrong. It's more what you never seem to realize. Everyone around you notices and sees it all the time. It's the way you react to women. I've told you this many times before, but I'm going to tell you again. You are going to have to pay more attention to how they react to you. Women keep falling in love with you, and you keep being oblivious to that fact. If you keep on responding to them the way you do, one of these days you're going to get yourself in some real trouble."

"I'm sorry, Lisa. But you know I don't mean anything about it when they get a little too friendly. All it is too me is a show of friendship. Men shake hands to show friendship. Women kiss. I think it would be awful insulting to them if I always pushed them away when they kissed me."

Lisa sighed heavily, then grinned. This was one discussion she knew she wasn't going to win with Mack. He just wasn't going to admit to her that he was, in truth, a magnet who constantly attracted women. It never seemed to occur to him how strong that magnet was.

Contrary to what Lisa thought, Mack was beginning to understand how right she was. Knowing that, he knew he'd have to start being more careful with the way he dealt with women. Especially when he was alone with them. So he waited until it was time to go for breakfast at Ben's before he met with Shanty again. Lisa was pleased that he did.

CHAPTER 6

Dasadist was not a happy man. Along with his anger, a natural state for him to be in. First, four of his best men were beaten by two men and their wives. He told himself it was highly improbable. No woman could possibly fight the way his men claimed those two did. It was imperative though, to learn as much as possible about them as he could. He sent a different four men to watch the women.

The four tough guys first looked to see if the women were in their homes. Since the research on where they lived was very incomplete, the men were soon confused about which women they were supposed to be watching. The quality of the photos they were expected to go by were of low quality. The men knew where their homes were located, but didn't know which house either one of them actually lived in. They were told that both women were beautiful, but there were several extremely attractive women among the people in the place they were watching. To add to the confusion, one of them looked almost identical to a famous singer, and the other looked similar to Dasadist's latest partner, Shanty Lucas.

When the men reported what they'd learned, Dasadist was extremely upset with them. "How," he asked his lead man, Kerry Mitchel, "could you even begin to think up the fantasy stuff you assholes have just tried to tell me. That singer you claim you saw. That Kathy Magee is one of the most popular singers in the world. She sells so many records, she's probably worth near a billion by now. So there's no way she'd be living around some two-bit, small time private dick-heads who probably barely make enough money to get by. And as for Shanty Lucas having anything to do with any of them, that would never happen. She's almost as rich as God. There's no way she'd ever have anything to do with any of those smalltime twits. So get your shit together, and next time, send me a report that means something."

When the call to Dasadist was done, Kerry Michell was not a happy man. He didn't at all appreciated being chewed out for reporting what he and his men saw. The two women he told Desadist about did look like the singer and the billionaire. What else could he do other than say that's what they looked like. And as far as the two women he was supposed to be checking on, the photos he had of them were not good enough to do it as accurately as they were supposed to do it. That meant the only way he could learn what he was there to learn, was to do some research himself. So he left his three men to watch, and went to town.

The first place he stopped to see what he could learn was Katie's Kafe, located on Main Street, in Kingsburg. He figured that if he treated the waitress extra nice, he might be able to get some information about the people he was checking on. Having the office of a private detective agency out in the country, and in the middle of some decidedly middle class homes, was odd enough to make it something a waitress in a local cafe could know about. When he talked to the waitress, he pretended to be a potential customer for them.

"I was wondering," he said to her, "if you could tell me if you know anything about those private detectives from that agency near here. I've heard they are honest. I need to hire someone to check up on my wife. I think you would know why. Have you ever heard anything about them?"

"Only that they're good people," she answered, limiting her answer to him. She knew Mack, Lisa, and everyone else from Refuge Rescuers, but she wasn't going to tell a stranger that. Not until she talked to Mack first.

"Is there anything else you can tell me about them?" Kerry asked. "So many of those kind of people can be dishonest. That leaves me kind of wondering about hiring anyone. I can't really afford to be ripped off. Especially if I end up divorced, which I probably will if she's doing what I think she's doing." He was sure his story sounded real enough to convince the waitress to talk about them.

She disappointed him though, when all she would give him was the contact information he would need to make an appointment with them. When he left the cafe, she took it a step further and called Mack to tell him about the man. He took that information seriously enough to put everyone on the alert, including Shanty's bodyguards. It was one of them who spotted one of the three men off in the distance, watching everyone as they went about their business.

Knowing that the person who could ultimately end up in the most danger from whatever it was that was going on was Shanty, they were immediately careful to do what they needed to do to be sure she wasn't recognized. That caution paid off when Kerry took the bold step of visiting Refuge Rescuers. Shanty and Mack were meeting in her RV, so Kerry didn't get to see her.

All he got when he told Donna, who was the receptionist at Refuge Rescuers, about wanting to hire them to check up on his wife, was a referral to other agencies.

"Are you trying to tell me that you don't handle cases like mine?" he complained. "From what I know about the world, my kind of case is the bread and butter of an agency like this one. How do you folks think you'll stay in business if you don't take them?"

"Without those kind of problems," she answered. "We not only don't need that kind of work, we are currently so busy working on cases that matter more, that we are having a hard time keeping up with the load."

Kerry totally gave himself away than when he commented to Donna, "Oh, I suppose you people make up the difference overcharging billionaires, like Shanty Lucas. I heard you were doing some work for her."

Donna knew then, that it could lead to disaster for Shanty if this phony customer learned they actually were working for her. So she answered the question with a quizzical look and said, "I don't have any idea who you're talking about. But whoever it is, I can assure you that we definitely do not ever overcharge anyone. The only time there's any difference in what someone is charged, is when we reduce or eliminate the charges."

"Well, if you're so honest, then why won't you take my case?"

"We just don't handle domestic cases like yours. There are a large number of honest agencies who do. I will be glad to provide you with a list of those, if you want one."

Kerry decided to push her some then. "You know, ma'am, if you won't tell me why about my case, maybe you could tell me what the hell it is that you people do? Are you even a detective agency, or is that a cover for something else?"

Donna knew it was time to stop answering any more questions from this man. So she picked up the phone, pushed a special button on it, and within seconds said, "I need you at the reception desk."

A couple of minutes later, Mack stood next to Donna. He stared Kerry, who was on the other side of the desk, and asked, "What can I do for you?"

Kerry knew then, from Mack's tone of voice alone, that he was busted. He'd pushed too hard, and now he needed to try to worm his way out of there without making things worse than they already were for him. When he finally answered Mack it was a feeble one. "I was just trying to find out why this agency won't handle my case."

"What is your case?"

"I need someone to check up on my wife. I think she's cheating."

"The thing is, Donna already told you that we don't handle domestic dispute cases. I also know, without having to ask, that she offered to give you some referrals. Yet you continue to ask questions which are not relevant to your problem. That tells me you are likely here for some other reason. Do you care to explain?"

"There's nothing to explain, other than it seems strange to me that you don't take cases that are usually the main source of income for a detective agency."

"That might be true for others, but it's not us. So if there's nothing else you need from us, it's probably a good time for you to move on. If you actually do need someone to do some surveillance on your wife, try one of the agencies on the list Donna gave you. If you don't, then you can tell whoever it is who hired you to check up on us that we don't appreciate this kind of bullshit. You can also tell Dasadist, who I am quite sure is the one who hired you, that it is our definite goal to hang his ass. One way or the other."

Kerry realized then that his cover story about the wife he didn't have wasn't just blown. It had never worked to start with. He also knew now, that Mack and all the people in this agency were not particularly afraid of Dasadist. That meant only one thing. It was time to get the hell out of there. Without another word, that's exactly what he did.

He also decided on his way out that even though working for Dasadist paid good, it wasn't good enough. He was one of the few people in his line of work to see how much trouble the entire Refuge Rescuers was going to be. The time to move on was now, so that's what he decided to do. He stopped to tell the men with him that he was leaving and why he was. Once they heard his explanation, the other three men agreed with him. They were already leery of the job they were supposed to be doing anyway.

They'd been paid recently, so they didn't bother to try to collect the remainder of their pay. They all simply left the area. Two of them returned to Canada where they were originally from, and Kerry and the other man decided that a visit to Mexico was appropriate. They wanted to be as far away from Dasadist's reach as possible.

It took three days of no contact with the men before Dasadist realized the men had walked off the job. When he did, he couldn't believe it. He was paying them what he considered more than a decent sum of money, and the work they were doing for him was vital. He was bitterly disappointed that anyone would walk out on such a fine christian man like himself, who was doing God's own work.

Mack, on the other hand, found the fact that the men walked out on their jobs to be delightful. He followed Kerry out of the Rescuer's office when he left, and managed to keep tabs on him until all four of the men were gone. Above all else, it meant that Shanty's identity was safe. At least for a while. Even so, one of the major things they decided was that in the future, meetings she would have with Dasadist would be using computers. Meetings in person with him now held too big an element of danger. Their excuse for the change was to save travel time.

Dasadist didn't argue about it. There was no way he wanted to leave Wisconsin to meet with her anyway. At least, not until he started his official run for president of the United States. By then, he was sure, he would be so popular for his great work with books, other media, and schools, that it would be far less dangerous to travel than it currently was.

Upset as he was about his deserters, he was pleased with his progress with Shanty. She was assisting him with the planning of the next school raid, and was continuing with her donations, even if they were slower than what he would have liked. Their meetings via computer were working, as far as he was concerned, just fine. He had no idea that they were being recorded.

That left him with one big concern. What to do with Refuge Rescuers. He knew they were a big problem. They were continuing to snoop into his work, and he was certain that if they gathered enough information, it could hurt him in his presidential run. People simply didn't always understand some of the very good reasons he had for doing God's work the way he often did it. The end result of what he wanted did justify the means he sometimes used to get to that end. He just couldn't expect the average follower of his to be intelligent enough to understand.

That left him with one solution when it came to those trouble makers at that horrible detective agency. Take them one or two at a time. It didn't matter when, who, or how. When it was possible to take any of them out, that's exactly what he was going to have his own people to continue to try doing. From this moment on, the dark of night was going to be the devil's own hell for each and everyone of them.

It was the dark of night that gave him what he considered one of his better ideas. Mack Thomas had demanded that any meeting between them, had to be on neutral ground. He could agree to that, but he could insist that it be at night. That way Mack wouldn't notice until it was too late that he wasn't there. Someone would double for him. And when Mack was close enough to know he'd been tricked, it would be too late. His men would kill him. They'd do the same to his feisty wife too, if she was along. He was sure his plan would work, that he made sure that Mack received his proposal right away.

Sure it was some kind of trap, Mack accepted Dasadist's invitation anyway. He knew it would be a good way to test the book banning governor's ability to pull off something more difficult than attacking innocent people with hordes of goons called a swat team.

Since Dasadist's research on Mack was incomplete, he was never made completely aware of his relationship with the wildlife refuge. That meant he didn't have any problem with using it for their meeting place when Mack requested it. The truth was, as far as he was concerned, Mack had to be such a simple minded creature that he would feel safe in the refuge. If for no other reason than he thought he knew more about it than Dasadist's people.

The advantage Mack had was exactly what Dasadist considered irrelevant. He did know the refuge better than anyone else. He was familiar enough about it to know of an ancient oak tree that had somehow survived the massive fire that burned nearly all of the refuge years before.

It was a stubborn old tree that had appeared to be dying, even years before the fire. When the fire came and its hot flames licked the land around it, and even parts of its trunk, it managed to survive. It now stood as a sentinel, keeping watch on all the surrounding land. It was also the perfect place for a person to keep watch. All that was needed to do so was an easy climb up the massive limbs provided by the tree. A climb so easy that carrying a high-powered rifle with a night scope wouldn't be any kind of a problem. Another plus would be if the person up in the tree was one of those rare people who never missed what they are shooting at. Wanda was one of those people.

The designated meeting place was about a hundred yards from the tree. That was no problem. She could easily hit a target much smaller than a human head from four or five times that distance. The night of the meeting, Mack, Lisa, Wanda, and Roy arrived early. They knew the area well, but wanted to double check all the ambush places the Dasadist people might try to use. Finding them empty, Roy picked a hiding spot with a good view of the meeting spot, and Wanda climbed the tree. Due to the size and age of it, she quickly found a comfortable place to sit and shoot from, if she found that shooting was required.

When the opposition arrived, they came in two large, black SUVs with heavily tinted windows. Two big men got out of the front of the lead vehicle when they stopped.

"We need to scope things out," one of the men said, "before Dasadist gets out of his car to meet with you."

Mack just shrugged and waved his hand, telling them to go ahead and look. Which they did. They never did get close to Wanda's tree, and when they got near Roy's spot, he just temporarily moved farther back into the brush he was hiding in.

When the two men finished their sloppy search, one of them waved his hand at the cars they came in. The fake Dasadist was the second man out of the first car. Six men got out of the second car. They were all heavily armed.

"We'll keep this meeting short," the fake Dasadist said. "What we're here for is to tell you to stop sticking your noses into things that are none of your concern. What we want to do, rather than kill the bunch of you, is to tell you that you and your agency will be a million dollars richer if you're willing to do what we ask."

"To start with," Mack answered, "you aren't Dasadist. So you have already proven to me that none of you can be trusted. Second, right now you have a lot less chance of killing us than you can begin to realize."

"We'll take that as a no," the fake one said. "So we are done here. Take them out."

Mack lifted his hand in a prearranged signal. Before any of the men who were there to commit the murders could do anything, a shot rang out. Wanda pulled off one of her favorite tricks, and took of a large portion of the fake Dasadist's ear. She instantly fired a second shot, and eliminated the gun from the hand of the man next to the fake.

Mack told them then, "You all have ten seconds to drop your weapons."

Of course, they didn't. Wanda rapid fired three more shots. Three more weapons were on the ground. The rest followed without another shot being fired. Mack gave Wanda another signal. Four more shots were fired and the front tires of the two SUVs went flat.

Lisa spoke up while Mack collected the weapons on the ground. "It's like this guys," she said. "We will be watching you until you get your tires fixed and leave our county and our state. If you ever again try to do anything to any of us, it will be payback time. Whatever you do, we payback double or more. If you kill any one of us, we will kill all of you. It might take a few years, but we will hunt you down and kill you. We do have the resources to find you no matter where you go. You can tell Dasadist, that if he comes after us, he will be number one on our list. There's not a one of us who won't enjoy the chance to put a bullet in his head."

One of the men, who was still suffering from the illusion that they'd somehow get the upper hand, laughed. "You're forgetting, Lady, that we outnumber you by the hundreds. You don't stand a chance against us."

"I guess not," she smiled, "but then, you don't understand just how much damage we can do." She gave Wanda another signal.

This shot more than terrified the defiant one who thought that numbers of people on each side was all that mattered. The bullet from Wanda's perfect shot ripped the cloth from his pants, between his legs.

"She didn't miss," Lisa told him. "So if you want to keep on irritating me with your half-assed threats, I can tell her to aim about an inch higher. Scumbags like you should be neutered anyway."

He looked this pants, then at Lisa, and shook his head no, as if to say he wasn't going to make anymore trouble. That wasn't his intent however. He reached behind him and pulled a small pistol from his belt. It did him little good. Wanda eliminated it from his hand, then rapidly clipped the outside of his arm with three more shots. They did no permanent harm, but did leave him in a fair amount of pain and a very bloody arm.

By then, Mack had collected all of the guns on the ground and dumped them in the back of his pickup. He was now searching their cars for more guns. He found a total of eight AR15s in the cars. After unloading them, he threw them into the back of his pickup too.

One of the Dasadist men objected to it. "You know," he complained, "those are some damned expensive rifles you're throwing around. You could damage them, treating them that way."

"It doesn't matter," Mack snapped back at him. "They are all going to be destroyed anyway."

"You can't do that. None of those guns belong to you."

"Don't they now? It looks to me like they do. They damn sure don't belong to any of you any longer."

"We can have you arrested for stealing our guns."

"You can try. But then I'll have you arrested for attempted murder. That will, I'm sure, piss off Dasadist some. Especially when everything that happened here tonight is on TV everywhere. Because we have recorded the whole episode."

That threat quieted down all of the Dasadist men. The last thing that any of them wanted was their face on TV. Mack knew then that it was time to leave the scene and go home. It would be long past daylight before the tires were repaired, and by then he would have gotten a few hours of sleep and would be back in time to watch them go. All the tire repair shops in the area were going to follow Mack's request and refuse them service before morning. Mack knew the wait would be good for the men.

It proved to be more than good for them. Only two of the men involved continued their employment with Dasadist. None of them appreciated being screamed at because their boss couldn't understand their opponent was far superior to what he wanted them to be. All of them left over the next week or so, without telling him they were leaving. They just disappeared. To say he was unhappy about it was an understatement. He was, as usual, extremely angry.

More than that though, he was confused. All of the men he'd sent after those Refuge Rescuers people were beaten by them, then had quit. And on top of that, those Rescue people had turned down a million dollars. That was a hell of a lot of money, especially for doing nothing more than tending to their own business and leaving his alone. It made no kind of sense at all.

He knew he needed to do something to stop them, but he was no longer sure what he could get away with. If he continued to try and kill them off, they might actually be able to retaliate the way they threatened to do. He might be able to escape their wrath now, but once he launched his presidential campaign he'd be out where he would be a lot more vulnerable to their threats. It would definitely be difficult to become president if he was dead. As bad as that, he wouldn't have to be dead to be really screwed up during his run. It would be hard to run a decent campaign from a hospital bed.

That left him a lot to try to figure out. Something that really taxed his brain. In the meantime though, he still could continue with his original plans. His swat goons were already scheduled for raids on two libraries and a school. There was nothing, he was sure, that the rescuers could do about those.

CHAPTER 7

Shanty was keeping them well informed about Dasadist's plans, so Mack and the rest of Refuge Rescuers knew what, where, when, and how he planned to make his next attacks. Mack knew he couldn't take the so-called Fahrenheit-now swat teams directly. There was just too many of them. The trick would be too somehow defeat their purpose without a direct confrontation.

After meetings with local authorities and the staffs of the libraries, and after they were guarantied they would get new buildings for no direct cost to the community, all the books and other materials were removed from the libraries. It took the efforts of over a hundred volunteers, but the local community managed to complete the job in time. The buildings were then boobytrapped.

When the Fahrenheit-now bunch made their mighty charge into the first library, they were met with an empty interior. The goons filled the building, then stood staring in disbelief. Where were all those books they'd planned to throw into the beautiful fire the were going to start.

They didn't get the books, but they did get the fire. While they hesitated about what to do next, all the interior walls of the building burst into flames. The only place free of fire was the area around the door they'd used to charge into the place. During the stampede the swat goons made to get to the door, more than a dozen of their men fell and were trampled by the rush. All but three of them did ultimately escape without serious burns, but none of them ever fully trusted the other men they were associated with again. The three who did end up seriously burned were never again of any use to the Fahrenheit-now bunch. They were left to pay their own hospital bills. A proposition so expensive it was impossible to do.

Again, Dasadist was driven into a temper tantrum to end all of his fits of anger. He blamed everyone around him for allowing his plans to leak. With his ego as big as it was, he absolutely couldn't even consider that he was the source of the leak. Which of course he was. Every time he met with Shanty, he leaked all of his plans. He was sure, beyond even the slightest doubt, that someone who donated a million dollars to him now and then couldn't possibly be the cause of any leaks. It meant he had no idea of where the leaks were coming from.

That left the group who had given him constant problems. Refuge Rescuers. The problem was, what to do about them. Since he was still shy about starting to kill them all while they were in Minnesota, he knew he had to do something about the next library.

He picked out six of his best swat goons to watch it. They split the day into three shifts and worked them with two men on each shift. They did an excellent job of watching, and the only books they saw leave the library were carried out by normal people checking out books.

So when it came time to make the raid, they were sure that this time they'd end up with the right kind of fire. A nice bonfire of the much hated books. They ran into problems, however, when they attacked. They once again found an empty building.

Mack, along with everyone else, knew all along that after the first library raid they'd be watching the second one. But they had a simple solution. They emptied both of them at the same time. While the Fahrenheit-now guys were watching, everything they saw was staged. And now they were so surprised by what they'd found, they momentarily forgot what happened to them on their first library raid. All of the swat goons were inside the building when the interior walls of the building exploded in flames.

The panic was the same and the results of it were somewhat worse this time. Five men ended up in the hospital as a result of this fire, and one of them was the captain of Fahrenheit-now. That meant that they would be without an established leader when they made their school attack, which was scheduled for early the next week.

Mack knew, from Shanty's reports, that there was a lot of chaos among Dasadist's troops. He also was confident in the preparations that had been made for the coming school raid. So he decided to take the next Saturday off, and do something that had been pushed aside all too often lately.

At a time when it was a much needed thing to do, he'd promised Kathy Magee that he would take her on walking in the refuge on a regular basis, which as far as she was concerned, would be at least once a month. Two months had gone by since the last one they taken alone. And alone, in her opinion, was the only way the walk counted as far as Mack's promise went.

Lisa never complained about those walks that he took with Kathy. Whenever he did, she spent the day with Sheriff Dale Magee, Kathy's husband. It was understood by the four of them, that for the most part, the Saturdays should be kept innocent. So they were. For the most part.

When it was time to start their day, Mack and Lisa went to Dale and Kathy's. It was only a few hundred yards away from their home. Mack and Kathy then left for the refuge in Mack's pickup, and Lisa stayed with Dale until they decided what they wanted to do with their day.

Kathy couldn't resist commenting on the lack of walks when she got into the truck. "It's been too damn long, you know. I hate going so long without my refuge time with you."

"I know, Kathy. So do I miss our time. But at least we got that walk a few weeks ago."

"Those walks might count for you, Mack, but for me, they only count when it's only me and you. You know damn good and well that I need my Mack Thomas time as bad as I need the refuge time. The truth is, I think even more."

"I miss you too. And I'm sorry we've been so damn busy lately. But at least you have Dale and I have Lisa. They do a good job of filling our lives when we don't see each other."

"I know. I love Dale dearly. But sometimes you are the only one who can fill the gaps. A lot of them have opened up since that day when you were the only one who could forgive me my big mistake. You didn't hesitate, even though you knew I was wrong when I asked Dale for a divorce. Everyone else did hold back that forgiveness. I fell in love with you then. You know that, don't you?"

"Yes, and it didn't take me long to fall in love with you. But you love Dale and I very much love Lisa, so we are destined to only share part of who we are."

"I know, but no matter what, Mack, don't ever stop giving me these days."

They were quiet then, for the short time it took them to get to the refuge. As she always did as soon as they were out of the truck, Kathy put her arms around his neck and kissed him with the built up passion from the long wait for her walk. She then took his hand and they started down the refuge hiking trail.

It didn't take long for the walk to get interesting. At the first pond they came to, a muskrat was swimming in the open water, from one tiny, grass covered island to another one. A mink quickly joined the muskrat in the water, swimming up close to it. It could have easily killed the muskrat, but instead just followed close behind it. As the muskrat tried to scramble up on an island to escape, the mink bit it's leg to disable it, then followed it up on the island. That's where it killed the muskrat. It knew that since it was much larger, if it killed it in the water, it would never manage to get it out of the water. So the mink let the muskrat do its work for it.

"That was a fascinating thing to watch," Kathy said as they walked away from the two struggling animals, "but unpleasant anyway."

"It was that. It was what nature is about too. Most people get the idea that when they come to a place like this refuge, it's supposed to be all sunshine and roses. Everything peaceful, with nothing of the day to day strife we call life. The problem is, all these critters need to eat, the same as we do. So every time one of them gets hungry, something either dies or gets injured. It's a hard lesson to learn."

"Sometimes, Mack, it seems to me that life is mostly a long string of hard lessons to learn. And there's always someone to tell us all about the rules behind the lessons. I do, more often than I normally care to admit, get tired of constantly following the rules."

"I can't argue with that. Yet, at the same time, we do our share of rule breaking. Hell, something as simple as what we're doing today is breaking rules according to a lot of people."

"How do you figure that Mack? Where's the rule that says we shouldn't walk in this refuge?"

"The one that says we are married to different people than who we are walking with. To make it even worse, we are holding hands. We even tease each other some. That's a bunch of rules to break."

"I guess it is. I think though, that since we are such terrible rule breakers, we should definitely consider breaking the big one before this day is over."

"I'm not going to say no to that right now, Kathy. I'm not going to say yes either. I think I'll have to talk to Lisa before I can decide. As much as I don't believe that you and I, or Dale and Lisa, doing exactly that is anything bad, I still don't want to do something that could lead to her not trusting either one of us."

"I know. The same goes for Dale. I do think it's kind of weird though, the way things have evolved with the four of us. If they went ahead and broke that rule today, and we didn't know about it until later, neither one of us would be upset. For those two, it's the other way around."

"At least, Kathy, that pretty much is only about the knowing or not knowing what we're doing. They haven't at all made it something forbidden. Which says a lot for them, considering they know we love each other. Their relationship is much simpler. They're just super good friends."

Their conversation was suddenly interrupted when the brown bear that Mack had seen in the meadow behind his house casually walked by them. It was only about twenty feet away from them when it stopped and sat down. It tipped its head to one side, as if to look at them from a different angle. It then lifted a front paw, moving it up and down like it was waving hello. Mack returned the wave. It shook its head up and down, then stood and went contentedly on its way.

Kathy was now holding Mack's hand about as tight as she'd ever done. "Now that," she said, her face unable to decided whether to show fear or amazement at what had just happened, "was something special to see. It was terrifying, but awesome. How come you aren't reacting to it, Mack. I know that you're well aware of how unpredictable bears can be."

"They can be. I've seen that one a few times before. She's always been friendly toward me and whoever I've been with when I've run across her. I even accidentally got between her and her cubs once. Instead of attacking me, she just walked around me, got hold of her cub, and let it know that it had misbehaved."

"You weren't afraid of it then?"

"No, Kathy, I wasn't. I'm still cautious around her, but I'm not afraid of her. I think it would take a lot to set her off. For whatever reason, she's somehow trying to be friendly. Maybe not what we'd call being friends exactly, but definitely not the natural enemies we usually are."

"Does that mean I don't need to be afraid of it either?"

"I don't really know. From her behavior today and in the past, I'm sure you're safe when you're with me. If you ever see her when you're alone, I think you should be very cautious."

Kathy gave him a mischievous smile. "I'm curious now, Mack. With the bear wandering around us, does that mean we will have to call off any extracurricular activities? They could put us in an awfully vulnerable position."

"It could do that. So maybe fate, in the image of the bear, is trying to tell us something."

"The way you just said that, Mack, makes me wonder. You aren't just trying to avoid me today, are you?"

Seeing her forlorn look, Mack knew he needed to reassure her. He took her in his arms and kissed her. "I will never try to avoid you. You should know that. It's just that now, I've been getting a strong feeling that you and I have to be careful."

Just then his cell phone went off. Normally he would ignore it, but when he looked at who was calling it was Wanda. For some reason they, and everyone who knew them, didn't understand, he and Wanda had shared dreams and sometimes gut feelings, before some kind of disaster struck. So he answer his cell.

"I don't know where you are," Wanda immediately said, "but wherever it is, be careful. Something's wrong."

"I'm having the same gut feelings. I'm at the refuge with Kathy. Maybe I should get her out of here."

"I think so, Mack. If it was just you, or you and one of us trained to deal with this kind of thing, staying might be okay. It's not a good idea, I don't think, to expose Kathy to whatever the problem might be."

"Damnit, Mack," she complained when Mack told her it was time to leave. That it might not be safe in the refuge. "I don't want to leave yet. We aren't even close to having the day I wanted to have with you."

"I know," he answered, "but when Wanda and I get these feelings, it always means something is wrong somewhere. The worst thing about them is that we don't always know what it is that's wrong. So to be safe, it's best if we leave."

Just then they heard a shot ring out and a bullet hit a tree near Mack. It was instantly followed by a mighty roar and a sudden blood curdling scream. It was quickly followed by a second roar and another scream. Mack fell to the ground, taking Kathy with him. He was careful when he did it, to make her land on top of him. He just as quickly rolled over on top of her to protect her with his body. When all he heard for the next few minutes was the wailing sound from what sounded like two human males, he told Kathy to stay where she was and went to check it out.

He didn't have to go far to find the source. The bear stood over one man, her giant paw high on his chest, holding him absolutely still. The man was bleeding from his right leg and some deep scratches across his entire chest. On the ground about five feet away from him his AR15 lay on the ground. The man was obviously terrified. His pants made that clear from the way he wet himself.

A second man was as high as he could get in a young poplar tree. His back had several gouges across it, and the back of his pants was missing. He was bleeding there too. A second AR15 lay on the ground at the bottom of the tree.

As soon as Mack picked up the rifles, the bear shook herself vigorously, raked her claws a second time across the chest of the man she was holding down, and stepped away from him. She looked hard into Mack's eyes, nodded her head at him, then turned and walked away.

"Thank you," Mack said to her back as she did. "You can come out now," he called out to Kathy then.

"What happened, Mack," she asked when she saw him with the two rifles in his hands and the men on the ground. "Did you call an ambulance for these guys?"

"Not yet. I think I'll call Dale first. He can call the ambulance. They might get here quicker that way."

"But he won't be able to give them as accurate directions as you can."

"Well, that might be true. But it will be more official if Dale calls."

"What if they bleed to death, Mack? We don't want that to happen, do we?"

"I guess it would be a sad thing if someone who just tried to kill us bled to death. But we'll just have to take that chance." He called Dale. When he finished talking to them, he told Kathy, "When Dale and the other deputies get here, make sure you tell them that you saw the pack of wild dogs who did this to these guys. There were five of them. They all looked like German Shepards. Can you remember that?"

"But I didn't see anything."

"Yes you did. You saw the pack of wild dogs. Five German Shepards."

"But I didn't…"

"Look, Kathy, that bear saved our lives. If we don't claim it was dogs, it will be hunted down by every gun lover who thinks he's a mighty hunter in at least five states. The bear deserves to live. We'll tell Dale the truth later. He will, I promise, understand why we are going to do what we are going to do."

"Okay, Mack. It was dogs that did this."

It didn't take long for Dale to get there, and the ambulance wasn't far behind. Both of the hired killers were seriously injured and lost a lot of blood, but they survived. When they healed enough to make a statement, they were severely frustrated when everyone ignored their stories about the bear.

Mack and Kathy had a few hours of daylight left after they finished their time with the cops, and they decided to spend it in the refuge. Lisa had gotten there a short time after Dale, because she was with him when Mack called. When Mack alluded to her that Kathy was somewhat upset by all that happened that day, and that it was possible things might get a bit out of hand, she just smiled and said that would be fine.

"Besides, I have to admit, Dale and I pushed the boundaries ourselves earlier. I thought about calling you to talk to you, but then I didn't want to interrupt your day with Kathy, so I decided I would tell you later."

"I kind of figured that. Dale's uniform is usually perfect. It wasn't when he got here today."

Mack and Kathy wandered off then. It didn't take them long to find one of the spots Mack knew was quiet and very private. When they left it, She felt really good about her day with Mack and the bear he was such good friends with.

Later that evening, when Mack let her tell Dale and Lisa what really happened when the men shot at them, the bear story came as a big surprise. But after talking about it for a while, they all decided that it really wasn't that surprising after all. It was the natural affect Mack had on life around him. And no one knew that better than Lisa, as she snuggled up tight agains him when they went to bed that night.

CHAPTER 8

Governor Rod Dasadist was seriously flummoxed by the disaster in the refuge. His two men who were there watching Mack Thomas and the woman who looked like the famous singer, were now in the hospital. Attacked by a bear, they claimed. Attacked by wild dogs, according to the official record.

Dasadist was far more inclined to believe the official story than he believed the bear story. Even if they were in a wildlife refuge, it was highly unlikely that there were any bears in there.

It didn't matter either, how deep the scratches were on their bodies. The dogs could have somehow given the men the scratches. What gave them to the men wasn't what was the most important anyway. What was important was the fact they had the perfect chance to kill Mack and the lady and they'd blown it. Instead of getting that job done, they were now laying in a couple of hospital beds, of no use to anyone.

Even if it was true that they stood a good chance of walking away from their crime, it didn't make up for their mistake. Their alibi that they weren't trying to shoot anybody. That they were only going to test the accuracy of their scopes, could hold up. Especially since no one was shot. It didn't satisfy Dasadist though. He still was out two good men, and as far as he was concerned, it was all the fault of the people who were part of Refuge Rescuers. No matter what else, they had to be taken out of the game. They were way too much trouble. The kind of trouble he definitely didn't need for his presidential campaign. In spite of their consistent failures, he was sure the needed to go ahead with their attempts on the lives of everyone who was part of Refuge Rescuers.

He knew he had to do something about them. The question was what? He was aware now, that they would not be easy to defeat. They didn't appear to be interested in money. They had to be smart, or they wouldn't be able to defeat his people every time they went after them. They most of all appeared to be tough, as they seemed to handle the situations they got into without much trouble. And worst of all, they seemed to be well known enough so that simply murdering the bunch of them at the same time might draw the attention of the wrong people.

All that left him back where he started with them. Keep his men watching them, and it the situation and timing is right, kill any of them that it's possible to do so. Young or old, male or female, it didn't matter. They were all bad for Rod Dasadist, and therefore didn't deserve to live. Anyone who didn't love and respect him had no place in his world.

And that was also especially true of schools, private or public, that were still allowing their students and teachers to read any of the books on his list of the evil books he'd banned. There were several thousand on that growing list, and he was determined to continue it as long as the people recommending the books for the list did their jobs. He would pick out the books himself if he could. But he'd never read a book. For him, it was a struggle to read a few articles in one of the newspapers each day.

Back when he was in high school, he did read a story about a man trying to build a fire out in the far north cold. He didn't quite do it. Dasadist found the story depressing, so he banned everything the guy, whose name was Jack London, ever wrote.

Another thing he was learning was that just banning books wasn't going to accomplish his final goals. He was never going to rid his country, and eventually the world, of all the evil books. They continued to publish them. That meant he would have to go after the publishers. He would start with the small ones, and as they were eliminated he could go after the big ones.

His goal there was to narrow the field down far enough so that no book that wasn't approved by the government censors would ever be published. And all the censors would be members in good standing in the evangelical church. And those churches would be chosen by his team. A team he would have firm control of. That way, he was sure he could control everything published anywhere.

With that kind of control, which as president he could enforce with the might of the American military, he was sure he'd be able to spread his own greatness across the world. And when he completed his goals for all of humanity, he knew without any doubt whatsoever that he would have pleased God. Not only pleased him, but made God love him enough so that he, Rod Dasadist would live forever. And forever rule the kingdom God had given him to continue on God's own path of greatness.

It was so simple. Eventually get rid of all the books, except maybe the bible, and control everyone else's mind. And live forever.

CHAPTER 9

After everyone one was at the table and eating their Sunday breakfast, Ben surprised them. He rarely sat down during those meals. This time he did. He asked everyone to make room for him across the table from Mack. The look on his face was dead serious when he sat down. He waited until Mack looked up from his plate and caught his eye before he spoke.

"I have something I need to tell you, Mack," he said. "It's not a bad thing, but it is a serious one. I have to warn you too, depending on how you take it, you might find it sad. And I guess it is, in its own way. It's a memory I could say I will carry forever. But since there's no forever for us, I'll just say I'll will remember it for as long as I live. And as important as anything, I have to tell you, Theresa and I talked this out last night, so what I tell you now won't be hurting her. As good a woman as she is, she fully understands why I need to do this. And finally, I'm telling you this now, because in one way or another, what I tell you will ultimately effect everyone here."

"As serious as you sound, Dad," Mack answered, "I think that the best thing you can do is go ahead and tell me, tell all of us, whatever it is you've got on your mind."

"To start with, it's about your mom, Mack. I won't go into all that much about her. I only want, right now, to point out one thing about her. She was an avid reader. She loved books. She loved a lot of things about life, but books were near the top of that list. She wasn't one of those people who read only one kind of thing, She read everything. When it came to fiction, there wasn't a genre she didn't read at least some of. She even read a few of my westerns. She also read a lot of history. She seemed to enjoy any good books on history, but tended to like American history the best."

Ben paused for a moment, reached out and touched Mack's hand, then pulled his hand back and resumed talking. "Even after she got sick and the cancer started taking the life out of her, she continued to read. It wasn't until real close to the end, when she was so close to helpless, that she stopped. She asked me then, to read to her. So I did, as much and as often as I could. When she came home after her last visit to the hospital, to spend her last days there, I read to her a good part of the time. Then the day came when we knew time was running real short. The day was over, and you were in bed already, Mack. I was ready for bed myself. She was still awake though, lying so still in the hospital bed next to the one we'd shared all of our married life. She asked me in a voice so soft I could barely hear her, to please read to her for a while. So I did. It was one of her favorite romance novels. One she'd read herself two or three times. It seemed awful quiet in that room, with the only sound I could hear was my own voice. I read several pages before I realized it was way too quiet. I stopped reading and looked over at her. She had the slightest bit of a smile on her face. But she wasn't breathing. She was gone. But she hadn't died sad or full of fear. She died listening to one of her favorite books. She was at peace when she went. I can't think of anything else that could have done a better job of giving that, than one of her favorite books."

Ben stopped then, his head bowed and tears flowing from the memory he'd just shared. Mack wasn't doing much better, but managed to take his father's hands in his own and hold them. Lisa, who was sitting next to Mack, wrapped her arms around him and held him tight. Other than the sound of tears flowing, there was no sound at the table.

Theresa was the first to speak. "As soon as he's able, Ben has more to say. I want all of you to know. I absolutely agree with what he's going to say. I also want what he wants."

After a couple of minutes Ben took a couple of breaths, then looked up at Mack. "I told you that story for a reason. Good or bad, right or wrong, I need to be part of the battle against that Dasadist bastard and all of his people. You've always known how I felt about your mother, but I wanted to be sure you understood that part of her, and the way she loved her books. Now we've got some Republican governor son of a bitch banning those books. So you have to let me be part of going after that useless thug. For the sake of your mother's memory, we have to take him down."

"I can't make that decision alone, Dad," Mack told him. "So we'll put it to a vote." He looked around the table. "Everyone who thinks Ben should be part of our war against book banners, raise your hand."

Everyone at the table raised their hand.

"That's great," Theresa said, "but what about me?"

All hands went up again.

Gradually the conversations around the table went beck to normal. As it did, it was easy for Mack to see by the look on their faces, that Ben's talk had left an impression on all of them. Lisa seemed to have felt his words deeply. They had served as a reminder of what was going on in her own family. Her own father, Bob Anderson, was suffering from serious heart problems. They didn't talk about it much, but they all knew that his time was limited unless he managed to get a transplant.

When the meal was done, and Lisa could see that Mack was all right, she asked him if it was okay if she go visit her dad for a while. He, of course, agreed with her going.

"There's something I should do today anyway," he told her.

She looked at him, and easily read his expression. "Okay," she said, suppressing a smile, "which one are you taking to the refuge for a walk today?"

Mack couldn't hold back his smile. "You know me too well, Lisa." He sighed. "I think it might be a good idea to take Theresa. If she does have something to say, or concerns about dad's story about mom today, it's probably best if she gets the chance to talk to me first."

"I agree with you. I know she understands how your dad feels, but it probably would be good for her to talk it out with you too. And you can tell her, that if she needs another one, I'm a good listener too."

"I will do that."

Mack stayed with Ben and Theresa, helping with the breakfast cleanup. When it was done, Mack didn't have to say anything to Ben. He spoke first. "Are you going to take her to the refuge to talk?" he asked, referring to his wife, Theresa, "or just go for a walk around here."

"I'm in the mood for the refuge today, Dad, so I think we'll go aver there. If it's okay with you, that is?"

"It is. I'll be hoeing tomatoes when you get back, if you have a need to talk to me them."

Theresa wasn't at all surprised when Mack asked her to come with him for a hike in the refuge. When she and Ben talked about what Ben was going to say at breakfast the night before, Ben warned her that

Mack would likely as not want to talk to her about it. So they went there without any further discussion.

As soon as they started down the trail, she took his hand. When he gave her a look of surprise, she said, "I know that this is the way you usually walk with the other women you take for walks here, so I can't see any reason I should be any different." Mack's response was a light squeeze of her hand. "Good, I like holding your hand."

"I fell the same way."They walked a little farther before Mack spoke again. "I guess it's pretty obvious why I thought we should take this walk. Other that the fact that I really like your company. So the question is, were you really okay with everything dad said at breakfast today?"

"More than okay. Sure, I sometimes get a little jealous of the way he still feels about your mom. He really did love her with all his heart, with everything that he was. He still does. What gets me past that every time is the knowledge that he loves me too. It's in a somewhat different way, I think. But that's okay. It's right that nothing should invade that place inside him he's reserved for her. He has such a big heart, there's plenty of room left for me."

"He does have that. I think he'd try to move heaven and earth to please you, if he thought it was necessary."

"He would. He'd do the same for you too. And there isn't any one of us who was at that breakfast table today that he would have even the slightest hesitation to help, if they needed it."

"That's very true. He's also very forgiving of all of us when we make mistakes."

"He is. He has to be, to be able to have forgiven the mistakes I've made."

"I don't think doing it was all that difficult. Anymore than any of us forgiving mistakes like that."

"You're very much like him when it comes to that. You've always been that way with me. You're also apparently able to forgive those kind of mistakes in all the women in your life."

"If you're referring to Lisa and Kathy, there really wasn't that much to forgive. They're just human, and given what life so often is, it's actually pretty unusual for that to never happen to anyone. Not to mention that when it happens, it's made out to be much worse than what it really is."

"Are you saying that it's sometimes okay to make love to someone other than your spouse?"

"Yes, I guess I am."

"You mean, you think it would be okay for you and I to make love, if spite of Ben and Lisa."

Mack couldn't help a bit of a chuckle. "No, I wouldn't ever say that. And I can explain that in one word. *Ben.* If we did that and he knew it, there's no way in a hundred years he'd ever understand. And he'd blame me, way more than you. But other than your relationship with my father, there are times on this earth, that between two people something different can be okay."

"Okay, Mack. I see your point. But as long as we're out here all alone. And in a spot where no one can possibly see us, I'd like to try something."

"Really," Mack asked, taking a step beck from her. "I hope it's nothing that would upset dad."

"It won't upset his because he'll never know. And I'm not thinking about breaking any vows. I just want to kiss you. Other women do, when you walk out here with them, so I want to kiss you too. You don't have to kiss me back."

Mack shook his head, this time not sure about the right or wrong of it. But before he could make a final decision, she put her arms around his neck, pulled him close, and kissed him. Without even realizing what he was doing, he returned it.

"I think I liked that," she said. "I like it a lot." She took his hand. "It's too bad we'll never do it again. It would be a nice thing to share with you now and then. But Ben comes first."

Mack didn't have to answer her. Ben and Lisa did come first. And because of that, he knew he had to try to figure out the best ways to keep the both of them from the worst danger when Dasadist and his goons raided the school.

CHAPTER 10

It was a private school, teaching grades ten through twelve. It was founded by a group of educators who saw the need for a place to teach gifted children who were largely ignored by existing systems. It leaned heavily on liberal arts courses, but offered a wide range of science courses too. Among the advantages it offered to gifted students was a huge library.

The school made ebooks and readers of all types widely available to all students, but the best part of the library were the many thousands of real books it held. It even had special shelves filled with all the books banned by Dasadist. All of those books were easily accessible as ebooks too.

That is why Dasadist carried a particular hatred for this school. Teaching smart kids in special classrooms and offering an extensive range of books was a major crime as far as the governor was concerned. Having an intelligent, well educated group of people who read books was the last thing he needed. People like that would never follow him into the utopia he intended to create. Asking questions always interfered with his version of perfection. A state of being that left him as the complete, total, and only leader. No one else on earth was even remotely close enough to his perfection to do the job.

Of course that meant the school needed to be eliminated. And it certainly would be. At ten AM this very morning, his Fahrenheit-now swat team would be storming the school. All of the faculty and students would be arrested and charged with a series of crimes against the state of Wisconsin.

Along with all the other charges, there would be the usual meth lab charges. There was nothing else as effective as drugs to frame innocent people. And to satisfy the desires of his goon squad members, most if not all of them females, be they teachers or students, would be charged with prostitution. That way, the huge numbers of rapes they would commit wouldn't be so obvious.

The best part of the day for Dasadist though, would be the book fire. That would come immediately after the raid, shortly before they burned down the entire school. It was with a deep sense of satisfaction mixed with excitement that he awaited the hour of attack.

His problem was the fact that other people were filled with similar feelings. Mack was the leader of those people. They were stationed all around the school. Not so close they were noticed, but close enough to be able to move in quickly to do their job once the action started.

The inside of the school was now empty of people, books and other media, and the entire science lab. Everything was removed, without the prying eyes of Dasadist's spies seeing the activity, via a tunnel built as soon as it was known the school was a target.

As students and faculty arrived that morning, they left the school through the tunnel. From there, they were bussed to their new school, already built and ready to use. What everyone liked the best about it was the new, expanded library, with an additional two thousand books.

Once again, the Fahrenheit-now swat team was shocked when they charged into the school waving their AR15s in the air, or wherever it was that they could wave them. Over a hundred men stood stock still in the empty building. Then before they could react in any way, all the doors into the school slammed shut. Heavy, two inch thick boards were jammed into brackets bolted to the building to hold the doors closed,

Slowly, but steadily growing stronger, the sprinkler system in the building began spraying. The problem it caused the raiders was the fact that it wasn't spraying water. It was emitting a fine mist of pepper spray. The men who still wore their helmets and plastic masks didn't suffer quite as much as the ones who'd removed theirs. But it was a painful experience.

The instant the pepper spray stopped, the school windows began to break. Everyone possible from Refuge Rescuers, along with two dozen men Shanty supplied, let loose with automatic paintball guns. They deluged the raiders with the bright red and yellow paint balls. The firing didn't stop until they were almost totally coated with with paint, especially covering their face masks.

Once the raiders were stumbling blindly, trying to find their way out of the building, tear gas was shot into it. As the mighty swat team Fahrenheit-now screamed in terror as they tried to escape the building, Mack, his entire group, and the twenty-four extra men, got into their vehicles and left. But just before they did, Ben Thomas, Mack's father, managed to get close enough to the armored SUV Dasadist was in, trying to observe the action. He had his window open, so Ben managed to hit him up side the head with a yellow paint ball. A perfect color for the kind of man he was. Ben managed to follow that with a canister of tear gas inside the vehicle.

Dasadist didn't look quite so powerful when he dove out of his SUV to escape the gas. In fact, he looked quite the fool as he landed on his face, then struggled to his feet. An event recorded by Sue, then immediately transmitted to every major news network in the country.

It was a video played over several times by every network. With the exception, of course, of Fox News. Real news wasn't something they were interested in. Instead, they played fake, prerecorded videos of a raid on a school that was supposedly a meth drug lab. It wasn't until the next day that Fox realized their mistake. After that, they ignored everything about the raid.

The other networks, however, managed to get to the school quick enough to film the swat team trying to escape the building. An event that took near twenty minutes. Some of the spectators who had gathered around to watch, thought it was a circus act.

Several dozen of the swat team were taken to the hospital. Mostly from injuries received in the mad rush to escape the school. A few needed their eyes treated, as a result of heavy doses of pepper spray. Dasadist was one of the casualties who was taken to the hospital. He broke his nose when he took the dive out of his SUV.

None of Mack's or Shanty's people who dealt with the swat team Fahrenheit-now were even slightly injured. Once they left the school, they took several routes home, and no police paid even the slightest attention to them.

When they left the school, Lisa got to Mack's pickup first, so she got into the driver's side and started it. That allowed them to get moving the instant he got in the truck. As soon as they were a short distance away, Mack called Shanty to fill her in on the raid.

"So how did it go," she said as soon as she answered her phone.

"Better than expected. We caught them totally off guard. They were so damn sure of themselves, that when they went in they didn't even see the brackets we installed to hold the boards that locked them in. And as we expected, they panicked as soon as the pepper spray hit them."

"How about the paintball, Mack? Did that work the way we hoped?"

"Probably better. The way they were dancing around from the pepper spray, we were able to pretty much coat them with the paint. The teargas worked great too. They were blind from the pepper spray and paint by then, so most of them had a hard time finding their way out."

"Did anyone get to Dasadist? He said he was going to be there to watch the raid. He was really excited about watching the book fire. That man surely does hate books."

Mack couldn't help but chuckle about what happened to Dasadist. "That was close to the best part of the day, Shanty. My dad, Ben, got him. He told us a couple of days ago that he wanted to be part of it when we went after him, so that was his assignment today. Find him and do what he could to him, without shooting him. At least, not with real bullets. Dad got him in the head with a yellow paint ball, then managed to lob a canister of teargas into his SUV. He landed on his face when he dove out of his car."

"I don't suppose anyone got a picture of that, did they?"

"Sue recorded it all. She immediately downloaded it to all the networks. So it should be on the news anytime now. Dasadist is going to look like a pure fool on this one."

"Awesome, Mack. As soon as I see it, I will contact him and give him hell. Make him think I'm real upset about his failure to accomplish anything today. Especially after I donated to his raid fund. I have no doubts that doing it will keep him feeding me his plans."

"I don't doubt it either. But I also don't doubt that it will be a lot more difficult to stop his next move, whatever it might be."

"Actually, it won't be. I've already done it. He's been planning to destroy as many publishers of his banned books as he can. I can't possibly save them all, but I've already purchased your publisher. I'm keeping everyone who worked there, so you won't have to put up with any changes in the way you deal with them."

"That sounds good, Shanty. But now that you own a publishing business, maybe you could republish a few of the better banned books which are no longer being published. And if you do, promote the living hell out of them. I think that turning banned books into best sellers would be one of the best things we could ever do."

"So do I, Mack. And Jasper's story is going to be put at the top of my list of books to promote."

"You know you don't have to do that. You've already done more than enough for us."

"I'm not doing it only for you, or for any of you guys at Refuge Rescuers. I'm doing it because I think the book is good enough, and means enough, so that a lot more people should read it. I think your sequel to it deserves the same treatment. So it's going to get it too."

"I could pretend to be modest about all this, and say that the books aren't that important. And in some ways, I'm sure that's true. At the same time, I think they do have a fair amount of value when it comes to pointing out how we almost totally waste a valuable resource in this country. It's senior citizens. For the most part, we just throw them away."

"I agree, and that's why I will be pushing the promotion of those books."

"One thing concerns me though. What's to stop Dasadist from going after your publishing business? He does have the resources to attack it, one way or the other. And he could turn around and go after you personally."

"We've already thought about that. The purchase of the company has been buried under so much paperwork that he'll never figure out who actually owns it. As far as the physical part of the company, it's being moved into a heavily fortified building. I've also purchased a large book printing company, which will be located in the same building. That way we will have control over every book we produce. From receiving the manuscript to shipping the finished book. We will also have everything we need to produce the ebooks."

"I think what you're doing will do as much to defeat that book banning bastard as anything that could be done."

"It's people like you and me working together that's going to do the job, Mack."

"You're right. It's going to be a long haul before we completely take him down, but I'm confident that in the end, that's exactly what we'll do."

CHAPTER 11

Mack and Lisa were careful the next morning to make it to breakfast reasonably early. They wanted to have more time than normal to go over the previous days events. They also wanted to catch up on Larry's activities, since he'd been carrying the bulk of the day to day cases they were involved in.

He was already there and obviously glad to see them when they got there. "I've just taken on what I consider an important case," he told them when they asked him about how it was going for him. "And I really need to talk to you about it."

"That's why we made it a point to get here at a decent time today," Mack answered. "So tell us about it."

"Yesterday, an extremely upset father, Max Foster, hired us to find out who raped his daughter. It happened during a party in a frat house at…" he went on to name the college and the frat house. "It's members are mostly made up of the privileged children of the rich and powerful. Mostly politicians, business leaders, and those at the top of the religious community. Those boys have been accused of rape before, but nothing has ever come of it. This time, I'd like to hang some asses. Shit like that just shouldn't be allowed to happen."

Mack knew instantly that they would be doing everything they could to solve this case. Given Lisa's history, she was kidnapped and raped when she was sixteen, there was no way she was going to allow anything less than a full effort being put into this one.

It was also no surprise when she immediately spoke up about it. "I agree that we should take the case," she said. "So what are your plans, Larry?"

"Well, this is the hard part. I want to put two people into that college. I doubt we'll ever get the evidence we need any other way but undercover. I've already enrolled in the college as an adult special, and I plan to spend enough time on campus to be able to worm my way into the parties that that frat house has. I also want to plant a female at the closest women's frat house. She needs to be someone young enough, and seemingly innocent enough, to grab their attention."

"Do you plan on hiring someone for that job?" Lisa asked.

"No, we already have someone who is as close to perfect to do it as anyone you are ever going to find. She wants to do it, but it's going to ultimately be up to you, Lisa."

"Why is it up to me?"

"Because Julie is the one who wants to do it." Julie was Lisa's younger sister, and was part of Refuge Rescuers.

Lisa looked across the breakfast table at her sister, who had wisely kept quiet during the discussion. Even so, Lisa could see the beginnings of a hopeful grin on her face. Slowly shaking he head at her sister, she turned to Mack.

"What do you think about that idea?" she asked him. "She doesn't have any experience in that kind of work yet, and it could get real nasty."

"But she has been in training to be a detective, and you've been training her in self defense. I think that if she wants to do it, we should at least consider it."

Lisa turned back to Julie. "Are you sure you want to take on a job like that?"

Julie quickly nodded her head yes. "I very much want to do it. It seems like no matter where you go, there's always some guy or guys who think they can do to a woman anything they want to do. Having the chance to do something about some of them is something I want to take advantage of."

"If we okay this, Julie, you are first going to have to agree to put in a week of some of the toughest training you can imagine."

"What kind of training. I'm already in pretty damn good shape."

"This will be something new. It's time you learn how to fight."

"You've been training me for that for a long time. I think I've gotten good at being able to defend myself."

"I agree. You are damn good a defending yourself. That's not enough now though. Now you have to learn how to fight. You are going to have to find the mindset where you are able to attack before your opponent is ready. You have to know how and be ready to use the skill required to take out someone twice your size. And when you do it, you forget the so called rules. You have to be ready to take him out, and to do it the surest and quickest way you can. When your life is on the line, you can't hesitate. Not even for a second."

"You sound awful serious about all of that. Why haven't you talked to me like this before?"

"Because I hoped I wouldn't have to, Julie. As much as I love what I'm doing, I've always hoped you'd find something different to do with your life. Something safer."

"Are you trying to say that it's okay for you to take risks, but that it isn't for me?"

"No. It's not up to me to say who can take risks and who can't. Anymore then it's up to Mack to tell me I can't or for me to tell him he can't. It's totally a matter of I don't want you to. Mack and I give each other way too much worry already. So it's hard to take on anymore. But if we have too, then you are damn well going to be prepared. Which means you have to go into some serious training for at least a week before you venture forth."

Before Julie could answer, Wanda, who had been patiently listening, interrupted them. "Julie," she said, looking hard into her eyes, "I think, given who you are, you should be anxious to do what Lisa wants you to do. Even if you weren't going into that undercover operation, what you're going to learn are going to be some of the most valuable skills you could ever have. Most especially if you continue with this line of work."

Julie smiled at them. "I'm not only willing to go into training, I'm anxious. For a long time, I've admired the way you two have been able take on just about anyone and beat them. I want those skills that you have mastered so well."

Lisa was pleased with Julie's enthusiasm for learning the skills she needed to protect herself, but still wasn't at all happy to have her younger sister doing undercover work. Especially not on a job that held the particular dangers this one did. At the same time, she knew she couldn't justify telling her no. She had no real choice other than to let her make her own decisions.

Lisa did, however, feel justified in pushing Julie's training. It started right after breakfast. It continued through the day, starting with Lisa. Wanda ended her training for that day. The next day, her trainers alternated between Lisa, Mack, Larry, Wanda, and Roy.

When Julie thought she'd reached the saturation point on ways of fighting, Lisa brought in the street fighters she'd learned from. They took Julie through every trick, dirty or otherwise, that could be used in a knock down drag out fight.

By the time her week was over, Julie was ready to take on any but the most skilled fighter. And skilled fighters weren't what she was likely to have to go up against at a frat house party. She might have to fight off more than one spoiled frat house boy at a time, but it was unlikely there would be any real fighters among them.

CHAPTER 12

Dasadist was going nuts again. His latest three raids were all disasters. Two libraries and a school, and no books burned, when there should have been three large bonfires. Worse than that even, was the way his men were so completely humiliated on all three raids.

Each time it happened it was bad. Having men die in the library raids was one thing, but what happened at the school was, as far as he was concerned, much worse. Each and everyone of his Fahrenheit-now swat team came out of that raid looking like idiots. The pepper spray and tear gas were definitely humiliating, but the paint bombs were the worst thing he could have imagined. Worst of all, he was hit in the head with a yellow one. And the video of it happening had been plastered all over the media.

Along with his disaster, well over a hundred men staggered out of that school building looking like a bunch of blind, red and yellow clowns. Over half his team felt so degraded and beaten down by the experience that they quit. And among those who quit, most of them simply disappeared.

They all knew enough about Dasadist to be aware of his passion for revenge. His love of torture was another of his strongest characteristics. He had managed to keep much of his past from the public, but those close to him knew much about him that he preferred to keep quiet.

Near the top of that list was the fact that early in his career as a lawyer, he worked for the U.S. government. He was stationed at Guantanamo Bay, in Cuba. His main function was finding legal loopholes that could be used to allow the torture of prisoners. And it never mattered to him at all that they might not even belong there. Torture was what mattered, and when he made the choice, that is what he always chose.

It was a job he was good at, and there was nothing he loved more than watching the results of his efforts. He always smiled as he watched, but the louder the screams coming from the agony of the torture, the broader was his smile. He also never tried to hide what watching the screams and agony of men and women did to the inside of his pants. He just kept one female prisoner or another at the ready to take care of it when the screams stopped. He especially liked that ending when the female was younger. Like under twelve years of age.

Because of who he was and the kind of past he was known to have, the men who quit on him left Wisconsin and got as far away from there as they possibly could. They scattered all across the US, into Canada, and even more into Mexico. There was one exception to that.

Jules Sapphire was a former high school science teacher. His parents were strong conservatives and born again evangelicals, so it was always drilled into his head that big government was an evil thing. That alone was all the proof he ever needed to know how wrong all liberals were. So he first followed Trump, then switched to Dasadist when he started to abuse minorities, women and nonbelievers, even more than Trump did.

He started to get uncomfortable with the Dasadist movement when the book banning and burnings started. Early on it was okay to ban some of the books, but for him banning books on science was wrong, as was banning so many of the classics. He hadn't read all that many novels, but he had read enough of them to know their value to society as a whole, even if that was a contradiction to his other beliefs.

When the two library raids failed, he wondered more about how Dasadist could be so easily fooled, then he did about the books that did or did not get piled up and burned. It was the school that did it to him. It was supposed to be filled with evil liberals. Both students and teachers. Dasadist had assured everyone that the library there was filled with atheistic and communist inspired books. Worse yet, were the books written by black writers who told lies. His best example of that was Uncle Tom's Cabin, written by Harriet Beecher Stowe. It never did occur to him that she was a white person. He'd never read the book.

So instead of finding all those dangerous people and evil written material, they walked into an empty building where they were sprayed with pepper gas from the sprinkler system. Another Dasadist intelligence gathering failure. The spray alone would have been enough for the school raid to be a total failure, but the paint balls brought it all to another dimension. It was as complete a defeat as could ever be expected. It wasn't enough for the school defenders though. Before anyone could escape the horrors going on inside the school, they all had the privilege of getting their lungs and eyes filled with tear gas.

That was enough for Jules. He was already beginning to be a bit leery of a lot of the Dasadist program anyway. More and more, it was sounding like big government. He was coming up with laws and rules against nearly everything a person might do. It didn't seem to matter who it was or what it was, Dasadist was hell bent on controlling it. At the same time, it didn't appear that he had much, if any, control when it came to something as simple as raiding a school.

So Jules decided to walk away from the man, even if it did put him in danger. He just didn't think it was that serious. If he couldn't stage a proper raid, he wasn't likely to be able to find Jules. Especially not where Jules planned on going. Dasadist just wasn't smart enough to look for one of his missing men hiding among his worst enemy.

Two days later he was standing at the receptionist's desk at he office of Refuge Rescuers. Donna, their receptionist, gave him her usual friendly greeting. Then she said, "I know you made your appointment to see Mack," she told Jules, "but he's running a little late today. However, Lisa will be starting with you until he gets here."

"So who the hell is this Lisa person? I specifically requested to see the head man when I made the appointment."

"You will see Mack, as soon as he gets here. Lisa is one of our lead detectives, and she will be able to start working on your problem in the meantime. No matter what it might be."

"I doubt that like hell. Why the hell isn't that Mack guy here now?"

"He used to be a deputy sheriff. On his way home from town, he witnessed a bad multi-car pile up on the four lane. Right now, he's assisting the sheriff's department with traffic control."

"Why the hell can't the sheriff's department do that on their own."

"You can never have too many experienced people working to control traffic at an accident as bad as that one apparently is."

"That might be true, but I want you to know, I don't like to be kept waiting like this. It seems to me, that if you want to stay in business, you should treat our clients a little better."

"You are probably right," Donna pretended to agree. "So if you are in that big a hurry, I can refer you to another agency. There are always some who are anxious for new clients."

"You sound like you don't care if I walk out of here. That's a lousy attitude."

"Not really. The lousy attitude is the one you have. Instead of arguing with me, you could just as well be working on your problem with Lisa. Everyone of us here puts in our share of overtime. We simply don't need more business."

"I can assume then, that you are not going to call that Mack person and tell him that I'm impatiently waiting."

"I certainly am not. Mack could, easy as not, be involved in some kind of life or death situation on that highway right now. As far as you're concerned, I don't see any chance in you dying simply because you don't want to talk to someone else while you are waiting."

"You just don't have any sympathy for me at all, do you?" He tried to smile, then pointed at the name tag she was wearing. "Aren't you at all worried, Donna," he said, "that my complaining about you making me wait might get you in trouble? Maybe even fired?"

"If you are trying the threaten me, Mister Jules Sapphire, you are wasting my time a well as yours. I can get Lisa for you, you can sit down and wait, or best of all, you can turn around and leave. But you can definitely not stand there and threaten me."

Jules didn't have to study her face to see she wasn't kidding. The fact that she meant every word she said was deeply etched into her expression. What didn't show there was something she didn't know. Lisa was now standing behind her with a definite frown on her face. The stare she laid onto Jules wasn't friendly.

"I hate to tell you this," she said to him, "whoever the hell you think you are, but we don't tolerate anyone coming here and giving any of our employees a hard time. Not at anytime nor for any reason. So you'd best tell me what your problem is, or turn around and hike your ass out of here."

A very surprised Jules dropped his mouth open, then closed it. He took a deep breath before asking, "You're not Lisa, are you?"

"I am."

"That was some pretty tough talk from such a beautiful young woman. You aren't planning on throwing me out if I choose not to go are you?"

"Only if you force me too."

He shook his head. "You sure are a weird bunch here. You don't seem to care whether you keep customers or not. Your service stinks. And now you seem to think you could actually throw me out of here. Such nonsense."

Donna stepped forward. She glared into Jules's eyes. "Please don't be stupid," she said, "and push Lisa until she's forced to throw you out. I don't want to see you get hurt."

Jules lost his patience then, and pushed Donna out of the way. It was a mistake. Before he knew anything was happening, he was on the floor. Lisa had her hand out to help him up before he could find any way to react to her.

"If you're not hurt," she told him, "I'll walk you out to your car."

Shocked as he was, he knew now that he didn't want to leave. "I apologize for my bad behavior," he said. "I was out of line. And I would very much like to talk to you, Lisa, if you're willing to listen. I do have a lot to say that I think you should know. It's all about Mister Rod Dasadist."

That was enough for Lisa. She took him into the office she'd been working in. "So what is it that you want from us," she asked as she pointed to the chair where she expected him to sit. "Given the lousy impression you've made so far, it better amount to something or we won't be taking you on as a client. We aren't very tolerant of your particular brand of bullshit."

"Well damn, you sure as hell aren't afraid of being blunt, are you?"

"Do you really believe there's a reason I should be?"

"Only one I can think of. Do you or don't you want to stay in business? It seems to me that you could be a hell of a lot more courteous to potential customers."

"To start with, Mister Jules Sapphire, it remains to be seen whether or not we want you as a client. As far as business goes, we are already somewhat overloaded. We flat out don't need any more than what we already have, because what we have now is becoming somewhat of a burden. So you can damn well knock off your not so wise criticism and tell me what the hell it is that you're looking for."

Jules decided then that the best approach was to be every bit as blunt as Lisa was. "I used to work for Dasadist. I was in all three raids. The two libraries and the school. I'm fed up with the man, so I decided to come here to see what you people are really up to. You keep on beating him, but looking around it's easy to see you ain't no where big enough to be doing it all on your own. Even so, I'd like to join up with you. I've come to hate that bastard. He's just put the ban on too many of the wrong books for me to be able to tolerate what he's doing any longer."

"The problem with that is, why should we trust you? We don't know anything about you. Are you willing to let us do a thorough background check on you?"

"I guess that depends on how thorough you plan on making the check."

"If we do it we'll be going into your entire life. And we will go deep. We have a technical expert who can dig like you can't even imagine."

"What happens if you don't like what you find?"

"We'll talk about it, then make our decision."

"You know, I think you're over doing it. I'm just a high school science teacher who has a deep faith in God, but who hates banning books. They are one of the few things in life that have much real value."

"I take it then, that you don't want us to do the background check?"

"I guess not."

"I'll walk you out to your car then."

"I can find my own way out to my car."

"I don't doubt that at all. I will walk you out anyway."

"Why?"

"To ensure that you leave when you get there. You said you worked for Dasadist. We have no interest in having one of his employees, current or former, snooping around here. The less he knows about us, the better."

"But I told you, Lisa, I'm done with him. Why can't you just take my word for it?"

"The answer to that is about a simple as an answer can get. We don't know if your word is any good or not. If you actually worked for Dasadist, that puts the odds in favor of you being a liar, not to mention someone who'd love nothing as much as somehow being able to bring serious harm to a group of liberals like us. But, that's enough said. I'll walk you to your car now."

"What if I don't want you too? What then?"

"Then I do one of two things. I call for help and we drag your sorry ass the hell out of here, or I get impatient, render you harmless, and Donna and I literally drag you out of this building. From there I call the sheriff and have you arrested. It's rare for the sheriff's department to not have someone close by."

"It never would have occurred to me before I got here, that I would believe you when you say you will render me harmless. I do now. Does everyone in your agency have your talents?"

"That is something that is none of your concern, Jules. And my patience is beginning to wear awful thin. It's time for you to go."

"Well, Lisa, you have managed to convince me that I shouldn't leave. There's something about you that tells me that if anyone in this country is ever going to be able to do something about the bastard's book banning, it will be you people here. I will now submit to your background check on me. I just hope you don't judge me too harshly."

"We aren't here to judge. We just need to be careful. We've dealt with men like Desadist too many times in the past to do anything else. I'm going to call our tech expert in now. She'll walk you through the necessary questions. While she does, keep in mind that she is not trying to do anything other than what she's supposed to be doing."

"I'll do my best to answer all of her questions. It probably doesn't seem like it to you right now, but I do understand why you need to check up on me. If I was in your shoes, I wouldn't do anything less."

Sue quickly joined them then, bringing her laptop with her when she did. As soon as she began her interview with Jules, Lisa left them. She was working at a desk in the general office area when Mack finally arrived. She filled him in on what she knew so far about their possible new client. Mack's initial reaction toward the idea of taking him on as one was basically negative. But Mack being Mack, he was willing to look at the results of the background check on him, then interview him. He wouldn't make any final decision on him until both of those tasks were completed.

CHAPTER 13

As unusual as it was, still no one paid much attention when Julie showed up at her sorority house in the middle of a semester. The professors teaching her classes were also careful to accept her starting her classes, even though they were halfway through them for this semester.

Attention, however, was paid to her personally. It didn't matter that she dressed relatively conservatively, her natural beauty and near perfect figure left a startling impression on nearly all the boys who saw her. Especially the boys from the frat house close by the one Julie was now part of. The leaders of it decided they would have her, one way or the other. Consensual or not. They were way too important to ever miss a chance with someone who looked like her. There were a lot of women who were pretty and some who were beautiful. But few in Julie's class. Like her sister Lisa, she was a rare one.

They planned a party for the first Saturday she would be spending on campus. Her entire frat house was invited. Half of the women accepted the invitation and the other half turned it down. That half warned Julie about the dangers of going to the frat house's parties. Especially for someone as great looking as she was.

Julie went anyway. That's what she was there for, but she was extremely careful the whole time. When she danced with someone, she was careful to not to take so much as a sip from the drink she left behind when she danced. Because it was difficult to get rid of her unsafe drinks, she switched to beer. There was a full keg there, so everyone was drinking it from paper cups. That left Julie with the opportunity to dump her beer into the cups of various frat boys.

It didn't take long for the drugs they were trying to feed Julie to take affect on several of them. It took a while, but even as slow and dense as the frat boys were, they gradually began to grasp what was going on. When they finally fully realized what Julie was doing, they decided to deal with her. Two of their largest boys, each of them over six feet tall and weighing more than two hundred fifty pounds, forced her to go outside with them.

The lesson they had planned for her was simple. Strip her completely, rape her, then tell her that in no uncertain terms, for the rest of her stay on this college campus she belonged to them. If she didn't go along with them, she would continue to pay dearly for it.

Then the last thing they expected happened. Lisa's training went into effect. Julie didn't bother to warn them or threaten them. She made no attempt to make it a fair fight. She just used every dirty trick Lisa had managed to teach her, and when both men were down and no longer able to fight back, she leaned down close to their heads.

She spoke to the one who was rubbing his eyes, hoping the blindness wasn't permanent. "That was just a start of what I will be doing to you. When you can see again, keep in mind that next time I do it to you, it will leave you blind for the rest of your life."

She moved to the second man. "You are never going to make a complete recovery. That broken kneecap of yours is never going to be what it once was. I think your football career is over. You'll probably walk with a limp for the rest of your life. That karate kick you tried on me was incredibly sloppy."

She left them there, then left the frat house. She knew that by defending herself, her cover was already blown. At the same time though, she was sure they would come after her in different ways. Ways that would be easier to prove in court than rape. And that was what she was after now. First get them into court, then locked up in jail. There was no place like the general population of a prison to teach some college boys what rape was really all about.

As soon as she got back to her room, she called Larry to inform him of the latest development. She explained what happened.

"From the sound of it," he said when she finished, "you have more than just a little Lisa in you, don't you?"

"If you mean you think we're a lot alike, Larry," she answered, "you are right. At least when it comes to crap like this."

"I was thinking more of the lack of patience. Are you sure there was no way you could have finessed those guys? It was your first time dealing with them."

"There wasn't. They were spiking my drinks, and they caught me feeding them back to them. Their plan was for the two of them that grabbed me to force me outside, rape me, then leave me for the rest of them to do with whatever they chose to do to me. I wasn't about to try to finesse my way out of that."

"Now that I know the details, I have to agree with you. It's best you didn't give them the chance to do anything. But we'll have to be doubly careful now."

"I think it'll take more than being careful. Those guys will be looking for revenge now. It's highly unlikely that we'll ever be in the position to go after them on just a rape charge. We'll have to figure out a way to prove what they are doing when they come after me, so we can get them on assault charges."

"The problem with that, Julie, is that it puts you over the top when it comes to the amount of danger you're in now. So I think the best thing we can do is get you the hell off this campus and find another approach to this case."

"You might be right, Larry, but let's give it a couple of more days. If nothing else, we can at least get some idea of how they're going to respond to us that way. I know they'll be looking for some way to get to me, but they are just a bunch of college kids. They might have the bodies of adult men, but inside they're still just a bunch of spoiled rotten boys."

"Okay, but you better be damn careful, even if they are just boys. You are more important than this case."

Not only was she more important than the case she was working on, she was in more danger than she could have realized. The boys in the guilty frat house weren't all boys. Two of them were followers of Wisconsin's Governor Rod Desadist. One was still healthy and ready to do his bidding, whatever that might be. The other was currently lying in a hospital bed, his eyes bandaged until his sight returned.

The men/boys were among a few others planted in the college to assist with the preparation of future raids that Dasadist had planned for this and several other Minnesota schools and colleges close to the Wisconsin border.

Added to the danger the males provided, there were two sorority sisters where Julie was staying who were Dasadist plants. Both of them were fervent followers of him. They were devout members of an evangelical cult who constantly preached the mythology that men always were and still are intended to strictly rule over women. They were also taught that women who resisted what men wanted, were daughters of the devil and must be hated. So they too, were a danger for Julie. They couldn't hurt her head on, but they weren't at all above shoving a knife in her back.

As did all of Dasadist's followers, the various degenerates who he had scattered around in schools and colleges all had one thing in common. They feared books. Some of them were terrified of books. Books contained what was for them the single most evil thing ever devised by mankind. Ideas! For them, any kind of an original thought was unimaginable.

So it was with total enthusiasm that they planned their attack on her. She was simply too suspicious to be allowed to continue her time at the school. If she had the ability to defeat the two frat boys, who were so big and strong, she had to be someone special. And that could be someone against their book banning leader, Dasadist.

The two sorority sisters followed her then, the first time she went out alone. It surprised them when she met up with a man at the local pizza joint. It was bad enough that they were already jealous of her, and the fact that she was so beautiful. What made their feelings toward her even worse was the fact that the man she met was so handsome. He also looked to them to be a real man's man. Someone not to be messed with. At least not without adequate support. So when they called the frat boys to tell them where Julie and Larry could be found, they warned them to be sure there were plenty of them.

They didn't listen. There were only ten men who came to join up with the two women. They then made the mistake of waiting in a group for the two to finish eating their pizza.

Larry and Julie knew right away that the bunch hanging around outside were trouble. So they made a few calls. Mack and Lisa were too far away to be of any help, but Roy and Wanda were just leaving an interview only forty minutes away. Close enough for Larry and Julie to wait for their arrival. They quickly became the slowest pizza eaters in that county.

It didn't take long for the waiting to start to bug the small mob of would be enforcers to get restless. They began milling around on the sidewalk in front of the place, often blocking the door when someone wanted to get in. Before long the manager of the place noticed. When he realized the crowd outside was waiting for the two inside, he approached their table.

"If those people out there are waiting for you," he said, directing his words to Larry, "I'd much prefer it if you'd eat up and go out there and see what they want. They're chasing customers away."

"If that's the case," Larry told him, "why don't you go out there and tell them to move on. We aren't blocking your customers from coming in."

"Maybe not. But I'm sure you're the reason that they are out there. I don't want any trouble, so it will be best if you leave."

"Not until we finish the pizza. We came in for a quiet meal and we fully intend to finish our quiet meal. In here."

"Look. I want to be fair about this. So we'll pack up the rest of your pizza for you, and you can take it home with you. There'll be no charge for it."

"If you are so concerned about those people out there," Larry told him, "I think you should call the police. They will deal with the situation."

"If I do that, then I'll have a constant problem with the college crowd. That's where the bulk of my business is. So please be reasonable and leave now."

Julie answered him this time. "In just a short time, a couple of friends of ours will be here. We'll leave when they get here. In the meantime, bring us the bill for the pizza. We bloody well don't want anything free from the likes of you."

"You're acting like my offer is an insult. It just was the offer of a peaceful solution."

"No, you're just too chickenshit to stand up for your own rights, not to mention ours. So bring us the bill, then stay the hell away from this table. We'll leave when the time is right for us to leave."

He wisely brought them the bill, then left them alone. A long fifteen minutes later Roy and Wanda arrived. Larry and Julie left the remaining pizza on their table and joined them outside. The four of them walked out to the parking lot and motioned for the ten men and two women to follow them. Roy was the one who talked to them.

"I know you all think you are going to teach us some kind of lesson," he said, a smirk filling his face. "But the trouble is, you are out numbered. There's four of us. That means that Larry and I each only need to kick the shit out of three of you guys, and Wanda and Julie only need to take two of you out. You two women don't count. You'll be knocked out of this contest by these two ladies with us so fast that you won't even know there's been a fight. And when it's all done we'll be pressing charges against you for assault, so you'll be going to jail as soon as you get out of the hospital."

One of the guys decided he should be the leader of his group and start what they were there to do. Which was to teach these mouthy people a lesson. It was time for them to understand that they didn't belong at this college.

Roy was the closest to him, so he decided to attack him first. Roy was a good four inches shorter and fifty pounds lighter. What the self appointed leader didn't know was the fact that Roy was far stronger and twice as fast. He didn't even have to dodge any blows. His fist took out the man before he could even lift his arms to swing them.

One of the two witless ladies went after Wanda, who really wasn't in the mood for this kind of nonsense. The witless one found herself sitting on the ground with a broken nose before she realized she'd been hit by Wanda.

A big men went after Julie. He was totally confident in his ability to control her, so he left himself wide open in many areas. She picked the most sensitive one, and buried her boot between his legs. He doubled over, sank to his knees, then puked his guts out.

Larry didn't wait to be attacked. one at a time he lit into the nearest three guys. They found themselves on the ground even before they had time to get confused. That's when the police arrived.

That was no contest either. When IDs were shown and Larry explained why they were hired to be there, the twelve were arrested. Two of the twelve were identified as the men who raped their client, and were kept in custody.

So it seemed as though they they'd quickly solved a serious case. There was one problem though. As a result of all that happened, Dasadist learned a lot more than what they wanted him to know about Refuge Rescuers.

One good thing did come out of it though. Julie learned, with no doubts now, how important her physical training was. She also understood now why Lisa considered her knowledge of down and dirty street fighting to be every bit as important as all of her traditional defense training. So even though she was somewhat disappointed that her first undercover job ended so quickly, she had every intention of being more than ready for the next one.

CHAPTER 14

Within hours of Mack and Refuge Rescuers's second book titled A Search For Jasper was banned by Governor Dasadist, Shanty Lucas called Mack.

"You know," she told him, "that useless son of a bitch really pisses me off constantly. But when he bans books as good as yours, I get so angry I could spit nails. We need to find a way to get at him right now. Something that will drive him about as close to crazy as we can."

"One thing I'm sure that would drive him nuts is if we could get a lot more of the banned books into the hands of the people he wants to keep from reading them. But he's got control of all the public school libraries, and most of the other libraries in Wisconsin. Same with the universities and colleges there that aren't totally private."

"I'd still like to figure out a way to get the banned books out there. There must be some way. I'd be willing to spend whatever it takes to just give those books away, if we could figure out a way to do it."

It only took a couple of moments for Mack's memory to kick in. He became a serious reader shortly after he learned how. As a kid he devoured every kind of animal and wildlife book he could get his hands on. The problem was, he read so much it often was difficult for Ben to keep him supplied with books. That's when he discovered the local libraries book mobile.

Once a week it stopped for three hours within a half mile of home. Mack rarely missed one of its stops. He soon got to know the driver of it, and after a couple of months the driver let him exceed the normal limit on the books he could check out each time. It was something that gave Mack the chance to do even more reading than he otherwise would have been able to do.

The trouble was, as he saw it, it wouldn't only be expensive, it would be near impossible to provide a service like that in a state ruled by Dasadist. If they tried to distribute any kind of books there, not to mention banned books, they'd get arrested. He decided to tell Shanty about it anyway.

After he explained to her about book mobiles, he said, "but even if we could do it without getting arrested, we'd still be pretty limited to the number of books we could distribute. And then we'd have the hassle of checking books out and back in."

"To start with, the money's no problem. The book mobiles don't need to be new, so instead of just one or two, we could put together a whole fleet of them. We'll search out school buses ready for retirement, rebuild them, and equip them with whatever it takes to turn them into book mobiles."

"But who would you get to drive them? You know there's bound to be trouble with the Dasadist bunch."

"The only people I know with the courage and the ability to do it are you and the rest of of Refuge Rescuers. I'm sure you will be able to find some others who will be suitable to do the job."

"There's still the problem of the book checkouts, Shanty. Most people aren't going to want their names associated with banned books. That's something that could come back and haunt them somewhere down the line."

"I'm well aware of that. That's why I think we should just give away the banned books. We'd have to limit them to maybe five books per visit per person, but we'd get a hell of a lot of books out there that way."

"What about royalties to the writers?"

"I'll pay them, Mack. And the most popular books, I might be able to convince the people involved to let my publishing company do the printing. The same with at least some of the books now out of print because of Dasadist. I know there are other problems we'll need to deal with too, but I know you well enough to be confident we can solve all of them as they show up."

"One more thing, Shanty. At the rate Dasadist is banning books, we may not have room for much else."

"You're probably right about that. So let's just fill the book mobiles with the banned books. That way we won't have any checkout problems. We'll give away up to five books per person per visit. And whether you like it or not, Mack, every one of those book mobiles is going to feature your two books. I am also going to publish both of them as audio books, and they will be available free too."

"One finale thing. We are going to have to figure out some kind of legal protection for the people working the mobiles. Or else we'll all be in jail almost as fast as we start."

"I have an idea for that. Because of who I am, or I should say, because I am as rich as I am, I know a lot of people in the right places. They'll never be friends the way you are, but I do have enough influence to pull something off. In the meantime, have Sue start researching Wisconsin laws for some kind of thing or another we can use to help our cause. It does't matter how obscure it is either."

"Well, Shanty, we do have one law on our side that about everyone knows about. It's called the first amendment to the constitution. He can maybe keep some books out of schools and libraries, but he can't ban them entirely. So get some of your lawyers working on that."

"I will. And I will also have them ready to bail out anyone who gets arrested. They will also, I am sure, get the paperwork started to file any lawsuits that might be needed. I've got enough money to keep the State of Wisconsin tied up in court for a very long time."

"Well, I guess we've covered about everything about the idea of banned book mobiles we can right now, which leaves the question. Do you actually want to go ahead with the idea now, or would you like to think it over for a while?"

"If I was talking to anyone else about it other than you, Mack, I'd say I think I'll wait. But because it is you I'm talking to, all I can do is ask you what you think about the idea. I need to know that before I can make a decision."

"I can't tell you what to do," Mack explained. "You know that. The plan will be expensive, time consuming, and might fail. Then again, Lisa and I will contribute our share of the money and as much time it takes to do everything possible to make it work. And finally, it damn sure would be a good way to stick it to Dasadist. So if it was only me, I'd do it. But for you, I think I'm asking way too much."

"I don't think so, Mack. You, your family, and your friends have accomplished so many things that others were afraid to try. That thing you did a few years ago to improve nursing homes. You didn't solve the problem, but you damn sure did manage to help a lot of older people. And what you started, Places Of Refuge, is still helping older people. It could have ended in disaster, but it didn't. I think this idea has an even better chance of working. So let's give it our best shot. It's time to raise some real hell."

"Okay, Shanty, that's exactly what we'll do then. I'll go over it with Lisa tonight, and that way we'll have a proposal for everyone at breakfast tomorrow."

"Good. In the meantime, I'll put people to work on everything we need to do to turn some buses into banned book mobiles."

Lisa's reaction to the new plan was all positive. She stayed up with Mack putting together a presentation for everyone in the morning. They were both pleased with it when they went to bed that night, and still felt good about it when they got to Ben and Theresa's for breakfast in the morning, only a few minutes after Roy and Wanda got there. They got almost as much satisfaction from seeing the surprised look of Roy's face when they did.

They enjoyed it even more when Wanda spoke up right away. "Okay, Roy," she told him, "they're here early. That usually means something important must be going on. So don't pick on them until you know what it is."

Roy laughed. "Okay, Wanda, I'll wait."

Mack laughed too. "It's okay," he said. "Lisa made up for having to get here early this morning, sometime in the early hours this morning."

Lisa just shook her head at Mack, but she couldn't hide her grin.

Ben, who knew Mack as well as anyone could, knew from his demeanor that he had something serious to talk about. "You want to eat now, Mack?" he asked, "or wait until after you talk?"

"I'll eat after, Dad. Sometimes it's hard to explain the details with your mouth full of food."

Ben and Theresa went ahead then with the early preparations for the meal, but only coffee was served until Mack finished telling them about the book mobiles. The idea was met with complete acceptance by everyone. There was one big question though. Jules Sapphire, who was a guest at the breakfast, was the one who asked it.

"What you proposed, Mack," he said, "sounds like a great idea. What's got me wondering though, is who the hell's paying for it? It's going to be one costly venture."

"That, I'm afraid, is confidential," Mack answered. "And it's going to stay that way."

"But if you want us to take part in it, don't you think we have a right to know who's sponsoring it?"

"No, I most certainly don't. It could put that persons life in immediate danger."

"What about those of us who are actually out there doing the job? What about our lives?"

"None of this will start until we know it can be done reasonably safe. It also will be done strictly on a volunteer basis. We won't be asking anyone to do it."

Jules frowned at Mack's answer, but knew he had no choice but to accept it. He also knew that he was likely the only one who didn't have any idea who was furnishing the money behind the idea.

While Jules was stewing over the idea of who was supplying the money, Mack was beginning to wonder if he should have even so much as mentioned the book mobile idea around Jules. The man was beginning to look like a wild card. Something they definitely didn't need in this deck, when what they needed to make it work was stability.

In order to achieve that stability, they all went into training on how to handle any of Dasadist's men when they interfered with the distribution of the banned books once the mobile units were ready. On the third day of training, Lisa watched Donna get surprised and taken down. The man quickly moved over her and wrapped his hands around her throat. He let her go immediately, but the act reminded Lisa of a weapon she was now sure any woman in one of the units should carry.

The weapon consisted of a switch blade knife, with a blade that popped straight out, rather than swing out. She had also designed a special pocket for the knife that could be installed in the waist band of either pants or a skirt. So each of the women who would be riding in a unit was supplied with it. They practiced until they could quickly pull out the knife, which was sharpened to a surgical edge, no matter what position they were in.

They were also each provided with the handgun of their choice. In Wisconsin, Desadist had passed a law making the open carry of any kind of gun legal, so they didn't need any special permits for them.

Once they had them, they spent enough time at the firing range to be far above average in accuracy. Wanda was their instructor, because she could handle a gun better than anyone else.

As they'd done before, the men as well as the women all reviewed their defense training, and then went through intensive training from the street fighters Lisa brought in. It was a relentless regimen of training, but by the time the mobile units were ready, so was everyone from Refuge Rescuers who would be operating them.

Finally, because of Shanty's influence, each of them was hired as United States deputy Marshal. Sue also managed to go online and apply for special Wisconsin permits to sell and distribute books. The clerk who issued the permits had no idea what he was doing, but they were legal anyway.

CHAPTER 15

Larry and Julie took the first mobile unit out when it was ready. To test the reaction, they picked a small college campus in Wisconsin, not far from the Minnesota border. When they parked across the street from the building the school's library was located in, the initial response to their signs for free banned books was a tepid at best. Only a few students and one teacher stopped in the first two hours.

Those who stopped though, were surprised at the number of books they had. They were even more surprised by the fact that they were all free. And they all loved the idea that they were all books that were banned by Dasadist. He was not at all popular on this college campus. The only people there, be they students or teachers, who actually liked him were a few ultra conservative business majors and their teachers.

It wasn't until after the lunch break that things began to change. Word about the unit spread rapidly while everyone ate, and there quickly was a lineup waiting for the chance to see and select books. By four o'clock that afternoon they were forced to close it up and head for home. The shelves were nearly empty of books.

There were soon four units out roaming Wisconsin, stopping at colleges, libraries, and high schools before Dasadis learned about them. He went a bit of his usual crazy when he did. It went way beyond his imagination that there were people who would so blatantly defy him. He was the governor. He ruled. What he said was law. No matter what means he needed to use, those people must be stopped.

He sent out his Fahrenheit- now swat team members, in groups of ten, to put a stop to what he considered a bunch of filthy law breakers. Mack and Lisa were operating the first unit they reached. It was crowded inside, with a lineup outside waiting to get in when they arrived.

Three of them forced their way in. The leader screamed at Mack, "This stops now. Get all these people the fuck out of here. You are officially shutdown."

Mack stood up and leaned into his face. "Not hardly, asshole. We have permits issued by the state of Wisconsin to do this." He waved at Lisa to come over to him. "On top of that, we are both US deputy marshals, so we can and will enforce those permits. That means you will now, and I mean now, take your bunch of morons and get the hell out of here. If you don't, we damn well will arrest the bunch of you."

"You don't seem to notice," the man argued, "that there are ten of us and only two of you."

"Maybe, but the two of us will near kill the three of you before any of those toy cops out there can so much as make a move. When they do, we will arrest all of them. I have no doubt that the men here to get their books will be glad to assist us. You will all then be charged with assault and attempted assault. In your case, when you get out of the hospital, I will personally see to it that you end up in federal prison."

Mack's speech flustered the man to the point he couldn't make a decision as to what to do next. While he worked at it, Mack took him by the elbow and led him outside. His two helpers followed.

Mack stood watch on the ten swat team men while people continued to flow through the mobile unit. They all went in empty handed, but few came out with less than five books. The swat people left after a couple of hours.

Before the day was over, all of the other mobile units were threatened by swat team members. None of them were among what you might call even somewhat bright, so the routine was much the same as it was with Mack and Lisa.

There was one exception. The bunch who went after the mobil Roy and Wanda were in. Because he was older than any of them, they were sure he would be easy to intimidate. They tried mightily to do so. Like most people who didn't know him, they grossly underestimated Roy.

The leader of that group of swats forced his way into the unit, then jammed his finger into Roy's chest. "You will shut this goddamn rig down now," he demanded.

Roy looked at his finger, then into his eyes. "Move it," was all he said.

The man laughed. "No way in hell."

Roy took a deep breath. "Yes. Now."

The man instead tried to push his finger deeper into Roy's chest. Before he was even aware Roy was moving, his finger was broken to the point his bone was poking out through his skin. As the pain hit him, he was escorted outside.

"Time for you *boys* to be moving on," Roy told them. "We are here legally, so we aren't about to leave. I don't really want to break anymore bones, but if you don't go, I will be forced to."

The swat team wanted to push things further, but by then they were surrounded by a couple dozen people who were there to get books. None of them looked like they were about to give up the chance to do so. The swat bunch left.

That night, when Dasadist learned that everyone one of his swat team groups was defeated and run off that day, he knew that if he was going to maintain control of his state he had to stop the banned book giveaway. No matter what it took. And he was sure now, that violence would have to play a big part in it.

The thought of what he hoped to do, with all the pain and blood, got him super excited then. So he asked his mistress, congress woman Maggie Baylor Blue to come spend the night with him. Knowing though, that she alone wouldn't fulfill all his needs, he also called his good friend, Ted Crustiest. They would share Maggie, and that way could watch each other perform. Because for them, the performance was the most important part. For her, the only thing about it that was unfair was the fact there were only two of them. She would have liked it to be at least four more.

Dasadist had his own disappointment about the deal. He missed the past when he could watch someone being tortured first. There was nothing that excited him more than screams of agony and lots of blood.

Crustiest didn't care much about how it happened. He just did it to her until he dribbled a little bit on her, then fell asleep where he wet the bed. Dasadist thought he was her king then, but as soon as he fell asleep, she invited both of his bodyguards into bed with her.

In the morning, she told Dasadist that they were only there to protect him from her damaging him. He believed her. After all, he was a man among men. How could it possibly be otherwise. Besides, he now had a lot of killing to be planned.

It was something he still needed to do carefully. Even his loyal followers weren't quite ready for the wholesale amount of murder he wanted committed. It would be different, he was sure, when he was president and in complete control, but for now he had to be careful, and limit the number of people murdered at any one time.

The next decision was easy. Who should die first. The people of Refuge Rescuers of course. But before that, he knew he needed to call Shanty Lucas. The best snipers were expensive, and he was sure she would be happy to contribute to their cost. Especially when it came to killing those Rescuers bunch. So he called her.

She let him know that she was delighted that he did. She also recorded their conversation. The main reason for doing it was so when she gave Mack the information it was accurate. But she also did it as evidence to use against Dasadist in the future.

As soon as she concluded her conversation with him, she called Mack. "I hate having to tell you this," she told him without any preliminaries, "but Desadist is planning on hiring professional snipers to kill all of you guys. I promised to help pay for them, but I fully intend to make him wait for the money."

This was not news Mack wanted to hear. Especially since there was a female riding in each of the mobile book units. Mack was old fashioned enough to be more concerned about them than he was about the men. "Did he tell you who he was going to go after first? If we knew, I could make sure there was two men working it. I don't at all like the idea of snipers coming after us. I doubly hate if there are women involved."

"Given the kind of man you are, Mack, I'm not at all surprised by that. He said he hadn't decided. He thought it would probably work the best if he let the snipers decide that."

"What do you think about this? Should we stop passing out the books for a while? At least until we get a better picture of what Desadist is going to do next."

"I do. If you keep on doing it, and you pull the women out of the units, you will, without a doubt, have a revolution on your hands. Especially from Lisa. And even though I understand where you're coming from when you worry about the females first, she does have her side of it. The truth is, if something happened to you it would be just as devastating to her as it would be if something happened to her was to you."

"Okay, we'll hold off on the book distribution until we learn more about what Desadist is planning."

Rather than wait for their normal breakfast meeting, Mack called for one late that afternoon. Everyone made it there, including Jules Sapphire, who had spent the day riding with Larry and Julie while they distributed the free banned books at a community college in Wisconsin.

He spoke up as soon as Mack explained the latest problem. "One thing I didn't tell you guys about my time in the service when you interviewed me, is that I was a sniper."

"If we were planning on killing Desadist and his men, the fact that you know how to be one would be a big help. But what we're up against is the opposite. The snipers are out there to kill us."

"Actually, there isn't that big a difference as far as how my experience can help. Because of it, I know where one is most likely to position himself to make the kill. If, for a few days we just send out one unit and I'm along, there's a good chance I'll be able to take out any sniper or snipers that might be waiting for you."

"The problem with that is, they won't know for sure where we'll be. We could use up a lot of days before we connect."

"Not if I tell them where you'll be. I know several of the guys who are still with Dasadist. I can always inform them on what you're doing. We can take it from there."

"I don't know. You'll be sticking your neck out a long way. It won't take them long to figure out that you are the one who set them up."

"That's true, but I figure by then we will have taken out at least three, maybe as many as four, of their snipers. That should make them stop and think about what they can and cannot do."

"I guess it's worth a try," Mack agreed. "The thing now is, who's going to be the decoys in the unit?"

Lisa immediately answered him. "I thought it would be you and me, Mack. We can't hardly ask anyone else to do it."

"You sure as hell can," Ben told them. "You all promised that I would have my chance to help in this fight against those book banners. I think this is the perfect place for me to help."

"Are you sure you want to do this, Dad?" Mack asked. "I don't see you as someone who would be at all anxious to shoot anyone. Not even a sniper."

"Anxious no, but willing, yes. The thing is, all the crap the Republicans keep doing has got to be stopped. This is something you and everyone here is doing something about. I just want to help. Given my age, it's better that I'm the decoy than you or Lisa. You both have too much to live for. I've already had a pretty full life."

"I agree with Ben," Roy said. "You and Lisa are too young to be the decoys. I'm going to ride with Ben on this one."

Two rather shocked women shook their heads as their faces filled with the shock they felt. Theresa was also close to tears. The man who filled her life with joy, the man she loved more than life itself, had just volunteered to do something that could get him killed. Everything in her wanted to protest what he'd just done. But she knew she'd be wrong in doing it.

Wanda took the opposite approach. ""It's fine for the two of you to want to do this, but one person looking for the sniper or snipers isn't enough. Since I'm the best shot of any of us, I'm going to be with Jules when we set this thing up. And we're not having any debate about it."

There was no further discussion about who would or wouldn't be directly involved. Not even Lisa argued the point, even though she still wanted to be in the book unit when it went out.

CHAPTER 16

Wanda and Jules arrived a full hour before the book mobile. Their trap was being set at a private college with its own campus, so they were able to watch the movement of people enough to spot anyone acting suspicious.

In the center of the campus a century old catholic church was the most dominant building. An old fashioned bell tower rose high above it, so it was naturally the place they suspected the most for harboring a sniper.

Watching the tower with binoculars, it didn't take long before they spotted the sniper. He was watching the campus with his own pair of binoculars. An AR15 lay on the floor next to him. A high powered sniper rifle rested on the tripod in front of him.

They were now faced with a dilemma. How to stop him without shooting him before he started shooting someone else. Jules thought he should go inside the church and climb up the tower. Wanda wasn't too found of the idea, but agreed to it because she was sure she could distract the sniper if he appeared to be going after Jules.

Their plan went well, until Jules got close to the top of the tower. Something alerted the sniper to Jules, and he picked up his AR15 and turned to see what it was that he heard. Wanda didn't hesitate. She put a bullet into the heart of the sniper's rifle, and he dropped it.

That's when they got their surprise. A second gunman came into Wanda's view. He aimed his AR15 in Jules's direction and fired twice. Wanda now had no choice but to shoot back. She quickly shot the man in both shoulders, completely disabling him. The first sniper then picked up the second sniper's rifle and started a rapid fire in her direction. She ended it with a perfect shot into his kneecap. He went down hard.

As soon as he fell, Jules appeared in the tower. The man who shot at him had apparently missed him completely. He waved at Wanda, and made motions for her to call the police. Because they were in Wisconsin, and the two men she'd just shot were working for the governor, it was close to the last thing she wanted to do. But she knew she had no choice.

The local police, most of whom were conservative republicans, were slow ing getting there. An ambulance had already arrived by then, and the two snipers were already patched up and ready to be taken to the hospital. The lead cop was just about to ask them a few questions when Ben and Roy got there in the book mobile. The cop shook his head in total disgust when he saw them.

Before he could do or say anything though, several shots rang out. There were two more snipers. One was on top of the auditorium, and the other was on the roof of the library. Two cops and Ben went down with the first round of firing.

The cops who were not wounded returned fire, but were ineffective. Jules was much closer with his shots, but the two snipers left little of themselves open as targets. For Roy, there was little he could do to stop them. He was too busy with Ben, trying desperately to stop the flow of blood from the bullet hole in his leg.

Wanda didn't have any chance of a shot at either of the two snipers who had everyone pretty much pinned down now. As she watched them, she realized her only chance would be from a completely open spot in grassy courtyard they were in. She also knew that if she tried to take them out from there, the odds of her making it were not good.

Taking a deep breath, she ran for her chosen spot anyway. When she reached it, she did the fastest shooting of her life. The sniper on the library was so shocked by what she did that he moved his head up some to get a serious look at what she was doing. It was a fatal mistake. She put a perfect round in his forehead.

Every bit as shocked by her actions as everyone else, Jules only hesitated for a second before following Wanda. He managed to squeeze off a quick shot at the last sniper only a moment before he was about to put one in Wanda. It didn't kill him. Instead, it stood him up. He lost his footing on the steep roof, and screamed as he fell to the ground.

The medics from the first ambulance ignored the three snipers still alive at that point, and concentrated on Ben. As soon as they got him patched up enough to transport him, they loaded him into the ambulance. With sirens blaring and lights flashing, they took him to the hospital. Roy rode with him.

The cops who were shot weren't as serious, but they were taken care of right away too. That meant the snipers were not in the best of shape by the time they got to the hospital. Their condition had deteriorated enough, so that none of the three still living could even begin to answer any questions.

The cops were anything but pleased by what had gone down, but there was no way they could call the shooting Wanda and Jules did anything but self-defense. Even so, the cops strongly suggested that they stay out of Wisconsin in the future.

They agreed to do that, but insisted on checking on Ben before they left the state. He was in surgery when they got to the hospital. The bullet in his leg went deep into the muscle in his left thigh, and the doctors were in the process of removing it. Wanda and Roy sweated it out as they waited for the doctors to complete the operation. Jules was less concerned about Ben. All that he had on his mind was better ways to go after Desadist.

He tried to talk to Wanda and Roy about it, but they put him off until the doctors finally told them about Ben. Once they did, and were assured that he would fully recover from his wound, they made arrangements to have him transferred to the Kingsburg hospital by ambulance. Roy rode with him on the trip, and Wanda drove the book mobile back.

Theresa was waiting for Ben when he arrived. She took his hand and held it while they moved him into his room. He was more than happy to see her when he finally opened his eyes after he was settled in his hospital bed. The kiss she gave him was gentle, but telling.

Because they all knew and understood what an ordeal he'd just been through, they stayed in the waiting room until he felt up to more company than Theresa. Mack was the first one he asked to see.

"I think," he told Mack, "that Desadist has gotten real serious about stopping your book mobiles. There were four snipers in that attack. We were lucky we weren't all shot."

"You're right about that. There was some luck involved. But having Wanda there was more than luck. She took three of the snipers out. She tried to not kill any of them, but had no choice on the last one. The problem right now though, is the fact that Roy is upset with her.

She put herself at great risk, trying to take out those last two snipers. He thinks she pushed it too far. Maybe now, all of you will better understand why I sometimes get upset with Lisa. It really is hard to watch the woman you love put herself in danger."

"We all understand better than what you might think, Mack. But let's leave that discussion for another day. Right now. Roy and Wanda are who I'd like to talk to next."

Mack left Ben and sent Wanda and Roy into see him. He knew that Ben would need rest after his visit with them, so he and Lisa left the hospital. They were hungry, and because neither one of them was in the least bit in the mood for cooking, they decided to stop for a burger and fries before going home.

They both wanted a quiet meal alone. As much as they could enjoy and appreciate other people, all they wanted at that moment was to eat a good burger and not even think about putting any effort in a conversation with other people. Just being alone together was all they wanted or needed. So they decided to eat at a sports bar out on the four lane they rarely went to. The food was adequate, and they were far less likely to see someone they knew there than they would somewhere closer to town or in town.

They were wrong. Shortly after they were served their bacon cheeseburgers and fries, three Minnesota Highway Patrol cars stopped, and the officers came inside the bar. As soon as they saw Lisa and Mack, they decided to join them. Two of the cops used chairs already at their table, and the third cop took a chair from another table. He moved it to the table close to Lisa.

"We are both tired," Mack told the patrol men. "So don't expect much of anything in the way of conversation from us. All we want right now is some peace and quiet."

"No problem," the patrolman closest to Lisa said. "Just having the company of this beautiful wife of yours will be enough." He pulled a french fry from her plate and pushed inside his mouth.

Lisa kept quiet, and left her objection to what he did to a simple dirty look. When he tried to take a second one, she grabbed his wrist. "If I wanted to share my meal with you, I would have told that I did. The thing is, I don't."

What she said didn't mean anything to him. He reached for another fry anyway. This time Mack, none too gently, grabbed his wrist and squeezed it as hard as he could. Then, rather than simply letting go of it, he pushed it away from her plate hard. Very hard.

"I think," Mack said, "it's time for the three of you to find your own table."

"So what the hell's with you?" the cop with the grab hands asked. "We were just trying to be friendly when we sat down here with you."

"That's fine, but you could have asked if we wanted company before you sat down. You didn't. I probably would have said yes if you would have asked, but now that you didn't, I'm saying no. We don't want you here at our table."

"If you don't like sitting with us," the cop snarled, "the two of you can move."

"We were sitting here when you came in. The table is ours. You are leaving it now."

"You know what," the now arrogant cop argued, "if you aren't careful, you are going to have to settle this with me outside."

That was all Lisa was prepared to listen to. She suddenly stood up, knocking her chair over as she did. She grabbed the cop by his shirt front, and leaning in close to his face said, "It's like this, Asshole, I'm not at all in the mood for your style of pure bullshit. And I'm just not in the mood for you. So you will move. Right now."

"We both know there's nothing you can do to make me do anything I don't want to, so you can back off with your threats. Not to mention, there ain't no way I can figure out why you're acting this way about a goddamn french fry."

'It's got nothing to do with my french fries. It has everything to do with your arrogant attitude. You sat down without asking, you comment about having the company of Mack's beautiful wife were enough. Then you think you can start eating my food without even asking. Something I would never do with you is share a meal or anything else on earth. So I will only tell you one more time. Move!"

The cop opened his mouth to argue. Then his eyes met hers. He stood up and walked away from Mack and Lisa. The other two cops followed him. They sat at a table on the other side of the room.

Mack and Lisa managed to finish eating without further interruption. But before they emptied their beer mugs, eight highway department men came in the bar. Six of them were wearing highway department shirts that showed the results of a days hard work in the sun. The other two wore suits, and appeared to be foremen of some type or another. They, far more than the working men, started to eye Lisa real closely. She knew what they were doing, but chose to ignore them.

Everything stayed peaceful until Mack and Lisa decided to leave the bar. The problem started because in order to get out of the bar, they needed to walk close by the table where the highway department people were sitting. As they went by the table, one of the foremen types suddenly grabbed Lisa and yanked her toward him. Because she was off balance, she landed in his lap.

She was out of it in an instant, and spinning around to face him she slammed the side of her fist into his temple. He and his chair landed on the floor with a resounding thud. He didn't get up. But the other seven at the table did. Lisa glared at them.

"Be best if all of you sit down," Mack told them. "Unless you are all in the mood for a night in jail. As for as your friend on the floor, if he doesn't wake up pretty quick, you might call him an ambulance or something."

"You had no call to hit him like that," the second, still standing, foreman type said. "He didn't do anything to you that justifies hitting him."

"He put his hands on me." She looked at the seven, one at a time. "Any of the rest of you want to try putting your hands on me?"

The men answered with a low grumble, but none of them answered her directly. Instead, they started to leave their table and move around Mack and Lisa. It was obvious they had no intention of letting them leave.

Mack sighed, shook his head, then turned to Lisa. "If you will take out the three between us and the door," he told her, "then I'll see what I can do with the other four." Mack knew that it was unlikely that he and Lisa could beat all seven of them, but he also know that before they went down, the condition of them would leave them wishing they'd never started any trouble.

Then they got a pleasant surprise. They had reinforcements. The three highway patrolmen joined Mack and Lisa. The cop who had aggravated them earlier put his hand on Mack's shoulder, then smiled.

"It's like this," he said. "These two people are good friends of ours. All they wanted was to eat a simple meal in peace and quiet. Now they want to go home. So unless the bunch of you want to go to jail, you will all sit back down." He used his foot to nudge the guy on the floor who was coming awake. "That includes you." He turned to Mack. "First off, I am sorry about earlier. I was out of line. Second, you two can go ahead and leave now. If there are any complaints, it will be me filing against them, not them against you."

Mack and Lisa were quiet until they got home. She was in and out of the shower before they talked. He found it a bit disconcerting when she joined him out on their deck wearing a pair of well worn, form fitting short shorts and a light blouse within a couple of washings from being see-through. The top three buttons were left open, and the way her nipples were standing out, it was obvious that she wasn't wearing a bra.

As it always did when she dressed that way, just for him, it left him wondering how he could be so lucky. So he told her how she made him feel. "You are you know, Lisa, beyond beautiful. The way you look right now, sitting out here with me, makes me feel like the luckiest man alive. I have to tell you too, that knowing who you are inside is even better than what I can see, makes me love you far beyond any dreams I might ever have had."

Lisa, whose smile said she was on the verge of laughing, stood and moved to his chair. "Does that mean I can sit on your lap?" Without getting an answer, that's exactly what she did. She laughed before she kissed him and moved his hand inside her shirt. "I know you'll want more right now, but will it be okay if we just sit here like this for a while? I've kind of been thinking, since Roy told us, about what Wanda did when she went after those snipers. I've done things like that, and so have you and Roy. Sometimes it scares me. So if you don't mind, I'd like it if you could just hold on to me for a while. We can make love later."

"I think I would hold you forever if I could, Lisa."

"That's good. I'm kind of wondering though, how Roy is feeing about Wanda right now? You and he are a lot alike, and you've been known to get pretty upset with me a time or two."

"I have no doubt that he is plenty upset. But he loves her and cares so deeply about her that they will have made peace with each other before they go to bed tonight."

And they did. Before Roy even got the chance to say anything about the reckless moves she made going after the snipers, she settled it with a short explanation.

"I know I upset you, Roy. I knew before I did it that I would upset you. But there were two snipers up on that roof. Shooting at all of us. You were busy trying to save Ben's life. Both of you could have been killed. I couldn't have let that happen. If I did, then my life meant nothing. If you died that way my life could never again have any meaning. So it's simple. I didn't have a choice. I didn't do it because I'm brave or because I wanted to. I did it because you mean more to me, Roy, than life itself does."

Roy knew then, that he could do nothing other than accept what she said. So he took her in his arms and kissed her, telling her she was forgiven.

That left only one problem. Having Wanda forgiven or not, everyone involved in the war against book banning still couldn't help but wonder, "what was going to happen the next time one of them was caught in a similar situation."

CHAPTER 17

Rod Desadist was wondering much the same thing. But his wondering, of course, was dominated by a wish for a different outcome. He wasn't concerned about anyone's life other than his own. He, more than anything, wanted Mack and Lisa Thomas and everyone connected to them dead. They started out as a huge annoyance, but had proved to be an even bigger road block in his process toward becoming the president of the United States. They were even more of obstacle, at that time, than his major opponent in the race for the office, Donald Trump.

He decided that this time he would have his men go after them first and hit them hard. But since he wanted his men to catch them alone, or at least close to alone, he was sure twelve of his best men should be able to do the job. So that's the delegation he sent to Minnesota to specifically murder Mack and Lisa Thomas.

Shortly after the men were dispatched to do their job, he was having a conversation about it with his good friend, Ted Crustiest. Ted liked the idea of going after Mack and Lisa until they were dead. They were the leaders, and it was always best to kill the leaders. Unless he was a leader someone else might be after. In that case, going after leaders was grossly unfair. Either way, he was in a hurry to bring up another, what he considered just as important, subject he wanted to discuss with Desadist.

It took quite a while, and Crustiest's patience was wearing thin, when he finally got the chance to talk. "I don't think anyone's told you about this, Rod," he said to Desadist, "but there's a person of interest in that group we should have our men capture alive and bring directly to us. She'd be a real treat to have around here for while. Even Maggie will enjoy her. You know how she likes to lick her victims when they bleed."

"Yeah, well, maybe. But what's so special about this one? We can get lots of broads."

"She's special because she's really damn cute. And you know how we like them ten to twelve year olds when they're cute."

"True, but we've always gotten them when we wanted one. So what else is so special about this one?"

"Her name is Emma, by the way. She belongs to two of them Refuge Rescuers people. If we take her away from them, we'll be accomplishing two things at once. Getting some revenge with them people, but just as important, adding some real fun to our lives. Poking that little bitch will also be like poking that Lisa bitch. Something else I'd like to do before we kill her."

"So would I, Ted, so would I. The thing is though, it's more important for us to bring a stop to their trouble making. We need them out of the way so I can get on with my run for president. I'd hate to have to wait another four years to get his country into some kind of decent shape."

"I don't want to wait that long either. I'm looking forward to being vice president. One of the best things will be, I think, all the young stuff we'll be able to take out of the schools when we want to. And without any retribution. When you get all your new rules in place for the public schools, the pickings will be easier than even buying a gun is."

"You are right about that. Because with my rules, buying a gun in Wisconsin ain't no different than buying a gallon of milk. But enough of that. I agree that we should go after that Emma girl. You are going to have to be in charge of that one though. I'm too busy with leading the bunch going after the the Thomases, not to mention my more frequent public appearances."

"Yeah, you have been busy with those, haven't you. When are you going to have me start with my share of them?"

"I think it'll be best if you don't do any that are directly on my behalf until after the convention and we are both nominated."

What Dasadist didn't explain, was that Maggie Baylor Blue was his first real choice for vice president. A truth that Ted wasn't supposed to learn until he, Dasadist, had won the nomination.

That thought started to have an effect on him then. Something about Maggie often did that to him. But knowing he had a busy schedule for the rest of the day, he called his secretary into his office, rather than try to get Maggie to join him right away.

Totally ignoring Ted, he unzipped his pants as she joined him. He point to the open zipper. "Fix it," he said.

He'd forgotten she was new and not yet fully trained. So it was a shock to him when she tried to fix his zipper by closing it. He grabbed her arms and demanded, "Don't try to be funny. You know what I wanted and that wasn't it." He pushed her head down where he wanted it.

Being his secretary wasn't enough reason for Kelsey Real to do what he wanted. She didn't want her head there, and because she'd had extensive training in selfdefense, she was able to escape his grasp. She ran out of his office, picked up her purse and the device she'd used to record all of his conversations he'd had since she started working for him, and fled the building.

She went home, not knowing what else to do. To kill time, she played the recording of the conversations Desadist had the previous couple of days. Most of them conversations she'd never heard. It wasn't until she was listening to the conversation he just had with Ted Crustiest that something really got her full attention. Just the talk of killing someone wasn't it. She'd heard Dasadist talk that way before. It was much more who he was talking about. She knew Lisa Thomas. Lisa was an occasional instructor where she had gotten her defense training. She remembered Lisa because she taught some things other instructors were hesitant to do. With the most memorable thing being, don't ever be afraid of seriously hurting your attacker. Do whatever it takes to stop them, even if the injury to them results in permanent damage. And without saying it, Lisa made it clear that in most cases, she included death as an injury.

The threats sounded real enough, so Kelsey decided that she somehow needed to warn Lisa. But before she could, she needed to learn more about her. She not only didn't have any contact information for Lisa, she didn't know much of anything else about her either.

Kelsey was more computer savvy than most. She'd started to learn on her first computer at age three. So to find the information she wanted, she went online to see what she could learn. It didn't take her long to discover Lisa's connection with Refuge Rescuers. From there she read everything she could find about Refuge Rescuers and its people. It was all good, so she knew she had to provide a warning. Most especially since Dasadist and Crustiest had talked about kidnapping the young girl, Emma.

Kelsey wasn't sure how she wanted to approach Lisa on the subject, and after analyzing it near to death, she decided to just show up and talk to her the next day. It was Wednesday night, and when she woke up Thursday morning she was hesitant about going to see Lisa cold, the way she planned. So she used up the day fretting about it. It was Friday morning before she got herself together enough to pay Refuge Rescuers a visit.

CHAPTER 18

With the bulk of the stress over for the moment, from the book banning issues in Wisconsin, it felt real good to Mack to be able to wake up slow. He and Lisa only had a couple of rather simple cases to deal with that day, so he wasn't particularly surprised when she enticed him back to bed. What did surprise him though, was the leisurely way she extended their love making. It was well past time to eat breakfast with the family before she consented to leave the bed. That didn't matter though, because this morning there was no breakfast with the family. Ben was in the hospital, and that was their first stop. They kept their visit short though, because the doctors were worried about the number of visitors he was having. They worried he was getting too tired.

Lisa was close to Mack, holding his hand while they were there. All during the rest of the day, she would rest her hand on his arm or hold his hand at every chance she had. When they walked together anywhere that day, she walked close. One of their calls was out in the country, and after they completed it, she opened her blouse when they finished it and got back into Mack's truck. She wasn't wearing a bra, and made sure Mack noticed that fact.

He loved her dearly, and did enjoy what she was doing, but as close as they always were, he did wonder what she was up too. Showing that much affection constantly for a whole day was definitely something that wasn't normal. By the end of the day when they were on their way home, he knew something was going on. She wanted something, and his gut told him it was probably something he wouldn't like.

Normally, on a warm day of sunshine like this one, they would relax for a bit with a cold beer out on their deck. Not this night. As soon as they stepped inside the house, she wrapped her arms around him and kissed him with everything she had.

"I can't help it, Mack," she said, "but for some reason being with you all day today has got me totally turned on."

Without waiting for an answer, she took his hand and led him to their bedroom. There, she did her best to perform her sexiest striptease. When she finished shedding her clothes, she undressed him.

She gently pushed him down on the bed, then moved over him. He was ready for her, and she was turned on enough to be as wet as he'd ever seen her. Slowly, but with firm and urgent movements, she rode him. Every time either one of them grew close, she stopped long enough to kiss him.

When she finally relented, they exploded in unison. If anyone would have been outside, but close to their house, they would have easily heard their moans of pure pleasure. She moved off him and snuggled close. They were quiet for a while. Then she took a deep breath.

"I have something to ask you," she said."

He pulled away from her. The look he gave her wasn't pleasant. "I've been expecting that most of the day. So ask."

"It's no big deal or anything. But Saturday you and Kathy are going to take your monthly walk in the refuge aren't you?"

"Yes, but you already knew that. What's the real question?"

She hesitated before answering. When she did, her voice was real soft. "Well, Dale and I were thinking that since you and Kathy always have that time together, we might have some time together too."

"You two always have the same Saturday together that Kathy and I have. We just do different things. So what is it that you really want?"

"You're starting to sound upset, Mack, and I haven't even asked you for anything yet."

"No, Lisa, you haven't. But you have been setting me up for something since we went to bed last night. So whether I'm going to like it or not, it would be a damn good idea for you to ask right now, and get it over with."

"It's nothing really, Mack. It's just that Dale and I would like to take one of the RVs we haven't used for a while, and go up north. It'll mostly just be a chance to get away and relax for a while."

"How long do you plan on being gone?"

"We thought we'd leave Friday night and come back Monday morning."

"Convenient. Three nights together in bed."

"It's not like that. We're just friends who like to spend time together."

"Tell me about it. Not so long ago you said you didn't ever want to spend even one night away from me. Now you want to spend a weekend alone with your boyfriend. Or maybe lover is a better way to describe it."

"Are you telling me I can't go?"

"Absolutely not. As I've said before, it's your body, you are the one who gets to choose what to do with it."

"But you still sound upset. Does that mean you don't want me to go."

"It does. But it means more than that. It means that I don't at all approve of what you are going to do. It also tells me that what you and I are supposed to be to each other is getting lost. Right now, I'm becoming less to you and Dale's becoming more. But shit happens, and I doubt I can do anything to change that."

"But you are going to let me go?"

"Of course I'm going to let you go. I've always told you that if you really want something, I won't stand in your way."

"The way you just said that bothers me. It sounded like one of your about to get out of the way claims."

"That's because that's what it was. You are perfectly free to do with Dale anything you want to do with Dale. At the same time, there's nothing to stop me from doing what I think is the right thing to do when you do it."

"Meaning what?"

"Meaning that tomorrow I will be prepping the other RV for quite a long trip. All the legal stuff we need to take care of can be done on the phone and online. As I've always promised you, you will get half of everything. Except Refuge Rescuers. I want to give it to everyone who works there. We owe them that much."

Lisa's face was now sheet white and her hands were trembling. "My god, Mack," she said, barely above a whisper, "All I did is ask to spend a few days up north to relax. And now you want a divorce? That makes no sense."

"It makes every bit of sense. Without asking or talking about it, you and Dale make plans like you have. What's next? A month in Mexico maybe? Or regular sleepovers a couple of nights a week? An open marriage with the two of us living two separate lives. Ain't gonna happen."

"All this for one short weekend that hasn't happened yet. This is crazy, Mack. I don't want a divorce. I don't ever want to break up with you. I want you in my life forever."

"I don't think so. If that was true, you wouldn't have tried so damn hard to convince me to quietly let you run off with Dale. You made your choice, Lisa. Dale won. I lost. But I'm not going to spend my life dwelling on it. Time is too short. We both know that. So after I spend the day with Kathy on Saturday, my new life will be starting. And you can go ahead and make love to Dale, now knowing that your times doing that with him will be from then on be a lot more frequent. Unless Kathy somehow stops him."

Lisa turned her back on Mack then, curled into a small ball, and cried. All desire to go anywhere with Dale was washed away with her tears. She gave Mack a few minutes when she felt him leave the bed, then followed him. She stopped in the kitchen for a beer, then joined him on the porch. She sat on the love seat across from the rocker he was in."

When their eyes met, she could see the love for her that was still there, but overriding it was the hurt she'd inflicted on him. She knew he was right about her reasons for wanting to have the weekend with Dale. The two of them had made love in the past, and Mack was okay with that, but he was wise in objecting to their relationship being carried any further than what it was.

The truth was, she wasn't as sure as she should have been about her relationship with Dale. There was no doubt that she cared deeply about him. But was it only a strong friendship as they constantly claimed, or were they actually in love.

For Mack and Kathy it was different. They were in love and they knew it. They also never made any secret of it. They were always open and up front with Dale and Lisa. At the same time, they knew and followed the boundaries. Their walks together in the refuge, even if they took all day, were nearly always platonic. If they weren't, what they did was never hidden. Dale and Lisa weren't always that honest.

Finally Lisa told Mack. "I won't be going. I was wrong to even consider it. The absolute last thing I ever want is to lose you."

"If that's true, Lisa, then why would you want to do it in the first place?"

"I know this is going to sound really stupid, but the reason is really simple. It sounded like something different that would be a lot of fun. Kind of like a new freedom for a little while. Where it's true that I would have enjoyed the sex, that was not the main reason I wanted to do it."

"Maybe not, but it's going to be a long time before you stop resenting me for objecting to your going. That's not going to be much of a way to live. So maybe you should go and have your new kind of freedom."

"But if I did that, you'd leave then, wouldn't you?"

"I would. You know me well enough to know that the last thing I ever want to do is get in anyone's way when there's something they really want. I think what you want right now is what Dale's been giving you. It isn't anything I can give you."

"That's just not true, Mack. You give me everything I want or need. I didn't want to go with Dale to fill some hidden need. I wanted it for a silly, very childish reason. Just to have a fun, stress free weekend."

"Something I apparently can't give you. So you'd best go with Dale."

"I'm not going with Dale. And you, Mack Thomas, are not going to leave me. Besides, if you did leave me, you'd probably die from being lonesome alone. What the hell would you do if you left me and all the rest of what's here. You'd go nuts from the boredom."

"Actually, I wouldn't. I've had a lot to do with writing two good books now, so I know I can write if I want to. I can also learn how to use a good digital camera. So what I would do is go out in the wilds somewhere and shoot pictures. It would beat the hell out of being shot at. Then I'll write for magazines. It's the kind of thing that could keep me real busy."

"That sounds to me like something you've already put a lot of thought into. Is that what you really want to do?"

"A lot of days, it is. Sometimes, when things get really difficult, I think about talking to you about us quitting. We'll never have to worry about money, so we could travel from place to place and take pictures and write. It wouldn't all have to be in wild places either. There are a lot of cities that would be interesting to explore too."

"I think I'd really miss this place though."

"Maybe. But it's not like we'd be traveling by covered wagon. Hell, if we go too lonesome, we could always hop a plane and come back for a visit. But all of that is a moot point. You could never leave Dale."

That comment, coming from Mack, shook Lisa. It wasn't only what he said, it was the way he said it. He sounded as if he'd given up on her. And it was possible he had. She'd pushed him before, on issues not all that different from the one they were facing now. She also knew that he'd lost a lot in his life, and maybe now the thought of losing her was more than what he wanted to deal with. So instead of fighting it, he was ready to walk way and let it happen. Doing it that way would hurt, but it would be less pain than losing her the other way.

"I don't know what to say, Mack," she told him. "You are the one I could never leave. You are my life, Mack. You're my refuge. You are the only one who can keep me believing that there's enough good in this world to keep me fighting for it. If you want to quit what we're doing right now, tonight, I will quit. I think I can do almost anything you might ask me to do. But I can't let you go. I won't let you go."

"Those are easy words to say. They are not so easy to live by. You've said them before. But it wasn't but a little more than an hour ago you were ready to throw it all away for a weekend with your lover."

"No, Mack, I was never ready to do that. I admit I was ready to argue the point that it should be okay for me to go, but I was damn well sure not ready give up you over it."

"If you weren't, then why the hell did you ever get the idea to run off with Dale in the first place?"

"The truth is, both Dale and I thought there was a good chance you'd welcome the idea. It would give you and Kathy all that time together. The feelings you and her have for each other are stronger than what Dale and I feel about each other, so that idea made sense at the time."

"I hope you know now, that they didn't."

"I do. But please stop holding it against me, just because I sometimes get goofy ideas like this last one. I need you to understand that there's a part of me filled with a burning fire that sometimes destroys all logic in my brain. I makes me often hates almost every man alive. Then, other times I feel a need to be loved by more than just one man. That's when everything in my head goes to hell. I know I hurt you Mack, when I came up with the weekend with Dale idea. But hurting you was the last thing I wanted to do. So even though it's probably a feeble excuse, this kind of thing still goes back to when I was sixteen. I don't think, Mack, that I'll ever get over getting raped the way I was. So I will probably always bounce back and forth from wanting more revenge to wishing I could better accept the idea of a man, any man, being able to make love to me the way you do."

"The thing is, Lisa, that you have to understand is the fact that no matter what I do, I can't fix those things. All I can do is be there for you when you want me and need me to. And the those other times, like now, I can only get the hell out of your way when I am in your way."

"This is where we have to stop this conversation. You are never in my way, Mack. It always seems that when you stand in front of me and stop me from doing something, I was doing something stupid."

"I don't think though, that the feelings you get are stupid. As far as the revenge goes, you have gotten a fair share of that. The other thing. The wanting to be able to accept love from someone other than me, maybe we should experiment with that in the future."

"Really? How?"

"Maybe find a few men you feel safe with, and set up a situation where you can be alone enough with them to do what you want to do, all the time knowing you are protected."

"You mean have sex with more than one man at a time?"

"Either that, or one after another."

"How many men would that be?"

"As many as you might think you need."

"That might be a good idea, Mack. But I won't do anything like that. What I will do though, is work my butt off so we can cut the number of cases we have. I'll also go with you tomorrow to buy a couple of cameras. After we have a week or more learning how to use them, I will go with you anywhere. We will then take lots of pictures, and see what kind of articles we can write. Who knows, maybe that's what we'll end up doing. In the meantime, we will still have this to do too. Either way, it'll be you and me, and I won't be sleeping with anyone else."

"Not even Dale?"

"Only an occasional nap, Mack. Only an occasional nap."

"That part's okay. Running off for days at a time definitely never will be. You have to promise me you will remember that."

"I promise."

"Good. But your occasional nap comment gave me an idea. How about the four of us taking this weekend off? You and Dale can go ahead and go North Saturday morning. Kathy and I will have our day at the refuge, then meet you later at the campgrounds. One of the things we can do is practice taking pictures with our new cameras. How does that sound?"

"But that will leave Dale and me up north all day without you. Won't that bother you?"

"You are always alone with Dale all day on the walk days in the refuge Kathy and I have. This is pretty much the same thing. So no, it won't bother me."

"When do you want to tell them, Mack?"

"How about now?"

"Should I call Dale then?"

"Sure, but if they want to come over for a while, I want you on my lap when they get here. And it would be nice if you put some clothes on. A skirt and blouse would be nice."

"Are you trying to prove something, Mack?"

"I'm not sure. I only know that I want you close, whether or not they come over. I think we both need that right now. We need to be close, the same way we always do when we've just been so far apart. Especially when one of us forgets just how short what we have might be."

"I guess I did sort of forget that, didn't I. I forget sometimes that you are never trying to own me. You do anything but. I know how lucky I am to have you, Mack. How lucky we are to have each other."

"We are. And we should always remember, most people want what we have."

"And most of them will never have it. Not even Dale and Kathy. As much as they love each other, they don't quite seem to ever get to the places we do."

"They never will either, Lisa, if you don't call them." He laughed and the sound of it drew away the tension she'd felt since their conversation started.

CHAPTER 19

Lisa was working at the reception desk so Donna could take a break when Kelsey walked in. Lisa recognized her as one of the students at the selfdefense school where she occasionally donated some time. She remembered Kelsey as an enthusiastic student. Enough so that Lisa had shared a few fighting secrets with her that she only did with a few she considered special.

Lisa gave her a big welcome smile and asked, "What is it that I can do for you today, Kelsey?"

Kelsey blushed slightly, cleared her throat, and said, "It's not what you can do for me Lisa. It's what I can do for you. I recently got a job over in Wisconsin. I had to move there, but the pay was so good I took the job anyway. I was forced to quit that job already, and that's what I'm here to talk to you about."

"Were you getting some kind of harassment or something?"

"Yes, but it's much more than that. Can we talk somewhere private? I was working for Rod Dasadist. I think that what I have to tell you is important."

"We sure can. But if this is about Dasadist, I'd like to have my husband hear what you have to say too."

"That would be Mack then?"

"It is. How did you know his name? I don't think I ever mentioned him to you."

"I went online and looked you up. I read a lot about you, Mack, and this detective agency of yours before I finally decided to come and see you. At first when this happened, I was kind of afraid to do anything. But now that I know about you, I'm not quite so scared."

"Okay. Now if you'll give me a minute or two, I'll get someone to watch this desk. Then I'll take you back to the private office where Mack is."

Lisa went to the tech center where Sue and Julie were doing their mysterious workings with computers and other stuff, and brought Julie back to watch the reception desk.

She then took Kelsey back to Mack's office. He stood up when they went in, and as Lisa introduced him to Kelsey, he looked into her eyes and gave her a wide smile. Lisa had to have been watching her close to see it. She was watching her close and did see it. When Mack took her hand to shake it, Kelsey took a sudden, sharp breath, and her eyes lit up with tiny sparkles. All Lisa could think of then was, "Mack's hooked himself another one, and odds are he doesn't even know it. Not yet, anyway."

"I know this might sound strange," Kelsey said as soon as she started talking. "But Governor Dasadist is planning to kill you guys. I've been recording his conversations, and after I quit working for him, I listened to them. He's going to kidnap a girl called Emma too. They plan on raping her. After they kill you two and kidnap Emma, they plan on killing everyone else who works here. I guess you guys are making it a lot harder for him to run for president."

"Did you bring that recording with you, Kelsey?" Mack asked, working hard to not show too much excitement. He was afraid he might scare her off if she knew the effect her words were having on him.

"Yes, of course. I thought you might want to listen to it."

"Do you mind then if we take it back to the tech lab and listen to it there. Our lead technician is great with things like that, and the sound quality will be better if she plays the recording."

"No, that will be fine, Mack." She gave him a wisp of a smile. She loved the way he looked directly into her eyes. More than that, she could see the kindness and concern in his. In the short time she was there, she was already envious of Lisa.

They went to the far end of the office and met Sue and Julie (already back from the reception desk). Mack gave Sue the recording device, explaining to her what it was. Without needing to be told, Sue immediately copied it onto several other devices, along with a cloud. She did it without Kelsey knowing she did. They'd wait until it was safer to tell her.

They only listened to a couple of hours of Dasadist's most recent conversations to start with. They then went back to Mack's office where they listened to Kelsey's story. When she finished, Mack was concerned over her safety.

He had no doubts about what Dasadist was likely to decide her fate was. So the idea of leaving her alone was out of the question. As they considered all the possibilities, none of which looked good,

Theresa came home from the hospital. She needed a short break, and even more, a shower. But first, she checked to see how everything was going. When she heard about the problem with where to put Kelsey, she saved the day.

Kelsey would be staying in Ben and Theresa's house. At least for the foreseeable future. With that news, Mack breathed a sigh of relief. Lisa would be spared the disappointment of losing her freedom weekend. A time she sorely needed.

So they continued their preparations for the weekend, but spent even more time telling everyone one what they learned so far from the Dasadist recording. They especially warned Sue and Larry about Dasadist, so they would be super careful with Emma.

Mack was still uncomfortable about going anywhere over the weekend, but at the same time he knew that it would be a good thing for Lisa and him to get away where there would hopefully be peace and quiet. He knew her well enough to know now that at least half her reason for wanting to go away with Dale was to show Mack that she needed a break. It also served as a reminder to him that the time they had together could so easily be cut short. And that was enough to allow him to overcome his discomfort and go ahead with the weekend plans.

Mack was surrounded by enthusiasm for the weekend ahead when they got together Saturday morning. Dale was his natural calm self, but his positive anticipation about the days ahead showed in his eyes and with his slight smile. Lisa looked both excited and a bit guilty. She was more than happy to be going and had no problem with the way it was arranged, but worried that Mack might be somewhat unsettled about it. Kathy was simply anxious to have Lisa and Dale get on the road so she could start her day with Mack. She loved Dale and her life with him, but she always felt that her best days were the ones spent with Mack while they walked the refuge.

It didn't matter so much what they did or what they saw. What mattered to her most was just being close to him and holding his hand as they walked. Kissing him frequently went beyond just pleasant. And those rare days when they made love were to her something that went way beyond the physical act. It took her to places no one or nothing else ever had or could have.

As soon as they started their walk, she took his hand, stopped him, and said, "I love you, Mack Thomas. I know that these walks you and I have are the only thing we'll ever have that are just ours, but I want you to know that if the time ever comes it could change, I would be all yours."

"I love you too, Kathy. And I admit there have been days that have been close to that. We came close again the other night. But the truth is, I could never leave Lisa. She's definitely one of the toughest people any of us have ever known. At the same time though, she's pretty fragile. In most ways, she's made an incredible recovery from being raped. Even so, it still haunts her. And that haunting is what makes her go after Dale the way she periodically does."

"That's probably true. But whatever the reason, he doesn't even seem to do the slightest thing to discourage her."

"Why would he. He has to put up with our relationship. Add to that, he's no longer completely sure of the relationship he has with either you or Lisa. You scared him enough to change him when you asked him for a divorce. What happened then changed all of us. Mostly for the better, I think. But sometimes there's a negative side of it too."

"By that, do you mean who Dale and Lisa now are? Or are you talking about you and I. Which is what I would hope you think of as a positive thing, not negative. Because if you don't, my life will have a lot less meaning. I've had a lot of luck in my life, Mack. Now though, if you were no longer in it, a lot of my life might just fade away. My music has taken me beyond my wildest dreams. Yet, what I have with with both you and Dale has more meaning."

"Well, we can't let anything happen to lessen your life. You deserve every good thing you've ever had. So let's see if we can convince Dale to take a year's leave of absence, or maybe even quit his job. Then how about the four of us just go somewhere. You can still do a concert now and then, and we can all take lots of pictures everywhere. Every so often, we can write an article about something and try to get it published. We already own the RVs, and can afford to do it either way."

"I don't think Dale could get a leave that long, so he'd have to quit. He might not like that."

"He could always run for sheriff again. Or we could go to work for Refuge Rescuers. And if that didn't work, we could start our own agency. Not to mention, we might decide to stay on the road until we get too old to do it."

"Are you really serious, Mack? You want to quit what you're doing and travel around the country taking pictures and writing about them?"

"Yes. Actually, I'm very serious about it."

"But why?"

"I'm tired of the violence. I'm tired of trying to solve problems that can't be solved. Lisa's beginning to feel the same way. We've already bought a couple of cameras, so we can learn more about photography. I'm talking to you about it, because I think the four of us have something special. It might be interesting to take it into another dimension. Give it some thought."

The only answer Kathy could give him then was a deep sigh. She took his hand and they resumed their walk. As they did, Mack felt a slightly disappointed at her response. At the same time, the more he thought about it, the more he felt that it would be the best thing he and Lisa could do. They could, after all, always come back home if it didn't work out for them. So he decide to talk to her about it when he and Kathy joined her and Dale that evening. That made him start to hope that Lisa would be thinking about it some before then.

She wasn't though. She and Dale had just arrived at their campsite, and they were busy arranging the inside of the RV for their stay. They didn't get far before someone in a huge class A RV started to back into the campsite next to them. The campsite they had reserved for the RV Mack would be driving when he and Kathy got there later. Dale rushed out and waved at the driver to stop.

"I'm sorry," Dale said when the man rolled down his window, "but this spot is reserved for another party. They will be here later."

"If it's reserved, you should have a sign saying so. You don't, so this is where I'm going to park." He moved to finish backing his RV in.

Dale again blocked his way. When he refused to move, the driver of the RV jumped out of his vehicle and charged Dale. He weighed about three hundred pounds and had a belly on him that carried his waist line close to sixty inches.

"You get the hell out of my way," the man yelled, "or I'll knock you from here to hell."

"It's like this," Dale told him. "This spot is reserved. So it's time for you to go to the spot you were told to park in when you signed in."

"I didn't like it. I like this one much better. So I'm taking it. And I'll do to you whatever what I need to do to make it mine."

"The only way you can do that is to go back a couple of days and reserve it before I do."

"You're a real smart ass ain't you. Well, that'll get you no where with me."

Lisa joined them then. "What's going on, Dale?" she asked.

"This jackass," he answered, pointing at the fat man, "thinks he can take this spot just because he wants to. Now he thinks he's going to knock me all the way to hell."

"We both know he can't do that. But even if he could, he wouldn't get this spot. Because then I'd be required to beat the living shit out of him. Or if that wasn't enough, break his neck." She looked at Dale and smiled. "There's lots of coyotes around here. How long do you think it will take them to eat his bloated body down to the bones? Burying him will be far easier if all there is is bones."

"That it would be. But instead of burying his bones, it will be easier to just scatter them out in the swamps somewhere. It's unlikely he'll ever be found there."

"True. But either way, which one of us is going to do the job? And it is best we get on with it. I've pretty much had it with him."

"I agree. Let's flip on it." Dale took a coin out of his pocket. "You call it," he said as he flipped the coin.

"Heads," Lisa called out as the man climbed into his Rv. She laughed, then asked, "You leaving now?"

He didn't bother to answer her before driving away.

"Why is it," Lisa asked as she watched him go, that there is always has to be at least one person like him everywhere you go. He just didn't need to try to do that."

"No, Lisa, he surely didn't. But it'll be better for us now. I'm just hoping it's a good day for Mack and Kathy too. They need their refuge day together even more than we need our day."

"I'm sure they're doing just fine," Lisa said.

And they were. They were making it an especially slow walk on this day, and stopped often. Sometimes for no other reason than so Mack could stare at the horizon and wish the rest of the world could offer the same peace this place did.

Kathy picked up on those feelings some, but they were for the most part overridden by other feelings. Feelings being fed by the kiss she got from him at each stop.

Her passion didn't go unnoticed. Without saying why, Mack gradually steered their walk off the path. He led the through a thicket of poplar trees until they reached a small, but grassy meadow.

This time when she kissed him he said, "Let's rest a bit."

When she kissed him again, the buttons on her blouse became fair game. She didn't argue. Instead she started on his shirt. There was no hesitation on the part of either one of them, and soon the clothes were gone and he was pulling her over him. What followed lasted far longer than the clothes wrestling did. Far far longer.

It was well into the afternoon before they resumed their walk. When they did, they must have carried some kind of special aura with them. As soon as they left the poplar thicket a red fox crossed the path in front of them. Rather than dart away as fast as it could, it sauntered along in front of them for a while before disappearing into some tall grass.

At the river, they were given the chance to watch a pair of otters play, in and out of the water. Their walk was an especially quiet thing, brought on by the overwhelming contentment they were finding in each other, so they went unnoticed by a small herd of about fifteen whitetail deer. There was virtually no wind, so their scent wasn't traveling far. They were within a few feet of the herd before they were noticed. But even those skittish animals failed to run away. They only walked away without a one of them raising their white flag. Next came the best, even if it was the critter they least expected to see. The bear came out of some brush no more than ten feet in front of them. She sat down on the trail facing them. She lifted a front paw, as if to say hello, then proceeded to watch them. As she did, she sometimes tilted her head from one side to the other. She also made some bear sounds that come out much more like she was trying to say something, than the growl that would be normally expected from her.

Mack felt a strong temptation to walk up to her and pet her, but held back because of Kathy. It would be one thing if he got himself in trouble doing something like that, but much worse if he got Kathy involved in it. So they stood there watching each other for a while, until the bear decided it was time to move on. She shook her head, lifted a front leg again, then slowly moved off into the brush.

"I wonder," Mack finally asked Kathy, who was smiling broadly from what she'd just witnessed, "if Lisa and Dale are having near as good a day as we are."

Lisa was, at the same time, wondering the same thing about Mack and Kathy.

CHAPTER 20

It was close to suppertime when Sue and Emma went out into the garden to pick what they needed for a salad. Larry was still at the hospital with Theresa, so he could give her a ride home. Everyone who was a part of Refuge Rescuers was being extra careful now, because of what they had learned from Kelsey. That meant they weren't about to let Theresa drive to the hospital and back without someone along with her.

That left Roy as the only male close by. And he was in the shower, washing up after a day of working in the vegetable fields Ben would normally be working. Wanda was busy with supper preparations for her and Roy, and everyone else close by wasn't trained to be as vigilant as the rest of them, so it didn't matter what they were doing. It wasn't likely they'd notice much, even if it was something of a suspicious nature.

Sue was constantly looking around, but when she bent over to pick a choice tomato, the three men came from what seemed like out of nowhere. One of them stood guard while the other two grabbed Sue and Emma. The men were confident of their own abilities, and had no doubts that they had secure holds on Sue and Emma, so they didn't hold on to them particularly tight.

It was a grave mistake on their part. Both Sue and Emma were wearing what was referred to by all the women of Refuge Rescuers as Lisa pants. Sown into the back of each waistband of every pair was a special pocket. Inside of the pockets was a special switch blade knife, sharpened to surgical precision. The blades on the knifes popped straight out, rather than swing out.

All the women of Refuge Rescuers had practiced pulling out the knife until they could, in almost any situation, remove it in little more than an instant. And that's exactly what they did as soon as the men grabbed them.

Sue pulled her knife out with her left hand. She didn't hesitate to do what she knew she had to do. Swinging her arm as hard as she could, she lifted her hand with the knife in it and swiped the blade across his throat. It went in deep and instantly blood was spraying out of him. He dropped to the ground and was very quickly dead.

Before Sue could assist Emma, she was defending herself. Throughout too much of her life, she'd been raped by her father and some of his friends. That made her automatically distrustful of strange men, and made her react in a very defensive manner if one so much as touched her. The one holding on to her was even worse. He grabbed her.

She pulled out her own knife. Like Sue, she didn't hesitate, and her knife went deep into his right forearm first, then his left. He howled in pain and let her go. She quickly moved behind Sue. It normally would have been a good move, but that's where the third man was standing. He grabbed Emma. She screamed as loud as she could.

That brought Roy, fresh out of the shower and wearing nothing but a pair of jeans, out of his house at a run. Wanda was close behind him, with a rifle in her hands. She raised it to her shoulder to aim and shoot it at the third man, but before she could pull the trigger a shot rang out.

Mack and Kathy had just gotten back from their refuge walk, and when they heard Emma scream he automatically grabbed the rifle hanging in the rear window of his pickup. Because he couldn't see Roy and Wanda come out of their house from there he was, he didn't hesitate to shoot the man trying to hold on to Emma. He knew it was a safe shot, because the man's head towered more than a foot above Emma's. It was also a great shot for Mack to make. It hit the man in the middle of his forehead, killing him instantly.

With Kathy at his heels, he ran to join Sue and Emma. Sue was standing over the man with the bleeding arms when he got to them. She looked up at Mack.

"We're going to have to thank Kelsey again for warning us the way she did. That's the reason we were wearing Lisa pants. They might have been able to take Emma if we weren't. I think they would have just killed me."

"I think you're probably right," Mack agreed. "Has the bleeding one had anything to say yet?"

"Not yet, but then, I haven't had the chance to question him. I don't suppose I could talk all of you to disappear for a while, could I. He should never have gone after Emma. This is the last thing she needed. I won't need much time with him. Even if I can't make him tell me what we want to know, I do have a few things to say to him. Things like whether or not he should continue to have the ability to breed. Personally, I don't think he should."

Hearing Sue scared the bleeding man. He was now weak from the loss of blood, and he started to whimper. Sue nudged his head with her foot.

"Shut the hell up," she told him, "or I damn sure will cut your nuts off."

"I agree with her," Mack said. "You should lose them. So unless you tell us who hired you, you will lose them."

"Dasadist," the man said in little more than a whisper. "We work for Dasadist. He wants that kid real bad. You'd better watch her close from now on."

That's when they heard the sirens. Wanda had called 911. As soon as Mack heard them, he called Lisa. She answered right away.

"What's wrong, Mack?" she immediately asked.

"Why do you think something's wrong?"

"Because you should be on your way here, not calling me. Aren't you coming tonight?"

"Yes, we are. But something's come up that I'll explain to you when we get there. If you'll wait up for me?"

"Of course I will. We had a good day, Mack, but I miss you anyway. Is everything okay with Kathy?"

"Yes, Kathy's fine. So don't worry. We will be there tonight sometime. We'll tell you and Dale all about it then."

"Okay, Mack. We'll be waiting."

Mack hung up the phone just as the first deputy sheriff pulled in. She was a long time veteran in the sheriff's department, so she and Mack knew each other real well.

Mack was, in fact, well acquainted with nearly everyone who was part of the Clayborne County Sheriff's Department. He knew most of them from the years he was a deputy himself. He knew the rest because since he left the department he did his best to get to know anyone who was new there.

That meant the deputies who were dealing with the attempted kidnapping and the deaths of two of the kidnappers were willing to listen to the explanations of what happened and why it happened. They also got a boost from the confession the bleeding man gave them.

Larry and Theresa got back from the hospital while they were in the middle of the investigation. He didn't say much when he learned what happened, but it was easy to see that he was extremely upset over it.

It wasn't until the investigation was over that he said anything to Mack. "I know you might not approve of what I'm thinking," he said. "but we are going to have to do something about Dasadist now. And I damn sure don't mean just more harassment. We need to do something to bring this shit to a stop. If one of us is hurt or even killed, that's one thing. But Emma. *No!* We just can't let something like this happen again."

"I can't argue with you about that. I totally agree with you. It's something we'll have to figure out soon. In the meantime though, I'm really tired. Kathy and I had a longer day at the refuge than we usually do. And now we are anxious to meet up with Dale and Lisa at the campgrounds. They're waiting up for us."

Mack was wrong though. It was later than he realized, and Dale and Lisa also had a long day. So instead of waiting for Mack and Kathy sitting up, they laid down on the kingsize bed in the back of the camper where it was more comfortable. As they grew more sleepy, Dale turned over on his side and moved his arm around her. They then fell into a deep sleep.

That's where they were when Mack and Kathy got to the campground. Since they were both as tired as they were, Kathy went directly into the RV she was planning on sharing with Dale for the rest of their stay at the campgrounds. She immediately left it.

Shaking her head, she said to Mack as she joined him in his RV, "So much for anyone waiting up. They're both sound asleep on the bed. They're still dressed, but they are snuggled up real nicely."

"You sound upset, Kathy. Are you?"

"No, not really. I just find it interesting that they can be so open about it. Most of the time I get the feeling that if there is any jealousy between any of us, it's them with that feeling. So what do you want to do? Should we wake them up?"

"No. Let them sleep. I know Lisa well enough to know that she had to have been really tired to have fallen asleep after promising to wait up for us. And whatever they might do with the rest of the night, we can be sure they did with part of their day too. The same as we did."

"Where do you want me to sleep then?"

"I prefer you do it in my bed, but there's other places if you would be more comfortable in one of them."

"I think, *Mister Mack Thomas*, that you were being a complete ass with that last comment. I'm going to take a shower now. I'll meet you in bed. But I have to warn you. All of my nightwear is in the other RV. So I'm going to have to sleep tonight without it."

"Well, so be it. And to be sure not to confuse things, I'll dress the same way. Does that sound sensible to you?"

"No. I think the word delightful fits the situation better than sensible."

"Me too. Now go take your shower. I'm anxious to take one too, so I can prove to the both of us that delightful really does beat sensible."

Kathy giggled all the way to the shower, no longer caring about sleep. Something they didn't get much of that night.

Mack was the first one up in the morning anyway. He was on his second cup of coffee before Lisa came out of the RV she slept in. She smiled as soon as she saw him, but she somehow seemed sad.

"You look really nice this morning," he said to her right away, because she did.

Her hair was tousled from sleeping in it. All she'd done with it so far was run her fingers through it. On her, it looked good anyway. Added to that look was a freshly washed face, and a quick glance gave Mack a nice view of her bare legs. She wore a yellow cotton dress, just tight enough for him to notice every soft curve of her body. It quickly told him that she wore nothing else under it.

"I like your dress," he said.

She blushed a little. "I put it on last night. For you. I wanted to look nice for you. I wanted you to know that I miss you sometimes, no matter what else is happening. I love you, Mack. I'm sorry I fell asleep. I was just really tired, There was no other reason. No matter where I slept, there was no other reason."

"I understand, Lisa. So why don't you come and sit in my lap for a minute."

"I would, but you're wearing your gun. I thought we were going to try to stay away from that while we were here."

"We were, but you'll understand why I'm wearing it when I tell you what happened last night."

Lisa made just two steps toward him when the shots rang out. Bullets rained around them, slamming into the ground and sending chunks of sod flying out of the grass Mack's chair was on.

He jumped from his chair and tackled Lisa. He covered her with his body as he franticly tried to see where the shooting was coming from. Dale was out of his RV by then, with a rifle in his hand and his eyes scanning the land around them, searching for the shooters. The door to Mack's RV opened then, and Kathy literally crawled out.

Mack looked around again, then told them what to do. "Don't stand up. Crawl around to the other side of this RV. When you get there, one of you lean with your back against the back tire. The other one of you, sit in her lap. There's duel wheels in the back, so they should give you fair amount of protection from the shooting."

"I don't want to leave you here alone, Mack," Lisa agued. "I want to help, not run."

"You're not armed, and there's no way you can get into the RV to get your gun without getting shot."

Kathy nodded yes, then took Lisa's hand to get her moving. There was still no way she wanted to leave Mack there at that moment.

"Please, Lisa," he begged, "go now. I need you both to be safe."

Dale, who was silent with his concentration to find the shooters now said, "Yes, for God's sake, go. We need you safe."

Knowing there were no good choices, they both made the desperate crawl to the other side of the RV. A storm of bullets flew by them just as they rounded the corner of the RV. This time though, Mack spotted one of the shooters.

He knew Dale was in the wrong place to get a view of him, so he knew he had to take the man out himself. The problem was, there was no place with any kind of cover between him and the man. He paused for a few moments, thinking about his situation. He knew how totally dangerous any move he might make would be, but decided to make the move anyway. He knew that even if he was killed, it would be better than any harm coming to Lisa or Kathy.

He thought about crawling in a wide berth to sneak up on the man, but knew his chances of making that work were slim to none. That left him with one choice. Get up on his feet and charge the man. So far the man had proved to be a lousy shot, so that gave Mack hope that his bad aim would continue.

He checked his guns magazine to be sure it still held all twelve bullets, then took a deep breath. When he stood up, he was running for his target before he'd even straightened up. The man he was after was so startled by Mack's move that he hesitated for just a moment. Long enough for Mack to make a dive for the ground. By the time the man was ready to shoot at Mack, he already had the man in his sights. He put two bullets in his heart.

He then quickly moved into the place where the dead man was laying. To Mack's surprise, it gave him a view of six of the shooters. He thought, for just a second, about giving them a warning. Then decided to not do something so stupid. Aiming carefully each time he pulled the trigger, he shot all six of them.

When the last of them fell, he heard the rifle fire coming from Dale. He left his position, but by the time he reached Dale the shooting had stopped. He was dialing 911 on his cell phone.

Lisa and Kathy came out of hiding. Lisa spoke first. "Did you guys get all of them?" she asked.

Dale just stared at Mack, shaking his head. "Not me," he told Lisa. "It was all Mack. I've never seen anyone do anything that brave before. It was nuts, but really brave." He looked at Mack. "I can't believe you survived that. Charging out in the open like that. He had every chance of killing you."

"I guess he could have, but I didn't do anything brave. I just didn't want to let anything happen to Lisa or Kathy."

Kathy looked at him with a heart full of love then, as tears streamed down her cheeks. She gave him a quick hug and kiss, then turned her attention to Dale.

Lisa just stood there looking as if someone had just stuck a knife in her. She started to shake, trembling so hard Mack had to hold her up. She raised her head until their eyes met. It was easy to see that hers were filled with guilt and regrets. She dropped her head again and her shoulders shook as the tears finally started to fall. She lifted her head again, struggling to meet his eyes.

"I'm so sorry, Mack. I was so wrong. I should never have wanted to be away from you. I'm so sorry. I could have lost you. And I didn't spend our last night with you. How could I do that? I'm so sorry, Mack."

He took her in his arms and held her. "There's nothing for you to be sorry for. We both know that no matter what we do, as long as we keep on doing the work we do, we can easy lose each other at any time. So what happened today wasn't your fault. Neither was what happened last night."

Mack went on to tell Lisa and Dale about the attack on Sue and Emma. He finished with, "And I didn't tell you guys about it earlier last night because I wanted you to be able to have a full weekend without any of the usual concerns we normally live with."

"I appreciate that, Mack," Dale told him, "but if anything like that ever happens again, tell me."

"I will. I know now that if I'd have told you last night, you probably would have cut this trip short. That would have avoided this morning."

"It might have." They heard sirens off in the distance. "One good thing though," Dale added, "this campground is on the edge of Clayborne County, so it's my department that's on its way. It's going to make our explaining all the bodies laying around a little easier."

Kathy gave Dale's arm a little tug. "I know that this is a terrible time to say anything like this, but I want to anyway. Mack has an idea for the four of us. When this mess here is cleaned up, I want you and I to talk about it. I think it's something we need to consider doing."

Dale gave her a slight hug. 'If it's with you, Kathy," he told her, "I'm open to almost anything."

Lisa guessed accurately about the topic Kathy was referring to. She moved her head up and pulled Mack's down. The kiss she gave him was filled with all the love she had inside her. All she could do then was wonder how she could ever have wanted four days and three nights away from him. Especially when there was always the chance to lose him forever at any time. Or, as far as she was concerned, he could lose her. Which would be almost as bad.

CHAPTER 21

After the investigation of the shooting at the campground was completed, Mack and Lisa decided to take the RV home, then go visit Ben in the hospital. To their big surprise, they found out he was out of the hospital and home.

The doctors there told him that going home already was a bit premature, and that it could be dangerous. That wasn't about to change his mind. Being home and sleeping in his own bed with his wife that he loved so dearly made it easy to override any concerns anyone might have over his health.

Having him home also brought a big benefit to everyone at Refuge Rescuers. Breakfast at Ben and Theresa's was again scheduled. And it was to start right away, on Monday morning. Ben still wasn't strong enough to help with it, but Theresa had an unexpected volunteer. Kelsey was still staying with them, and she was more than happy to have a way to pay them back for taking her in.

The breakfast also gave Mack the chance to turn it into a meeting about Dasadist. There was no doubt now, after the events of Saturday night and Sunday morning, that they needed to somehow render him harmless. And for that to happen they knew, there were very few options. He also knew that it would be best to not discuss some of them at this meeting. He didn't want Emma to hear them talk about killing. He also wasn't sure how far they could trust Jules Sapphire, who was there for the breakfast.

He knew that whatever they did, Ben and Roy would prefer something nonviolent if it was possible. He also believed that all of the women there would want the same thing. He wished for something that could settle the problem peacefully, but he couldn't make himself believe it was going to be possible.

On the other side, Larry's anger was too deep to hide. Dasadist did the one thing he could never, under any circumstances, be even slightly forgiven for. He went after Emma. For Larry, there was only one solution for the problem of what to do with the Wisconsin Governor. Death! A bullet from a high powered rifle to his head. The problem he knew he was facing was mostly Mack. He just didn't have it in him to become a sniper and assassinate Dasadist. Nor was he likely to want to be part of any plot to do so.

That meant that he'd probably have to do it himself, without any help from Mack or anyone else. Which was something he knew he would have no problem with his conscience about doing. He could easily sacrifice his own life, if that's what it would take to protect Emma. Not to mention everyone else at Refuge Rescuers. So he had no fear of being caught or killed if killing Dasadist proved to be the only way to stop him.

He was left then, with just one big hangup with the whole idea. *Sue.* It would break her heart if something happened to him. In the short time they'd been together, they'd fallen deeply in love and hoped to have a life together.

Larry was deep in thought, searching for some kind of solution for the problem that wouldn't take his own life in the process, when Jules approached him.

"I know," he said to Larry, "that I will never quite fit in with, or be a real part of, Refuge Rescuers. I'm too conservative. But I do completely agree with all of you when it comes to book banning. I don't like Dasadist's trying to create big government at all either. I was a high school science teacher, so I believe that education is important too. Too boil it all down, what I'm really trying to say, is that I have an idea on how to get rid of Dasadist."

"But you'd like some help from us?"

"No, not directly. And when it comes time, I'll only want some help after the fact from you. So I'm wondering if there's anyway you would?"

"I guess, Jules, it would depend on what kind of help you might want."

"I only want one simple thing. When it's all said and done, you will get me the hell out of this country. I have no interest in going to Mexico. What I'd like is for you to get me into Canada. Then far enough away enough so the powers that be are highly unlikely to find me, even if they ever do look for me there."

"Are you talking about trying to live in the wilderness, or just some kind of town?"

"What I'd really like, Larry, is to get lost in a city. But one that's a good distance from Wisconsin. Like in Australia."

"That shouldn't be a problem for you. There's damn sure a lot of ways to get to any Canadian airport. You could drive, take a bus, or even travel by rail."

"I know all that. But I want to get to one via a lot of ways, part of which will be walking. And I don't mean along some highway. I'm talking about making part of the journey in the wild country, where there's little to no chance of seeing another human. If I travel that way, I can get out west before I buy a ticket to Australia. I'll have a better chance of getting on plane there."

"And the rest of the trip to get that far?"

"Mix it up, Larry. Short bus ride. Hop a freight. If there's a river running in the right direction, go by boat. Anything to make it as difficult as possible for anyone to track me down."

"What about money? You'll always have a need for some of that."

"I know. I've already cashed in everything. Most of the money I've been constantly moving around and through all kinds of money markets. I've also kept enough cash to get by for a few months. I know how to do a lot of things, so I should be able to find some kind of work about anywhere."

"It sounds like you've given your plan a lot of thought, Jules. There's one flaw in it though. If you're going to do what I think you're going to do, there's damn little chance of you being able to escape. So it's highly unlikely that you will ever need my help for anything."

"The truth is, I'll have an excellent chance of avoiding capture. The distance from where I'll be when it happens, and the actual event will be considerable. I'll be in a spot where no one can possibly see what I'm doing. Before anyone's able to figure out what happened, I'll be on my way out of there. I won't be carrying any kind of damning evidence with me when I go. And what I leave behind, won't be traceable. So I will have a much better chance of long term survival with your help."

"If I decided to help you, do you have a plan for where we'll meet up after it happens? What about our first mode of transportation? We're damn sure going to want to get you the hell out of the country in a hurry."

"That part I'll tell you now, Larry. We're going by boat. It's all going to go down near Lake Superior. You'll pick me up in a car that can't be traced back to either one of us. From there, it'll only be a couple of miles to the lake. Our boat will be capable of high speeds. By then it will be dark, and we'll make the run across without lights. Only some unexpected bad weather can trip us up there. At the boat landing, there'll be another vehicle waiting. By then, we won't be needing speed or anything else special. It will be traceable, but its registered to a man in prison who was convicted of the rape and murder of two teen-age girls. We'll drop it about a mile from the place where we'll start the first part of our journey on foot. From there, what we do and how we do it will mostly be up to you."

"What about food, water, camping gear? Have you thought about that?"

"There'll be a couple of backpacks in the boat. Before we start any of this, you can give me a list of what we'll need inside them. I'll see to it that they are there."

"This sounds like it could work, but there's no way you can do all that prep work without help. How do I know I can trust whoever it is that's helping you?"

"All I can tell you about her is that she's got damn good reasons for wanting to help in this. I trust her with my life. But I'm not going to tell you who it is. She wants to disappear when it's over, the same as me. I think it's best we let her do that."

"Okay, we'll do that. As far as helping you, I'll have to talk it over with Sue. I can't just disappear with you without her knowing enough so she knows I didn't run out on her. If that bothers you, tell me now so I can back off on the deal."

"No, I trust her. In fact, I pretty much trust everyone here. I just think it's best for all of them and for us, if we can keep the people involved to a minimum."

"Good enough. I'll talk to you later and tell you what I've decided."

Larry left Jules and got together with Sue. They took a break and told everyone they were going home for it. Larry told her about Jules's proposal.

"You know how much I hate violence, and that normally I wouldn't approve of something like this, But this time I'm not all that sure what the right thing is. Normally, assassinations neither solve problem nor do they bring about anything positive. But with this one, I'm not so sure any of those things matter. He sent killers here to steal Emma from us. And from what we've learned about that so far, all the evidence points to the fact he planned to rape her multiple times, then kill her. He sent ten or twelve men to kill Mack and Lisa. And if they would have managed that, they would have killed Dale and Kathy too. All that makes me think that as bad as assassinations can be, maybe this time it's justified."

"To tell you the truth, Sue, I pretty much agree with you. I normally wouldn't want anything to do with it, but he went after Emma. When he did, he got rid of any and all rules. He doesn't deserve a fair chance. He doesn't deserve anything. Not even the chance to go on living. But that still leaves us with a problem."

"I know. Just as I know it will likely be more than one problem."

"It will. The thing is, there's one very big problem you aren't going to like at all. If we do this, it will mean I will be gone for an indefinite amount of time, which could turn into a long time."

"You won't let it become permanent though, will you?"

"Not if there's anyway not to, Sue. The last thing in this world that I ever want to do is lose you and Emma."

"Well, then I think we should move on ahead with our plans for Rod Dasadist. What I will do for Jules is set him up with a totally new identity. He'll even have a couple of credit cards. He'll still have to pay any bills he might run up, but they'll be real and part of his new identity. I'll make it deep enough, so he can use his new ID for the rest of his life. I'll set you up with a short term one. It'll just be enough to get you wherever you go, and then home again."

"That sounds really good. We still have one big question. How much are we going to tell Mack and Lisa about what we're going to be doing. Not to mention, everyone else here?"

Sue pondered his question for a couple of minutes. "I don't think," she decided, "that we should tell them anything. If things go wrong, it will go better for all of them if they don't know anything about it. The last thing we want, is for someone to end up in jail because of something we did."

Larry agreed that she had the right idea. If no one there knew what they were doing, then it was much less likely that someone else would be blamed for it.

CHAPTER 22

Dasadist wasn't just upset and angry about the failure of his men to kill Mack, Lisa, and the rest of the people he wanted dead. The inability of his people to kidnap Emma wasn't only a disappointment. All that happened the previous weekend scared him more that anything else.

If that damnable bunch at Refuge Rescuers could take on that many of his best people and win, what else might they be able to do. They weren't only competent at their jobs, they were apparently great at them. So good, that he knew he couldn't continue doing things the way he had been. It was time, he knew, to do some real planning.

Before that though, he needed to find out who was leaking so many of his plans to those damn Refuge Rescuers. That leak, he knew, was the single biggest problem he had when it came to eliminating the Rescuers. So he put his entire staff to work trying to find it.

In the meantime, while that search was going on, he had a serious meeting scheduled. His biggest contributor was paying him a visit. Shanty Lucas was planning being there for a couple of days. She was going to arrive the next day. It was a mistake, but she made it because she was anxious to learn even more about Dasadist's plans. Especially anything concerning Emma.

Because of his serious losses, Dasadist had reached the point of employing nearly anyone who could handle a gun and was willing to use it. One of the many he hired was an a person who had worked for Shanty, but was found to be rather incompetent and fired. The problem was, he was one of the people who was with her the very first time she met with Mack.

When he learned about Shanty's coming visit, he asked his immediate boss why she was coming there when, after all, she was good friends with Mack and Lisa Thomas.

When that news reached Dasadist, the news shocked him. But it also gave him an idea. As soon as she arrived for her visit, they would make her a prisoner. Dasadist owned a home on the south shore of Lake Superior, where he was planning to visit soon anyway, So they would take her there for safe keeping. It was rather isolated, and almost completely surrounded by trees, but it also afforded a beautiful view of the lake.

So his plan was to hold her for ransom. But money wasn't the only thing he wanted in exchange for her life. He wanted Mack and Lisa. He, of course, had no intention of letting Shanty go no matter what kind of deal he made with anyone, but no one else could know that for sure.

This time, things went well for him. Shanty didn't suspect anything, and because she'd had several successful meetings with Dasadist, her people were a little too relaxed. That allowed them to be taken hostage without even any blood shed. Demands were immediately sent to Refuge Rescuers. Mack wasted no time in calling everyone into a meeting. There was only one question to answer this time. How to free Shanty?

A lot of ideas were proposed in a short time, but each and everyone of them had flaws. None of them seemed to offer odds of success high enough to try. Larry, Sue, and Jules didn't say anything for a while, but when no one else could come up with any kind of answer, they knew they had to speak up.

Larry did the talking. "I was hoping I wouldn't have to tell any of you about his," he said to start his explanation, "but we need to get Shanty home safe. She's our friend, so we have no other choice. What I'm about to propose might not sit well with all of you, but I think it's the only option we have."

He went on to tell them about the plans he and Jules had already made to assassinate Dasadist. Then explained how he thought those plans could be expanded into the rescue of Shanty.

Instead of being upset because Larry and Jules had developed the plans, Mack was relieved to know that they had at some ideas to work with. He had one major question though. "How can we be at all sure that Dasadist will take her there?"

"There's no way we can be absolutely sure he will," Jules explained, "but it has been his place of choice for most of his nasty activities. Some of the people I've talked to about him, think that there are probably a few graves scattered on his property. Young girls mostly, that he and Ted Crustiest have raped and murdered."

"So how do you think this is all going to work?" Mack asked.

"I think the best way will be to take Dasadist out first. I think I should be the one to do that. It should cause enough confusion for a couple of you to go in after her. A couple more of you can try to find her personal guards, there were likely only two of them, and all of you can then get the hell out of there. All through the action, I will continue to shoot at the Dasadist people. From there, I'll meet up with Larry and we'll follow through with our plans. To throw law enforcement off your track, Sue is going to send a tape, to as much of media as is possible, of me claiming responsibility for killing Dasadist, and my claim that I'm flying to Mexico."

"What about Shanty. How the hell are we going to keep her out of it?"

"I think, with some luck, you will be able to convince all of the Dasadist people to disappear before the law gets there. If she gets clean away, it shouldn't be difficult for her to prove she was never there anyway. She has more than enough money to keep it quiet if she needs to go that route.

"When do we do it?"

"Late tomorrow afternoon."

Mack asked for volunteers, but they needed to draw straws to see who would be part of the raid. Everyone at Refuge Rescuers volunteered, but some of them needed to stay behind and run the agency.

Those who were going to take part in the raid spent their time getting ready for it. Both physically and mentally. By evening they were ready to go. They were a quiet bunch who ate supper together that night. All of them went to bed early. They were leaving for northern Wisconsin in the small hours of the morning.

When everyone arrived at Dasadist's getaway place, Mack was surprised at the lack of security there. Only three guards stood watch outside what Dasadist referred to as his cabin. Although it actually was a six bedroom, four bath house. A house that strangely had few windows with curtains. Mack could easily see too, from the uncovered windows, that the guards inside were minimal.

Dasadist had the habit of standing outside on his attached wood deck, which faced the lake. It was designed to keep him almost totally hidden from anyone on the ground outside. So if anyone tried to shoot him, he was sure they'd have to do it from the lake. Something he didn't worry at all about. If anyone tried to do anything from the lake, the odds were good he could get undercover before they managed to do it."

There was one problem with his reasoning. There was one small spot that was never found by his landscapers or anyone in his organization, that a person could get to from the ground. It was just large enough to set up a high powered rifle with a scope on a tripod. It was also far enough away from the spot Dasadist would be standing to give the shooter ample time to escape.

It was a spot Jules discovered the one time he served as a guard at the cabin. It was where he was now settled into. He was ready to wait all day if that's what he needed to do, but he hoped for an early appearance by the governor.

His original plan was to wait until near dark, so they could cross the lake without being seen. But with Shanty now held prisoner waiting was not an option. They needed to free her before any harm came to her.

That was another place it soon appeared that Dasadist's ability to plan was on Mack and Lisa's side. Shanty was allowed to move around on the main floor of the house. Not even her hands were tied. The time saved because of that could alone make getting her out of that house quick enough or not.

That was now Mack's biggest concern. Because he still had a big problem. Even though he could see inside the house in spots, he had yet to catch so much as a glimpse of Dasadist. And he couldn't see any of the deck Dasadist would be standing on. That meant he and Lisa would have to go in after Shanty based on hearing rifle shots, not by what they could see. So when they moved in after Shanty, it could all go wrong if it was someone other than Jules doing the shooting.

What Mack didn't know was that the main reason Dasadist hadn't been seen by anyone, was because he was busy in his favorite upstairs bedroom. He had his two favorite bed partners with him. Maggie Baylor Blue and Ted Crustiest. So it was a couple of hours before they appeared on the deck.

Jules wasn't happy to see that they had company. He was hoping he wouldn't be forced to shoot anyone other than Dasadist and possibly a guard or two. Now he was stuck with shooting three people who were part of the Government, and the guards who were there to protect them.

Jules was a good shot with the rifle he used to kill Dasadist, but it was a bolt action he'd chosen for its superior accuracy, so he couldn't shoot fast enough enough. Baylor Blue and Crustiest, along with one of the two guards on the deck survived, although they were both unconscious.

Mack and Lisa responded immediately. They quickly realized that they'd lucked out when all three of the outside guards ran in the direction the shots came from.

Inside the house, they found Shanty standing over one of the guards with a metal vase in her hand. He was facedown on the floor, very still, and bleeding profusely. A second guard faced her, his gun held high with a shaking hand.

"It would be a good idea to drop the gun," Mack told him.

"Not likely," he answered. "You drop yours or I kill her."

Mack didn't debate the question of what to do with the guard. He knew that any kind of discussion would prove to be futile. So he shot the man. It wasn't a kill shot, but it instantly took him down, and he dropped his weapon on his way to the floor. Shanty quickly scooped it up.

"Where are your guards?" Mack asked her. "We should take them with us."

"They're both dead, trying to do their job. I considered both of them to be friends, so you'll have to forgive me if I'm none to gentle with anyone who might get in our way before we get out of here."

"No problem. Our only goal is to get you where it's safe."

"I appreciate that, Mack. But a big part of me says that you and Lisa are more important than I am. You guys are always doing good things. I just have a lot of money."

They were out of the house by the time she finished talking, and following the animal trail that took them to the house earlier. They were belted in their getaway vehicle before Shanty asked, "What about Dasadist? How do you think he's going to respond to what you guys just did?"

"It's not at all likely that he will. If things went according to our plan, he should be dead."

"My God, you guys assassinated him?"

"No, we didn't. We just know that someone did."

"And I don't suppose you are going to tell me who did, are you, Mack?"

"Not quite yet, Shanty. We will though, as soon as the time is right."

"Okay. As much as I'd like to know, I'm not going to push it. You guys just saved my life. The least I can do for you is not give you a hard time."

And she didn't. Not even when it was time for her to get on her plane for her flight home.

CHAPTER 23

Larry and Jules had every bit as much good luck to start their escape, as Lisa and Mack had freeing Shanty. Jules made it out of the woods without any problems. Larry was waiting for him when he got to him. They made the ride from there, in near record time, to where the boat waited to be launched.

Larry wiped down the inside of the vehicle they used to get rid of any prints, and they were quickly on their way. The boat they were in was relatively fast, but the crossing was a long one, so it quickly began to feel slow.

The lake itself wasn't angry. Instead, it was just agitated enough to make for a rough ride, with swells as high as three feet. Even so, they reached the other side of the lake, and Canada, almost as fast as they'd hoped to.

They unloaded their gear from the boat, then pushed it out into the lake. Superior wasted no time in dealing with it, and the boat was out into the lake and floating freely. With a little luck, it would soon be far away from the spot where they landed, and no one would ever know where they entered the vast forest in front of them.

Jules looked at what they were facing. "Are you sure you can get us through that?"

Larry smiled. He was in his element now. "Nothing to it."

Jules looked at him, and tried to pick up on his confidence. He didn't quite manage it. Larry watched the look on his face, then couldn't help laughing.

"You know, Jules," he said, "this was your idea. And it's too damn late to back out now. We've only go two choices. Stay here and die, or start walking. Which do you want to do?"

Jules sighed heavily. "Let's walk. But you lead the way, All I could do is get us lost."

Larry did. Much to Jules's surprise, the walking wasn't all that tough. Instead of having to fight their way through an impenetrable wall of trees and brush, Larry proved to be a near genius when it came to finding various animal trails to follow. He also knew that Jules wasn't going to be able to make it out of the forest the first day, so that evening he watched for a good spot to camp.

When they crossed a clean flowing creek and found a grassy meadow, he knew he had the right spot. Jules questioned him though, when Larry told him they were stopping for the night.

"I thought," he said, "that you were going to guide me out of here as quick as you could? Why are we stopping early?"

"I was, but I've been watching you. If we push it any farther today, you are going to be in trouble. It's better, I think, to get a little behind schedule, then it is for you to end up so sore you can't walk."

"Are you sure you're stopping for me, Larry? Maybe it's you who has the problem."

"It's like this, Jules. We both know that's bullshit. So don't lay that kind of shit on me again. Because if you do, I damn sure will walk away and leave you on your own. You wanted me to guide you, so you'd best let me do that. In the meantime, until you know these woods and this country called Canada better than I do, you will follow my work direction. Understand?"

"I sure do." He shook his head. "And I do know that my chances of surviving this are much greater with your help than without it."

"It'll be a damn good thing for you to remember that, because without me, your survival chances in theses woods are close to zero. You have to realize that when I decide to make camp early or late, there's a reason for it. That goes for any other decision I make too."

"I'll do my best to remember that," Jules answered, knowing that his best chances of escaping, after what he did, were with Larry. Even when they weren't in the wilderness.

Larry further proved his worth when he retrieved a fishing line from his pack, baited the hook on the end of it with a nice fat cricket, and threw it in the creek in a spot the water was moving slower than the rest of the creek. The cricket was quickly attacked by a trout just big enough to eat. He caught five more before he cleaned them. He then found enough wild greens and mushrooms to fill out the meal.

He fried the fish first, then using the pan drippings left in it, he fried up the vegetables. Jules was very impressed with the meal.

"Now that meal," he said, "was something I never expected. I can't say that I've ever eaten fish that tasted better, and those vegetables were the best."

"I'm glad you liked it," Larry told him. "But you aren't likely to get many like it until we reach a town. I don't eat meat, and only rarely do I eat fish. So unless you catch it, kill it, clean it, and cook it, we won't be having any meat with our meals, and very little fish. There should be plenty of fresh vegetables though."

"Why don't you eat meat?"

"Because there's no need to. And we humans do way too much killing just to satisfy our cravings."

"I always thought that the purpose of the animals we eat was to feed us. That means eating them is the right thing to do."

"I don't look at it that way, Jule's. Each and everyone of those critters is a living individual that deserves to live out its life the same as we do. I think their lives have just as much value as ours do. So I no longer kill them just to fill my stomach. My stomach does just fine eating vegetables and only vegetables."

"Does that mean you will object to it if I do what I have to do to eat some fresh meat."

"No, I won't stop you from doing it, Jules. It's a moral choice. But I do object to you using a gun for hunting or any other purpose. Other than to save your own life. Out here, a rifle shot can carry for one hell of a long way. We don't want to attract attention, just because we think we can't get by with using a gun.

"What if I figure out another way to capture an animal?"

"Like I said, it's a moral choice." Larry paused a moment. He had lived a good part of his life since he made the decisions about other lifeforms than human ones, and he knew that the people who wouldn't question his ideas were few and far between. "The thing I will object to, is your killing anything too big to eat in a meal or two. Killing is bad enough. Waste is often even worse."

"You are saying then, Larry, that I should not even consider taking something like a deer."

"That's right. Unless you can eat one in a couple of days? But even if you could, I'd prefer you leave them the hell alone. You kill one of them, and you will be taking a valuable life."

"You know, Larry, I've heard people in the past talk about how they don't eat meat. It always seemed to me that they were trying to sound really noble about something that wasn't that big a deal. It seems different here when you talk about it. We are pretty much surrounded by critters who could provide us with a consistent supply of meat, and you won't kill them on moral grounds. I think, if I survive this adventure we're having, I'm going to need to rethink my diet choices."

"That's a good idea. Just don't be surprised if you find it to be something too hard to do. And if you dan't manage to change as much as you might want to, don't be too hard on yourself for it."

They bedded down early that night, slept sound, and were up and about early. They finished their breakfast, cleaned up the minimal mess they made while camped in their spot, and were on their way at first light.

Larry's years of experience out in the wild places generously paid them back. Using animal trails and walking around the high places, rather than try to go over them, made for a less strenuous hike too. By noon they'd gotten further than they expected to be at the end of the day, when they planned their trip.

"We're making good time," Larry said, "but we're going to take a short break now. I think we'll get farther today if we manage to get some rest, then we will if we try to push too hard."

"I won't argue with you about it. You could probably keep going at the pace you set this morning, but I'm not sure I can. For me, some rest is a good idea."

Larry started gathering what he needed for a light lunch. It proved to be an exorcise in futility. Jules was sound asleep by the time he was ready to prepare the meal. His initial reaction was to scrap the meal. Instead, he tore the vegetables he collected into bite size pieces, poured a packet of salad dressing from his backpack over them, and ate it all like a salad.

He took a short nap after eating, then woke Jules. He was groggy, and ready to complain about being woke up, until he remembered where he was. "Was I asleep long?" he asked, rubbing his eyes, "I didn't realize I was so tired when I laid down."

"No big deal," Larry assured him. "So far, we've been making good time. It's better right now to lose a little of the extra time we gained, than it is to get too tired to keep up a decent pace."

The were quickly on their way again, and didn't stop for anything other than short breaks until Larry found another good camping spot. This one was on the banks of a small river.

"If you want," Larry told Jules, "you can try your luck fishing while I gather up some fire wood and pick us vegetables for supper."

"I'm not sure I know what to do."

"It's simple. Take the line from my backpack, find a worm or bug that wiggles and put it on the hook at the end of the line. Then you throw the line in the water. When the fish gets hooked, you pull it in."

"What about cleaning it?"

"I showed you how, Jules. You can do it."

Jules went ahead with his fishing experiment. It only took a short time for him to catch a moderately sized fish, but he was rather inept with the filet knife. When he finished getting it ready, there was only enough meat not mutilated to serve one person.

Larry looked at the mess and laughed. "None of us are much good at our first try to filet a fish. That's okay. You go ahead and eat it. I'll be just fine with what I gathered."

It was Jules nature to argue the point with Larry, and to insist they share the meager serving of fish. The look on Larry's face however, told him that the wise thing to do was to go ahead and eat it himself.

They continued to make good time, and three days later they walked into a small town. It had a total population of eight hundred and thirty people, and was located on a moderate size river. They arrived late in the day, and camped on its banks.

The river was running in the direction they were going, so Larry made a deal on a canoe early the next morning. They bought a few supplies in the town's general store, and were on their way down river before noon.

They rode the river for two days. At the end of the second, after making camp, they pulled the canoe from the water. They stashed it back int the trees far enough so it couldn't be seen from the water. In the morning, they headed out across country again. It only took slightly more than a half day to reach a large town. It had railroad tracks running through it. They, like the river, were running in the right direction.

Larry picked a spot where they could hide under cover and wait, they hoped, for the train to slow enough for them to hop on a freight car. The first train through carried passengers, and didn't slow down much. The second one was a long freight train. It slowed considerable. It also had a half dozen empty cars with open doors. They managed to get on the second one.

The train surprised them, and carried them near seven hundred miles before the were forced to leave it. This time they were in a small city. They found a service station with a restroom to clean up in and change into fresh clothes they'd been saving for a time like this.

From there, they bought new clothes for their next change, and discarded the ones they'd just changed out of. From there they found a cafe that served breakfast all day. Jules ordered a typical breakfast, with the addition of an extra side of meat.

Larry ordered four over easy eggs, a double order of hash browns, a toasted english muffin, and sliced tomatoes. The both ate slow, savoring every bite, and enjoyed a second coffee when they finished eating.

They weren't sure what the town had to offer, but when Larry googled it, they found out it had a train station where a person could actually buy a ticket for a train ride.

When they checked it out, they learned that Jules could ride it all the way to the west coast of Canada, and from there could get on a plane to countries far far away. So knowing that Jules could complete his journey on his own, they parted company. He got on a train. Larry went to the local airport and bought a ticket. He landed the next day. Sue and Emma greeted him, and he never felt so happy to see anyone as he did those two.

CHAPTER 24

When federal marshals investigated Dasadist's assassination, the name of Shanty Lucas never came up. To everyone's surprise, neither did the Refuge Rescuers Detective Agency. The tape Sue sent to all of the major news media, including even Fox, was enough to convince authorities that Jules Sapphire was the lone perpetrator.

They also accepted his claim that he was going to Mexico, and that he would disappear from there. Every possible way for a person to get from the United States into Mexico was watched as intensively as humanly possible.

The Canadien authorities were notified about him, on the slim chance he went up north, but little was done to search for him. Partly because the Canadian authorities knew that trying to find him, on the slim chance he was in their country, would be futile. Mainly though, they were wise enough to know that the assignation of Rod Desadist was actually something that benefited all of mankind and the rest of planet earth. So why chase the man who did it?

When Jules reached the west coast of Canada, he used his new ID and one of his new credit cards for a flight to Australia. His plan was to say there for a while before he decided where to go next. He had no trouble passing as just another American tourist, and quickly melted into that lifestyle.

That all left Mack, Lisa and the rest of Refuge Rescuers free to resume their attack on Book banning. First in line to take one of the book mobiles out was Ben.

"I know you're going to try and tell me I haven't healed up enough yet, Mack," he said before Mack could argue with him, "but the truth is, it doesn't matter if I am or not. The only thing that matters is that we get back out there with the books. We have to show people that banning books is wrong. And you know damn good and well why I need to be out there, seeing to it that all of those banned books get into the hands of those who should be reading them."

"I'm not going to tell you not to go, Dad. All I'm going to do is ask you to be careful with your leg. It still has a lot of healing left to do."

"I will. And just so you know, Theresa's going to ride with me. For the first few days anyway. I guess she wants to show her support for what I"m doing, no matter what my reasons are."

"Do you think it's safe for her to go with you yet? We don't know what the reaction's going to be when we go out there again."

"I think it'll be safe enough." Ben gave Mack a grim smile. "I'll be riding shotgun and she'll be doing the driving, so we'll be covered."

"Are you sure you don't want another person along?"

"Not this time. This time it's best if it's just the two of us. Theresa needs the chance now to prove that she's okay with my doing what I'm doing. I need to show her that I can let go of the past enough to let her show me. She has to know how much she counts. Given all that's happened in her life, she sometimes forgets that she matters as much as she does."

"That makes sense to me. Just as long as you are both careful."

Roy and Wanda, Mack and Lisa, and even Dale and Kathy took out book mobiles. It took some arguing on their part, but then Julie and Kelsey Real managed to convince Mack into letting them take one out. Mack had to do the convincing when it came to Larry and Sue. They were all set to take one out when Mack asked them to stay with the office while everyone else was out.

"To start with, Larry," Mack said. "You've done enough for a while. Getting Jules the hell away went way above and beyond anything we had the right to ask you to do. And now I'm actually asking you to do it again. We do need someone with with your abilities to watch over this place while the rest of us are giving books away. And last, it'll be best if Sue is available while all of that is going on. We can never be sure what we'll need her for next."

Larry wasn't particularly happy about the arrangement, but accepted it. He was wise enough to know that it was a good idea too, that he not get out and about too much for a while. The less he was seen for a while, the less chance there was that anyone would put him together with Jules.

Each of the mobile units was given an area to cover, and a listing inside of their area of places that would be best for parking for giving away the books. At nearly all of them, people were happy to see them and to have the chance to get the banned books to read.

It wasn't quite as easy for Mack and Lisa. On their second day out, they stopped at a place they found less then friendly. Over half the crowd that gathered around them were members of the local evangelical church. They were all convinced that Trump was their new messiah and that Dasadist was his most important disciple. Which meant that banning books was God's will, and must be continued.

They even brought a couple of hanging ropes along, hoping to lynch Mack and Lisa. It was, they were sure, exactly what any good christian would do.

The rest of the crowd wasn't sure how to respond to the mob, so they just meandered around, hoping that despite the crowd, the books would be distributed. It didn't take Mack long to decide what to do. He opened the book mobile to those who wanted the books to read.

One of the first people to enter was an evangelical. He was a big man, standing around six foot six, and carried the arrogant look of someone who thought he could, because of his size, do about anything he wanted to do. He didn't get very far before he grabbed some books and threw them on the floor. Unfortunately for him, Lisa was within two feet of him when he did it.

"That's it for you," she told him. "Put the books back on the shelf, then get out of here."

He laughed at her. "Like an atheist whore like you can make me? I don't think so."

Mack wasn't that far away from them, and thought about interfering with their disagreement. He quickly decided to let it continue. Both he and Lisa were thoroughly tired of bullies, and if this guy was stupid enough to start something with Lisa, so be it. Let the son of a bitch get hurt.

And that's exactly what he did. He got hurt. Three broken fingers on his right hand. A broken right arm. Testicles that were going to be sore for more than a couple of days, and one huge black eye. When she finished with him, she asked a couple of women who were there to get books to read, to help her drag him outside. They let his head bounce a little as the dragged him out and the far enough away so everyone could move in and out freely.

One of the evangelical leaders then held up a rope and screamed that it was time for a good old-fashioned hanging. Lisa just raised a middle finger at him. Three of the religious ones moved in to grab her, but two big men from the other crowd stepped in between them and Lisa.

Before a fight could start, Mack joined them. He turned in a circle, looking over the crowd. "That's it," he told them. "The next person who threatens either one of us, or tries to damage the book mobile or any of the books is going to get shot. Man or woman, you pull any more of that crap, and you will have a long stay in the hospital. The rest of our time here is goddamn well going to be peaceful."

One stupid, but somewhat brave man, thought he could out maneuver Mack by grabbing Lisa from behind. He was very sadly mistaken. She sensed his movements behind her and turned around and was facing him at the same time he grabbed her. She slammed the palm of her hand onto his nose breaking it. While blood started to pour from his nose, she took his right arm and gave it just the right twist. As she pushed it around behind it, she lifted it until she heard a definite cracking sound as it broke. She then pushed him away, kicking him in the ass as she did so.

Mack laughed. "Oh, and by the way, if I don't shoot you, I'll let Lisa loose on you. It's a tossup on which would be worse. Now we're here to give away some books. So let's do it."

The rest of the day went far better. They gave away nearly all the books they had on the book mobile, so they got home early. Dale and Kathy had the same experience with their book give away, so Mack and Lisa invited them over for supper. It wasn't until they finished their salad fresh made from the garden, the hamburgers from the grill, and the baked potatoes from the microwave, that their conversation grew serious.

Lisa was the one who started it. "What do you guys think," she asked, "about Mack's idea about taking some time off and traveling?"

"It sounds like something that might be good for all of us," Dale answered. "It is a fact that there's been way too damn much violence in our lives. But I'm not sure I'm ready to just walk away like that. I'm going to have to give it a lot more thought before I can make a decision."

"What about you, Kathy?" Mack asked. "Are you at all interested?"

"I am. Even though I've seen a hell of a lot of the world during my concert tours, I think I'd see whatever places we go to differently traveling with all you guys, than I ever would during a concert tour. But like Dale, I'm not at all sure I'm ready to commit to something like you are considering."

"The thing about it is though," Mack explained, "we aren't asking for any kind of commitment. It's more like let's just try it. It might be only a couple of days, or maybe weeks. And we don't have to be gone from here the whole time, either way. I just think it would be a good thing to get away from what we've been doing, and just spend some time together being friends. I'd like to do some more writing too. Maybe I can continue to add to the banned book list."

"It will be good too," Lisa said, "to spend some quiet time with our husbands. I think Mack and I, at least, need that."

"It wouldn't hurt me and Dale any either," Kathy agreed. "And something else I probably shouldn't say out loud, but I'm going to say it anyway. I also won't mind having more time with Mack, and for damn sure we know you won't mind more time with Dale. It's become obvious that you and Dale love each other, the same as Mack and I love each other. In fact, I think that's part of the reason for this idea in the first place."

Mack laughed softly. "It's something Linda would have approved of, that's for sure." Linda was at one time Mack's lover. She was also Kathy's mother. Now she was only a memory. Dale was the one who killed the man who murdered her.

"Are you kidding me Mack?" Kathy laughed too. "She would have loved it. And thinking about her and how she lived and then how she died, what you guys want to do makes a lot more sense."

"To me too," Dale agreed. "But I'm still not sure."

"No matter," Kathy said, getting up and moving over to Mack. She sat in his lap, smiled and said, "go ahead, Lisa. Same as Mack and me, right now it's what you both want."

CHAPTER 25

Mack and Lisa spent another week working their book mobile. By then, they realized it was okay to stop. Libraries were beginning to be restocked, as were schools. In Wisconsin, all and any retail stores that sold books, now carried at least some of the banned books. A few movie theaters held special showings of the film, To Kill A Mockingbird, to celebrate the beginning of the end of book banning in the state.

After a second week of distributing banned books, all the book mobils were donated to libraries. They continued to bring books to people, but the books they carried included a high percentage of books not banned. And now, rather than give away free books, the books they carried were dealt with the same as the books taken directly from a library.

Wisconsin limped along with the Republican lieutenant governor, now governor, leading the state. He tried to continue with the book banning, but he wasn't near as good as Dasadist was at weaving his religion, hatred, racism and bigotry into one belief system. That left him with a broken system of banning books. That freed up Refuge Rescuers to go back to their normal routines.

Once they got into them, it left Mack feeling as if nothing was ever going to change. The first case they investigated was one brought to them by a mother who claimed her husband was abusing their daughter.

They were told that he had a habit of taking the daughter to the park, and while they were there, he'd put his hands on her in places they didn't belong. When they watched him with her over the next weekend, they didn't see any sign of him doing anything inappropriate.

He was a carpenter, so they spent a week watching him. His life appeared perfectly normal. He went directly to work every morning, put in a normal day of hard work, then drove straight home at the end of every day.

Given that they couldn't find anything wrong, they talked to the mother again. She acted upset when they told her what they'd learned so far.

"But I know he's doing it," she complained. "You just aren't paying close enough attention to what he does."

"We aren't here to argue with you," Lisa tried to assure her. "All we wanted to do is to let you know what we've learned so far. And that is, it doesn't look so far like he's doing anything he shouldn't. And the times we've watched him with your daughter, she seems to be having a good time with her father. We haven't seen any signs of any kind of abuse. One thing we've learned. With abused children, there's always something indicating that things are not quite right."

"Well, you're wrong. I guess I'll have to find someone else to get him."

She walked away from them then, and they assumed they were off the case. Something about the whole deal bothered them though, so they took it upon themselves to spend a day checking out the mother.

She worked for an insurance agent, who had his office in a store front in a strip mall. The plate glass windows in the front allowed them a reasonable view of what was going on inside.

Working along with the agent were three women. The mother and two others, both of whom were in their mid-forties. The mother was a rather pretty redhead, about thirty years old, with a noticeable figure.

When the two women left for lunch, the truth of what the mother was trying to do came out. She and the agent disappeared into a room in the back, and didn't reappear until the lunch hour was nearly over. She was still buttoning up her blouse when they did.

"I guess," Lisa said, sighing heavily, "that tells us a lot. The question now is, what are we going to do with what we know?"

"What I'd like to do," Mack answered, "is to walk away and forget we ever got involved."

"So would I. But we can't. You know what she's trying to do to her husband. If she can somehow pin child abuse on him, she'll be able to take everything from him in a divorce."

"She will. But what the hell are we going to do about it. We can't prove anything. Not yet anyway."

"I'd like to tell the husband, Mack, but we both know he isn't likely to react in any rational manner. So we are going to need to somehow get proof of what she's doing."

"We will. The trouble with that is the fact that pictures are about the only way to do it."

"I hate the idea of that. We decided when we started Refuge Rescuers that we weren't going to get involved in cases like this, and so far we haven't. It would be nice if we could turn this over to one of the agencies that handles cases like this."

"We could still do that, Lisa. The problem there is the fact that it would be us hiring them. I think we'd be way out of line hiring someone to get involved with someone else's marriage."

"Which leaves it up to us. Do you have any ideas on what we should do next?"

"Not really. About the only thing we can do right now is put someone else on it. If we follow her around too much, she'll sooner or later see us. So it'll be best if it's someone else from the agency that she won't recognize."

"I think, Mack, that the best team we could put on it right now is Roy and Wanda. They're damn good detectives, but look less like private detectives than anyone else in our agency."

"You're right, Lisa. They are the best choice."

Neither Roy now Wanda looked forward to the assignment, but accepted it without hesitation. They fully understood the concerns Mack and Lisa had about what the mother was hoping to do to her husband.

Roy decided right away to get up close and personal with her and the man she wanted, who was the insurance agent. He walked into the agency cold, just before the two older ladies left for lunch, and asked about car insurance. His current insurance company, he complained, had just raised his rates again.

The office was small enough, so as he waited as they checked out his driving record, he could hear their conversations. She told the agent that she was going to get free that evening. Roy even heard her tell him what bar they should meet in, and what time."

When they brought him the insurance information he asked for, he again said the price was too high and walked out of the place. By then it was too late for the lovers to make use of the room in the back.

That evening, Wanda dressed to attract men. Shortly before it was time for the mother to meet with her lover, she went inside the bar. The insurance agent was nursing a drink at the bar. She said on the empty seat next to him. She didn't make any kind of move on him right away, because she knew she could take her time. The mother would be busy for a while.

She was having trouble getting out of the driveway. An old man with a bad limp was looking under the hood of his pickup truck, which was parked in front of it.

She got out of her car and marched over to Ben. "You are in my way," she complained. "So move your truck."

"I will," Ben said, "as soon as I can get it started again."

She shook her head in disgust, then went back to her car to get her cell phone. She wanted to call to tell the man she was meeting that she was running late and why. It took her a while to accomplish that. While she was talking to Ben, Roy moved her cell phone from the top of the front seat of her car, to down between the seat and the back of it. By the time she made her call, forty minutes had gone by. It took Ben another twenty minutes to get his truck started.

That had given Wanda enough time to do her work on the agent. Within a short time, he was doing his best to get her complete attention. She let him work at it for a while, then flirted back at him. Shortly before the mother finally arrived at the bar, Wanda agreed to dance with him. The third song was a slow one, and he pulled her close. She allowed it until the mother was far enough into the bar to see them.

She then slapped the agent and yelled, "No, you asshole, I won't go up in your room with you." She then ran out of the bar.

The mother didn't hesitate with her response. She too slapped the agent. "You said you'd never do that to me," she screamed. "After all I've been doing for you, you cheat on me like that."

The agent threw up his hands. "All I did was dance with her. I didn't invite her up to our room. I was waiting for you. You are the only woman I want."

The mother was crying by now. "I don't believe you. I was willing to do anything for you. Even ruin my husband. And you do this." She turned away from him, and at that moment Roy managed to get a full, closeup view of her face on the video he was taking of her. He sent it to Sue.

She worked her magic, and within minutes had managed to interrupt the network the mother's husband was watching on television. He was shocked when the TV series disappeared and the video taken in the bar started on his sixty-five inch TV set. The video ended with the closeup of his wive's face.

He was waiting for her when she came home. Right after she came in the door, he did a replay on the video for her.

"You've got a hell of a lot of explaining to do," he said.

"I know," she said, and wondered why she ever thought a man in a suit was better than a man who wore a tool belt.

CHAPTER 26

After the episode with the mother, Mack decided that what he wanted most to do was take some time off. When he mentioned it to Lisa, she hesitated.

"I take it you don't really want to take some time off," he said. "I thought it might be good for us to get away for a while. Go somewhere to relax and just enjoy each other. I guess though, I'll forget it. There's no way I want to go anywhere without you along."

"It's not so much that I don't want to go, Mack. It's more like I'll feel guilty about doing it while we're so busy. And we do have quite a case load now, after we put so much of our efforts and resources into going after the book banners."

"I know. The trouble is, our lives are getting to be so tied up in this agency it's beginning to feel like it's taken over control of every aspect of them. I agree that what we do is often important. The thing is, so are we, and we are getting lost here. I'd like to take some time and get the we that is us back to where it should be."

"Aren't you satisfied with me anymore, Mack. When you say things like that, it makes me wonder if you really want me to go with you. Or are you talking about us losing who we are so you have an excuse to ask someone else to go with you."

"That's crazy, Lisa. I said what I said because I so very much want to have some time with you. Just you and I. There's no way I want to go with anyone else but you. And all I'm asking is that you think about it. I think we've earned some alone time."

"Okay, I'll think about it. I do have to say though, that if you decided to take someone else, there's a long list of women who would love to go with you. Be it a weekend, a week or a month. For some of them, I think they'd prefer a lifetime with you."

"That's crazy. Kathy's the only woman I know about who's in love with me, and she's said many times that she has no intention of leaving Dale for me. I've never asked her to either."

Lisa would have laughed at what he said. Given that she wasn't pleased with their conversation she couldn't. All she could manage was a forced smile. "Pay attention," she told him, "and you'll see quick enough what they all think and feel."

"Even if that's true, it doesn't matter. I only want you, and you are the only one I want to spend some real time alone with."

Mack kissed her and she returned it. "I will think about it," she said. "But if we do it, I want it to be because we are doing something to move forward. Not because we are running away from something."

Their discussion quickly became a moot point. The new governor of Wisconsin decided he wasn't getting enough attention in the media. He wasn't, he was sure, because he wasn't acting macho enough. So he decided to prove he was very much a macho man who could take on anyone.

While looking around for targets, he ran across some information that Shanty Lucas and Rod Dasadist were in the same meetings a couple of times. He did some research on her, mostly on far right wing web sites. They all pictured her as a gun hating, left wing socialist. Never mind that she owned and ran a multi-billion dollar corporation that manufactured guns and that she was considered by most of the media to be conservative.

The governor accepted the views of the right wingers, and decided to go after her. He thoroughly condemned her in his next speech. That set off wave of protests from various gun groups across the country. Several people were killed and dozens were injured.

While they were going on, people were beginning to mob up around Shanty's home. It didn't take long for her to get extremely tired of listening to their screaming threats and chants. Her home quickly began to feel more like a prison than a home. She knew that she needed to escape it.

Where to go? She could, she knew, fly in her own private jet anywhere in the world. Escaping her home and getting to the airport was easy enough. She had a helicopter that could pick her up and fly her to the airport, which would be relatively safe to do in the middle of the night.

The question of where to go kept coming back to her. Where did she want to go. The one thing she was sure of was that she wanted to be around friends. Something she did not have a lot of. And most of those who claimed to be her friends weren't people she completely trusted.

After mentally going through the short list, she realized there was only one group she felt comfortable putting her trust in. They were people she knew she could trust her life with. Of everyone she'd known her entire life, they were the people she most wanted to see now. So she called Mack Thomas.

He answered on the second ring. As soon as he said hello, she said, "I need your help, Mack. I need a safe place to stay for a while. There's a mob outside my property right now, and they're driving me crazy."

Mack's answer for her was simple. "When are you going to be here?"

"Early tomorrow. I want you to know, I really appreciate this, Mack."

"No problem. It will be great to see you again."

Lisa was smiling when he hung up the phone. "I guess," she said, "that with Shanty coming, it will be a while before you and I have our get away together."

"It does, but you don't have to look so happy about it. And how did you know I was talking to Shanty?"

"I'm not smiling because we aren't going. I'm smiling because she's coming. I knew it was her because of the way you sounded when you talked to her. Your voice is a little different with every woman who is your friend. Just like the way you treat them is. I think that's part of why they're all kind of in love with you. You treat each one of them according to who they are."

"I guess it would be better if I treated them more alike."

"Oh no! That's not what I'm saying at all. One of the very best parts of you is the way you treat people. It's part of why I love you so much. I wouldn't be near as happy or contented as I am if you treated me the way any other man would. You know I'm different. That I can't be like anyone else. You're a good man, Mack. And that's part of my smile too."

Since they were home for lunch, and since the case they were working on wouldn't be harmed any if they took a long lunch, Mack took advantage of Lisa's good mood.

She knew when he took her hand and led her to their bedroom that she was being taken advantage of. It was fine by her. What they always shared was something she was especially grateful for. He was the only man who would ever have been able to take her from the victim of multiple rapes, to a woman who always welcomed the sharing with him.

For Mack, it always felt like an endless surprise that a woman as beautiful, inside and out, would love him the way she did. On this day, their lunch break turned into nearly double its normal time.

It proved to be time well spent though. They'd been feeling a slight, but constant, tension between them. It was gone by the time they made it back to work.

No one at Refuge Rescuers said anything to either one of them about it, even though everyone who had any contact with them that day knew that something had changed. And changed for the better.

Mack and Lisa felt the affects too, and felt so much better with each other that they repeated their lunch break when they went to bed that night. It worked out so well for them that they woke up twice during the night to repeat the experience.

As a result, they were a more than a happy couple when Shanty arrived the next day. They were also a somewhat tired couple. Shanty noticed both things about them right away.

After their usual initial greetings, she stepped back from them. Shaking her head, she said, "It's good to see what you two have hasn't changed. When I see the two of you together, looking the way you look now, it always gives me a renewed hope for the rest of us. At the same time, I surely do envy you and what you have."

"I don't know that we're special enough for you to envy us, Shanty," Lisa told her. "But I do know how lucky I am to have Mack. Without him, I never would have been able to become a whole woman. He's the only man I could have ever trusted enough."

"That trust thing is something special with him. That's why I decided to come here when I needed to get away. For me, I not only trust Mack, I know that if he trusts someone, so can I. That means that this is a place where I feel like I'm safer trusting, than anywhere else."

"Well, we are all glad you feel that way. It's good to see you too. Do you plan on staying for a while this time?"

"I'm don't know how long it will be, but it will for sure be longer than other times. The right wing fascists are once again in the mood to raise their own special kind if totally ignorant hell, so I think I'll be here long enough for you to get good and tired of me."

Mack decided then, to get in the middle of their conversation. "I can't see that happening, Shanty. You aren't the kind of person any of us would ever get tired of. We all enjoy having you around."

"Even with that big RV of mine parked in your yard, and my two bodyguards living in it with me?"

"That's right. Even with all of that, we still won't get tired of you. You are welcome to stay here as long as you want. And for right now, what can we do for you?"

"You can give me a couple of hours to rest. Then what I want most is for you to take me on what Kathy calls walking the refuge." Shanty turned to Lisa. "And I'll be really pleased if you'd come along with us."

"I will, if you for sure want me too. But it can be a very special thing if you go alone with Mack."

"I don't doubt it is, Lisa. I just don't want you to ever feel like I'm trying to start anything with him. Not that I think I could. You're so much more beautiful than I am. But I don't want to do anything that doesn't seem right."

"It's okay, Shanty. I'll make Mack promise not to do anything to make me jealous. That way, we'll both be safe."

Shanty laughed. "You're right. If Mack makes that promise, nothing will happen. Not even if I try to push it. Which I have no intention of doing."

"Good," Lisa said. "That settles it. You get your first walk in the refuge alone with Mack."

Shanty sighed. It was a heavy sigh. "If only..."

CHAPTER 27

Shanty wanted to make her walk with Mack alone. She didn't even want her bodyguards along. They, on the other hand, had no intention of letting the two of them walk out in the refuge alone.

Mack understood why Shanty wanted to go without them, even though he understood their point of view. Since he didn't feel quite as strong a need for the two of them to be completely alone during their walk, he worked out a compromise with them. They would follow along on the hike, but keep more distance between themselves and he and Shanty than normal.

The walk started normal enough. From the very first time Mack took Kathy on a refuge walk, she'd taken his hand and held it. Something she always did on their walks now. Other women that Mack had walked the refuge with picked up on Kathy's habit and usually held Mack's hand. This time, so did Shanty.

They didn't get far before she gave his hand a firm squeeze and said, "You know, Mack, it wouldn't take much for me to become part of this way of life of yours. I hope, for her sake, that Lisa knows what she's got. Living the way you guys do, and having such a strong love to share is a beautiful thing."

"I agree that most of it is. I'd like to change some of it though."

"Really? What would you change? And why would you change it?"

"To start with, I'd like to take a lot more time off. First, I want a week or two with just Lisa and I. I don't care where it is or what we do. I only care it's just us."

"That doesn't sound like it should be hard to do."

"You're right. It shouldn't be. The trouble is, Lisa doesn't feel right about us leaving the agency like that. To some extent she's right. We are awful busy most of the time. At the same time, we both need a break and I think we deserve one."

"So what are you going to do?"

"Wait it out. Sooner or later she'll come around."

"What are your plans after you get some time off?"

"I want to work hard at training everyone at Refuge Rescuers enough so it doesn't need me or Lisa to continue to stay in business. Then I'd like to quit and spend a few years traveling. Lisa and I are learning photography now. I think it would be interesting to stay in different places, take pictures, then write about it."

"Wow, that is some big changes, Mack. It sounds like it would be a good way to live too. For a while anyway."

"You wouldn't ever actually want to do something like that, now would you?"

Shanty stopped walking. She let go of his hand, lifted her arms, and wrapped them around his neck. "In the life I live now, I probably wouldn't. If given the chance, however, to have that kind of time with you, Mack Thomas, I'd do it in a minute. Even it cost me every dime I have."

She kissed him then. It was filled with all the enthusiasm that could only come from a woman in love. Mack couldn't help but like what she did, yet it scared the living hell out of him. No one could ever replace Lisa in his life. And that life was already complicated because of their relationship with Dale and Kathy. And now Shanty was telling him that she was in love with him too.

Not knowing what to say, Mack took her hand and they again walked into the refuge. He was looking hard for some kind of wildlife that they could stop and study, when he heard a familiar, but unexpected sound. Before he could warn Shanty about what was coming, she marched out of the brush. It was the bear.

Shanty was seriously startled by her, but not afraid. She'd seen her before, and knew that as long as she was with Mack, there was little chance it would attack her. Her bodyguards didn't know that.

Actually glad to see her, Mack momentarily forgot about them. It was Shanty's scream that brought him around. About one second before they were ready to shoot and kill the bear, he stepped between them and her.

"No," he yelled, "don't shoot. It's okay. We're okay. The bear just wants to say hello. She's not here to hurt any of us."

"Mack's right," Shanty added. "I've seen this bear before. She and Mack are friends."

Shaking their heads, the two men reluctantly put their guns away. Then something happened that surprised all of them. Even Mack. The bear walked up to him, rose up on her hind feet, and gently touched his shoulder with her paw. The look on her face appeared to be a smile.

She then dropped down on all four feet, nodded her head as if to say yes, and ambled away into the brush. Shanty, who stared at Mack and the bear the whole time she was expressing her friendship with him, still had her mouth open when the bear had disappeared.

Mack looked at her, a big grin on his face. He touched her under her chin with his finger. "It'd be best if you close it," he said, "before any flies decide to land in there."

"That was unbelievable, Mack," Shanty said, her voice trembling from the excitement rippling through her body. "Has she ever done that before?"

"No. Not even anything close. I'm as surprised by it as you are."

"I'm not only surprised, Mack. I'm deeply impressed. You know, you and I talked about this kind of thing before. About what it would be like if you could work with this refuge full time. About how we could possibly expand it." She stared at the ground, her toes of her right foot trying to dig a small trench in the trail. "You can't quit and go away. You have to stay and do more with this wondrous place you've already done so much to preserve. We can make it bigger and better. There are so many things we can do. Things that need doing."

"That's easy to say, Shanty. It's not so easy to do. It has been a constant battle to keep what we already have. Do you have any idea how tough it will be to try to expand this refuge."

"I do. I know too, that we can start slow, and quietly. If we don't tell the world what we're doing, it's highly unlikely the world will know what we're doing soon enough to stop us."

"I'm willing to try. And this way, for now at least, everything will stay pretty much the same for everyone. Lisa can ease her way into the job of full time manager of Refuge Rescuers, while I at the same time am leaving it. It will feel good too, to be working on what I consider the most important part of our lives. The environment. As the world goes, what we want to do is a small thing. Yet it's still an important one."

They continued their walk then. Mack stopped them often to look at or study one thing or another. While doing it, he came up with another idea.

"I think," he explained to Shanty, "that we should start a small school that offers classes on wildlife management. If we can find the right instructors to teach there, we might even be able to award real college credits to our students."

"I agree. Add it to the list of things to do."

Mack laughed then. Not being able to help himself, he put his arms around her and held her close. "I don't know, Shanty, how much of this, how many of our ideas we'll actually accomplish, but doing it with you is going to be a pure pleasure."

"That goes both ways, Mack. The only glitch in the whole deal is how I feel about you."

"I have some strong feelings for you too. And those feelings we have could cause us some trouble. They might mean that we should forget our ideas, and go back to life as it is now."

"I don't think so. We are going to move on ahead at full speed. We are just going to have to control ourselves. Me more than you. And I have an idea about something I know will help."

"Are you going to tell me what that idea is, Shanty?"

"Sure. I'm going to talk to Lisa about it. I'm going to tell her to keep an eye on us at all times. That way she can get after us if there's a need to."

"And she damn well will do that. I'll talk to her too. I think she'll like our ideas well enough to go along with them, even if she does need to keep an eye on us. But that isn't the only glitch. The other is, how are we going to manage the decisions that we will have to make together. Every piece of property we buy will be one. There'll be lots of others. You live a long way from here, and there's just so much we can do online. It could mean a lot of traveling for you."

"That's not going to be a problem."

"You won't mind all that traveling?"

"No. I won't be doing all that traveling."

"How are you going to avoid it? There will be times when you'll have to be here."

"I'm going to move. Here. Mack, I want to live here."

"Are you sure? It's going to be hard to find you a place anywhere near here that will match what you live in now."

"That's not a problem. I don't want anything like that. I know that there's already a lot of homes built on that land of yours, but I think it could hold one more. And I'm not talking about some kind of mansion. I want something like you and Lisa, and Dale and Kathy have. I'm only one person. What the hell do I need a mansion for."

"Do you actually think you could be satisfied living in something like that? For us, it was easy to adjust to. We never had much, so what we have now seems like a lot. You might miss the luxury you have now."

"I might. The thing is, I'll be gaining more than I lose. All my life I've felt lonely. This is the only place I've ever stayed that doesn't give me that feeling."

"What about running your company?"

"I'm going to turn the management of it over to someone else. There are a few people to choose from that I can trust. I can keep close enough watch on it to still have some control. If the new management doesn't do it right, I will change it."

"That's a hell of a lot to give up. Are you really sure you want to?"

"The truth is, Mack, I hate being CEO of my company. I have since I inherited it from my father. What I really want to do, is to work for you as the assistant manager of our new and improved wildlife refuge. I want to be able to see on any given day, what I saw today between you and the bear."

"Okay, I'm game for that if you are. Where do you want to build your house?"

"Somewhere out of the way. I've noticed a small clearing kind of in-between your house and Dale and Kathy's. I would feel safe there, and I'd always be close to the meadow."

"One more thing, Shanty. We're going to need an office. Refuge Rescuers's office is already over crowded."

"Lets wait on that. Some of the property we'll be buying will have buildings on it. We should be able to find something on one of them."

They continued their walk then, but didn't get far before a huge turtle crossed the path ahead of them. Shanty dropped Mack's hand and rushed forward, with every intention of getting a very close look at the animal.

Before she got too close, Mack warned her, "Be careful. Those things have an awful bite. And they won't hesitate to use one on you if you piss them off."

"They're so cute though."

"Sure they are, if you can call something with a perpetual bad temper cute. It's a snapping turtle, and they're called that for a reason."

Shanty giggled. "You mean there's an animal in this refuge that isn't a personal friend of yours?"

Mack smiled back at her. "There's lots of them who aren't what you could call friends. They don't have to be. They aren't my enemy either. I have a healthy respect for all of them. The thing with the snapper, I don't only have respect for his life. Those powerful jaws of his tend to keep me respectful of who and what he is too."

"Is he really that dangerous, Mack?"

"He can be. I don't know if he could actually take your hand off if he bit it, but the damage he could do would be permanent. And you could end up with some parts missing."

"This is strange you know, walking with you. First we see a bear that I was taught could be something dangerous. It gives you what almost could be called a hug, then moves on. Now we see what I think is a cute turtle, and you tell me to stay the hell away from it. It seems like such a contradiction."

"Maybe it is, Shanty. Not as big though, as you being willing to give up a mansion to live in a relatively small house. Especially given your net-worth."

"I think I'll be improving my net-worth by the move. I may end up broke, money wise, after this new venture we are about to get into. My real worth will be a lot more from it, no matter what happens.

CHAPTER 28

Mack and Shanty decided to meet with Lisa together, to tell her about what they wanted to do with the refuge and the changes Mack wanted to make. Both in the refuge and his own life. Lisa wasn't surprised about his ideas for the refuge, but the changes he wanted to make in his life came as a mild shock.

"So you mean," She said, "that you want to quit Refuge Rescuers and stop being a private detective? You've been a cop of one kind or the other for a long time, Mack. What makes you think you won't miss it if you quit?"

"I'm sure there will be things I miss. And I intend on keeping my license, so I will be available if you really need me. I still want to go ahead with this. The refuge, and my concern for the environment in general, have always what I considered the most important part of my life. Aside from you, of course. You'll always be the most important part of my life, as long you'll let me be part of it."

"What about you, Shanty?" Lisa asked her. "Aren't you going to miss running a multi-billion dollar company?"

"I don't think so. Getting out from under that job will be a great relief for me. I'm having no doubts about my enjoying the work I'll be doing with Mack far more than what I'm doing now."

"The way you say that, Shanty, makes me wonder about your relationship with Mack. You don't plan on trying to take him away from me, do you?"

Shanty laughed. "One of the things I wanted to do today is to talk to you about that very subject. I freely admit it. I am in love with him. Even so, I have no intention of trying to take him away from you, as much as I'd like to have him. What I want you to know is that I expect that you keep a close eye on us. If you see anything between us that bothers you at all, I want you to say so. No matter what, I don't want to screw up what you two have. It's too perfect to ever change."

"I feel that way about it too, Lisa," Mack told her. "If I ever do something, anything, with Shanty that you don't like or that bothers you, I want you to speak up right away. Whatever it is, I'll do my best to correct it."

"I take it from what both of you just said, that the two of you already talked about how to deal with that subject with me. How can I be sure you didn't just rehearse what you were going to say so you could throw me off track about it?"

It was Mack's turn to laugh. "The answer to that is simple. I, better than anyone, know you well enough to know that we could never, not in a million years, get away with that with you. You are too damn smart, too aware, and too alert to my moods. We said what we said because we do want you to keep an eye on us so you keep us on the straight and narrow."

"I wasn't kidding, Lisa," Shanty added. "It is very important to me that I never do anything that would upset the life you and Mack have. Especially not that way. And not by helping him change what he's doing either. If you don't want him to go full time into the refuge work, all you have to do is say so. We'll back off on the idea."

"I won't ever do that. Mack has every right to do what he what he wants to do. The truth is though, I do have one big concern. I'm not sure I'm good enough to be able to take over management of Refuge Rescuers. Maybe Mack should train someone else to do it."

"No, Lisa," Mack told her, "I shouldn't. You are by far the most qualified to do the job. You are, as far as I'm concerned, more qualified than I am. Add to that, you have as good a bunch working with you as you could ever ask for. And if you get desperate, you can also always talk to me about any concerns. After all, we will still be sleeping together every night."

"I agree with Mack," Shanty added. "I work with management types constantly. I've seen you work. You have more ability to make good decisions than a large percentage of them. You have the ability to maintain your composure even in high stress conditions. I have no doubts about your ability to do the job."

"Okay, you guys have given me enough confidence to try to do the job. But I want you to watch me as close as I'm supposed to watch you, and if I screw up, I expect you to step in and correct me and the situation."

"Fair enough," Mack said. "So are you okay with us moving forward on this new setup, Lisa?"

"I am. I'll miss working with you, Mack, but I damn sure do understand why you want and need to do what you're going to do."

Mack and Shanty breathed a sigh of relief with that. She hugged Mack first, then Lisa, who also got a kiss on the cheek after the hug.

Shanty went to her RV then, and spent the rest of the day on the phone, making arrangements to interview people to take over her job. Mack and Lisa talked more about the changes that were about to take place in their lives. They didn't talk long before Lisa admitted that she was actually happy with the way things were developing.

"I was worried about your wanting to travel," she said. "This is a much better change for me. I wasn't ready to walk away from everything and everybody. Not yet. With this new plan, we will still be here and we will still be together, even if we aren't working together every day."

"That's part of what made me want to go with this plan. I didn't want to leave you. Not even for a short time. But I do need a change. I'm tired of the fighting just to get the simplest things done. And the all too often violence has gotten to be too much for me."

"When are you going to start implementing the changes?"

"Tomorrow. At breakfast. Everyone will be told that you are now the manager of Refuge Rescuers. Then, from that point on, that's exactly what you will be. I'll still be there to assist you if you need me. I won't be just walking away. The transition should be easier if I gradually phase myself out of the business, then it would if I suddenly walked away."

"I appreciate that. It definitely will be easier."

Breakfast in the morning proved to be the right time for Mack to announce the fact that he would be leaving Refuge Rescuers. Everyone who was part of the agency was there.

Mack was surprised at their reaction. Rather than getting a lot of arguments against his leaving, everyone thought it was a good idea. Especially after he explained, with some detail, why he was going. Two of the people there were the biggest surprise for him. They both filled their faces with wide grins.

Roy was the first of them to comment about his move. "I can't tell you how happy I am for you, Mack. I've noticed lately that you need a change. I think you've found the perfect one. Now you can spend your time doing what you love most. Taking care of the refuge."

Ben followed Roy. "I have to tell you, Mack. This couldn't be better news. You are finally going to be able to do something I've wished you could do since you graduated high school. I know you liked what you've been doing since you got back from rodeo, but a part of you has always wanted to do what you're going to be doing now."

Wanda said her piece then. "Everything you've done over the years, Mack, has had some meaning and for the most part positive results. But this new venture you're going into now is the most important. Spending all your working time doing what you can to preserve the environment. Nothing is more important than that."

As soon as Mack got his compliments, everyone turned to Shanty to thank her for her part in the new project. Before they were done complimenting her, she felt better than she'd ever before felt about herself.

After breakfast everyone took on their work, whatever it was, with a renewed enthusiasm. So much so, that Mack managed to spend the day researching the real estate market north of the existing refuge.

Shanty spent the morning setting up interviews with some of the few people she considered qualified to take over as CEO of her company. In the afternoon, she consulted with the people who were going to assist her in the purchase of Lands Magnificent, the resort built on what was part of the original wildlife refuge.

By the end of the day, Shanty and Mack were happy with how much they'd accomplished their first day working on the project. Lisa was equally satisfied with her first day as manager of Refuge Rescuers. Best of all, she'd already gained some confidence about her ability to do the job.

Shanty too, felt as if she'd accomplished a lot. She flew home after breakfast, and managed to interview five different men as her replacement. None of them were quite what she wanted, but she felt a sense of accomplishment just by eliminating them from her list of candidates.

It wasn't until she did her fifteenth interview that she found the person she wanted for the job. Addison Bardo originally applied for the job of executive assistant to the company CEO. She was the lead candidate for that job, but had so impressed the man who gave her her first interview that he recommended her to Shanty as her possible replacement.

As was normal in the world of top management, Shanty hadn't considered a woman when she considered who she would hire. So she didn't tell her which job they were interviewing her for. But this woman, along with her credentials, so impressed Shanty that she interviewed her three days in a row. At the end of the third one, she smiled and said, "You are now the CEO of a multi-billion dollar corporation. How do you feel about that?"

"I'm what?" Shock filled her face, along with total disbelief.

"You are now the CEO of this corporation. If you want the job, that is?"

"But I applied for the executive assistant job. I had no idea that you were considering me for that job. I don't know what to say."

Shanty couldn't help but smile. This Addison had all the skills needed to do the job, but lacked the conceit nearly all the men being considered for the job had. "You don't need to say much," she told her. "A simple yes, I'll take the job, or no thanks, I don't want the job will do."

"Oh my god, this is the last thing I would have ever expected. Yes, of course I want the job. Just as long as I will actually run the company. If you picked me just so I can be some kind of figurehead only, then I'll have to say no. I don't want to spend any part of my life having a bunch of old men on the board of directors trying to birddog every move I make."

"You'll be running the company. But there are two absolute rules of mine you will have to follow. This company will never again manufacture assault rifles, no matter how profitable they are. The same goes for cheap hand guns."

Addison smiled. "I'll take the job. I can understand the ownership of most guns, but the two you just mentioned are things I've hated for a very long time."

Shanty called the board of directors together the next day. To a man, they considered Shanty's decision to be the wrong one, but knew better than to argue with her. She owned too much of the company stock for them to be able to argue with her. She could get rid of any or all of them whenever she wanted to. They had no chance of getting rid of her.

CHAPTER 29

It was a long three weeks for everyone, but the training of CEOs and managers was over. Everyone involved knew there would be mistakes and problems with the change in management. At the same time, they were confident that they could and would be positively dealt with.

Lisa and Addison were excited and happy about starting their new jobs on their own, but Mack and Shanty were even more excited about their new venture.

Initially the most difficult task they faced was the acquisition of more land. So every time there was property for sale within what they hoped would be the new boundaries of the refuge, they immediately checked it out. It was rare when they didn't buy it. The few they skipped were properties priced outrageously high.

What the people who priced their land that way didn't realize, was the fact that Mack and Shanty could wait them out. They'd already made a deal with the county for every road running through that area. Once those roads were closed, the high priced land would lose most of its value.

Mack and Shanty had no intentions of cheating anyone out of their land. They would pay somewhat more than the market value of the land while it was still worth something, but they didn't have any intention of being gouged. There was simply too much land to buy and too many other expenses to consider.

Just as there was during the setup of the original refuge back in the sixties, there was a fair amount of resentment about the expansion if it. This time though, instead of the government, the blame was put on everyone involved with it in any way. And as word got out on who was in charge of the project, a large portion of the resentment was focussed on Mack and Shanty.

It was the age of Trump and Dasadist, even with Dasadist now dead. All their followers were completely against any kind of large parks or wildlife refuges. As far as they were concerned, all the money being spent on the refuge should be spent on churches and cathedrals and those people who rigidly followed the rules of their evangelical church. After all, God desperately needed more places where he would be worshiped. Just as bad, he needed ever more people to do that worshiping. He, after all, never got all the praise he wanted and needed.

It didn't take long for those God fearing evangelicals to work themselves into a frenzy of hatred motivated blood lust. They knew they had to stop the refuge expansion. After long discussions they decided that the best way to do it would be to catch Mack and Shanty out in the refuge and beat them as close to death as they could without killing them.

They picked out six of their biggest, strongest men, and sent them out into the wilds of the existing refuge to find them. Once found, they would simply be beaten. The six strong men were on the side of God, so they were confident it would be uneasy task.

They were pretty much wrong about that. Mack and Shanty had friends there that the good christian evangelicals would never have been able to dream of. One in particular saw the men coming. She instinctively knew they were trouble. She sat down among some heavy brush and waited. Mack and Shanty were working only a few yards away.

Mack heard them coming first. He put a hand on Shanty's shoulder and gestured for her to be quiet. But he wasn't quick enough, and the six men spotted them. Mack moved between them and Shanty. He would defend her the best he could for as long as he could.

The men came in swinging. Mack managed to take out the lead man, but then was hit by a large branch from behind. It staggered him, but he managed to stand his ground. One of the men had grabbed Shanty, and was trying to rip her clothes off. But she too was a fighter, and he was getting nowhere.

That's when they all heard her before any of them saw her. She moved up on her hind legs, and with perfect accuracy landed a blow on the head of the man trying to molest Shanty. It removed most of that side of his face. He naturally screamed and fell, trying desperately to put it back together again.

With four men still standing, the bear quickly dispatched three of them. Mack was working on the fourth one, throwing short jabs onto his head and into his body. It didn't take long for the man to become defenseless, but Mack worked him over for a while anyway.

After he let the man drop, he turned to Shanty. "Wild dogs did this. No matter what, it was wild dogs. We don't ever, no matter what, admit it was a bear. She deserves much better than what the rest of the world will want to do to her."

"No problem, Mack. I know she's not the same kind of friend to me as she is to you, but I love her just the same."

That's when Shanty got one big surprise. The bear moved close to her, lifted a paw, and gently patted her head. She smiled, dropped down on all fours, and did a little sashay into the brush around them. Shanty watched her go with a huge smile on her wide open mouth.

Mack dialed 911 then, and waited for the sheriff's people to come. Three cars from the sheriff's department arrived just minutes apart. Sheriff Dale Magee was in one of them.

"What the hell happened, Mack?" he asked as soon as he saw the six bleeding men on the ground.

"I guess someone is pissed off at us for something," Mack answered. "Those men didn't say anything. They just came here and attacked us. We were doing our best to defend ourselves when a large pack of wild dogs attacked them. The animals in this refuge know that Shanty and I are never going to harm them, and that we are here to protect them. So they helped us."

"From the looks of the injuries on four of those men, I'd have to say it was something bigger than dogs that attacked them."

"Sorry, Dale," Mack explained, "but you're wrong. It was dogs. I will sear to it under oath if I have too. So will Shanty. It was just dogs."

Dale shook his head. He knew Mack's story was false. He also was sure of the reason Mack told it. As much as he respected the law and the truth, he knew there were times to set both aside. He was confident that he knew what had done the damage to the men on the ground, and what the outside world would demand that it be destroyed. Dale, however, was wise enough to know that whatever did the damage to the men was a living creature with far more value than those men ever had or would have.

"Okay, Mack," he finally agreed. "Wild dogs it is. Do you have any idea where they went?"

"There's no way to tell. They all ran off in different directions. They're all likely to be miles away from here by now."

Dale didn't have anymore questions, and his report stated that it was wild dogs who came to Shanty and Mack's rescue.

All six men spent time in the hospital. As soon as they were able to talk, they told everyone they were attacked by a bear. Their stories were even published in both the Minneapolis and local papers. Not much attention was paid to them though, since no member of the public who had visited the refuge had ever seen a bear there.

Lisa only had two things to say to him about the incident when he went home that night. "It doesn't look like your wish for a less violent time has worked out the way you hoped, has it, Mack?" And, "I damn sure hope the rest of the world doesn't learn about the bear. I worry less about you working out there in the refuge, knowing she's around."

A little over a week later, after they'd been able to work without much in the way of interruptions Mack and Shanty decided to take a midday break and go out for some lunch. Mack called Lisa to invite her along, but she was tied up with an important case. So they went alone to a local bar called the Mystic Curve. Mack especially liked the place because they served excellent bacon cheeseburgers and fries. Close to his favorite meal.

Their waitress had just delivered the two glasses of beer they ordered when a man approached their table. Without a word, he slammed his fist down hard on it. He accomplished what he wanted and got Mack's full attention. What Mack picked up on right away was the man's size. He was huge. He stood about six-eight and weighed in at about two hundred sixty pounds. There was no fat on him.

Mack looked him in the eyes. "You want something?" he calmly asked.

"Damn right I do. You're Mack Thomas. You had your trained attack bear go after my friends. Then you lied about what it was that done it to them. Well, you ain't got no bear here now, so I plan on beating the living shit out of you."

"Do you plan on trying that yourself, or did you bring some help along?"

"I'll do it myself. I fought professional for a while. A little shit like you won't be no problem."

"What kind of fighting did you do?"

"The only kind of real fighting there is. Boxing. You'll never be able to stand up agains a real boxer."

"So you think I'm going to get up and have a boxing match with you?" Mack stopped to chuckle at the thought. "I have to tell you, it ain't going to happen. There's no way I'm going to have a boxing match with you."

"On top of everything else," the big man snarled, "you're afraid to fight me too."

"No, not really. I'm just not going to box you. You want a fight, we'll have a fight. It won't be fair though. I'll go after you in anyway I can. As I said, there won't be any fair about it either. I'll probably start by breaking your nose. Piss me off enough before I do I'll jam it hard enough into your brain to kill you. If I can gouge your eyes out, I will. The same goes for you nuts. I'll destroy them if I can. Any bones I can break, I'll break. If I'm able, I'll damage your head enough to cause permanent brain damage. I'll do anything I can to harm you as much as I can. And I goddamn sure won't be following any kind of rules to do it. Now, the question is, do you want your ass kicked in here or out in the parking lot. We go outside, and it'll save you the money it will cost you for repairs in here after I'm done with you. Unless you're dead, in which case it won't matter either way."

"Ain't no way I'll be paying for nothing. Not even your hospital bill after I'm done with you."

Mack knew then that the man wasn't smart enough to take his threats seriously. So he stood up and moved too close to the man for him to be able to take a proper swing at him. He tried anyway. Mack easily avoided it, then let the man throw another one. That meant he was defending himself now, and that he could do what he'd just promised to do.

The attention of everyone in the bar was on them, so he felt free to do whatever was necessary to end this conflict. Mack didn't wait for a third blow to come to him. Instead, his right hand flew up and his palm connected with the big man's nose. He howled as he went down, grabbing his seriously broken and bleeding nose as he fell.

Mack didn't fool with him. He grabbed him by the hair and vigorously shook his head. "You done boxing yet?" Mack asked, a grim smile on his face, "or do you want me to continue?"

The big man, being a trained ex-boxer and therefore very macho, shook his head no. He tried to stand, but Mack sat him down again when the side of his fist slammed into the man's temple.

"I told you this wouldn't be a fair fight," Mack snarled at him. "Every time you try to get up, I'm going to hurt you. Two or three more tries, and you won't be able to get up again."

"If you had the guts, you'd let me up so we could have a fair fight."

"Guts have nothing to do with it. I won't let you up because I'm not that stupid. It's easy to see that you're in good shape. You outweigh me by at least fifty or sixty pounds. Your arms outreach mine by six or eight inches. And you call me boxing you fair. Not hardly. So you are either going to apologize for being such an ass, then get the hell out of here, or I'm going to continue to hurt you until the ambulance gets here."

Mack was becoming discouraged. The last thing he wanted to do was seriously hurt the man he was holding on to. He had quit working as a private detective to get away from so much violence. At the same time, he wasn't about to relinquish the upper hand he was now holding.

Before he could decide how he was going to further hurt the man, it was no longer necessary to make that decision. The siren from the sheriff's car wailed for about one minute, then stopped outside the bar. The deputy was a veteran, and was one Mack had always enjoyed working with back in the days when he was a deputy. He waited until the deputy was close before he let the man's hair go.

Mack explained to her what had happened, and that the man had taken the first swing. Several people in the bar verified Mack's story. There wasn't much for the deputy to do beyond cuffing the man and hauling him away to jail. Mack stopped at the sheriff's office after lunch and signed a complaint.

On the way back to the refuge, Shanty asked him, "Were you really planning on doing to that guy all the things you said you would do?"

"I wasn't planning anything. The last thing I wanted to do was get into any kind of a fight with him. So I was trying to talk him out of it. The only way that ever works with assholes like that guy is threats. It would be highly unusual for common sense or logic to have any effect on him."

"That's what I thought you were doing. But if it came to it. would you have done those things to him?"

"If I had no other choice, yes, I damn sure would have. I don't at all like to get into that kind of shit. But if there's no way out of it, I will defend myself the best way I know how. Fights like that aren't game or a sport. They're part of real life. So I don't see much sense in getting my ass kicked because some stupid jackass thinks I should follow his rules."

"Good. I'm glad you think that way. I'd hate to see you end up hurt when you don't have to. I also always feel safer around you, than I do any other time." She reached up and touched his cheek. "I surely do wish," she said, tears now running down her cheeks, "that I could feel that way twenty-four seven. Lisa is I think, Mack, about the luckiest woman alive. I sure do hope she knows that."

Shanty left her hand on his cheek, closed her eyes and let the tears fall. Mack concentrated on his driving. He knew that at that moment the only way he could give her the kind of comfort she wanted and needed would end up in a place they should never go.

That meant that what was happening between them bothered him a lot. He loved working with her, and the joy of what they were doing and accomplishing was like a dream come true. At the same time, he was beginning to believe that he should turn over the refuge project too Shanty. He could hire technical people to assist her, and he would do enough so that she wouldn't feel as though he'd deserted her. She just wouldn't be constantly reminded of the limitations of their relationship.

Without further thought about it, he drove to the refuge and parked in an open meadow. He turned to her, and as she did to him. He reached up and touched her cheek.

"I think, Shanty, that as soon as we get the refuge up and running the way we want it to, you should take over the management of it."

She looked at him as if he was crazy. "What the hell are you talking about, Mack? I'm never going to do that. As much as anything, the reason for doing what we're doing is so you can finally live your dream. If you quit on this project for any reason, so will I. As much as I love what I'm doing now, I don't ever want to do it without you. So why are you talking about quitting?"

"This is going to be hard for me to explain," he said. "It's not so much I want to quit. It's more that I'm getting the feeling that the way we're doing things is hurting you. It seems to me that if I back off some,

I won't be constantly hurting you. It breaks my heart every time I see you cry because of me. I care a lot about you, Shanty, and I hate it when I hurt you."

"I know you do, Mack. But you can't quit. Not for me, not for anything. What we are doing does matter, but more than that, it doesn't matter how much I cry. You've made me happier than I've ever been. And that's my whole life. I might be rich, but I've been through hell and back. Now, for the first time in my life that hell is behind me. Most of the time when I cry, I'm doing it for a mixture of reasons. I do it a lot simply because you've made me so happy. Other times, it's true that I cry over not being able to have you. Sometimes, like today, it's a mixture of both. The thing is though, what I have now, working with you everyday, makes the sometimes sadness worth it. Please, Mack, don't change what we have. It might not be everything I want, but it's way more than I've ever had before. I sure would like to keep it."

"Okay, Shanty, we'll keep it. As long as you promise you'll tell me if all of this gets to be too much."

"There's only one way that will happen. If what we are doing gets to be too much for Lisa, then it will be too much."

"It's great that you feel that way. It's unusual though. Most of the time in situations like this, the person in your position would be doing the opposite of what you're doing."

"If things were different, I might be doing this different too. I could never do that to Lisa. Not to you either. You and her belong together. If I messed you guys up, I'd be fucking up three lives. Lisa's, your's, and mine too. That makes my doing anything other than to continue to love both of you not just wrong, but incredibly stupid too."

Mack didn't say anything more. He moved his hand to the back of her head and held her there as he kissed her. She sighed heavily as he moved away and started his pickup.

CHAPTER 30

He was an older man carrying a cane when he came in. Donna Slater, Refuge Rescuers receptionist greeted him. "And what can we do for you, sir?" she asked.

"I'm not sure you can do anything for me," he answered. "What I'm hoping, is that there might be some way you can help my daughter."

"I guess that'll depend on what kind of help she'll need. Did you want to see one of our detectives, or can you tell me what you need?"

"I think I'd like to talk to a detective. No offense against you. I just don't want to have to tell my story more than once. It's too unpleasant."

"No problem," Donna reassured him. "Right at the moment, Lisa's the detective in the office. Should I check with her to see if she's available?"

"Now I'm not sure. There are some pretty rough things in what I will need to tell her. It might be better if there was a man I could talk to."

"Why? Don't you think a woman can handle adult problems?"

"It's not just that. Part of what I need to explain is violent. I'll have to describe it. I don't know that I would want a woman to have to listen to what I'll be saying. It's some pretty nasty stuff."

"I can assure you," Donna told him, "that Lisa can deal with anything any man can. She's tough as nails when it's necessary, and can deal with any problem as well as any man. On top of that, she's our best detective, and all of our detectives are damn good. Add to all that, she's the manager of this outfit, and anyone who works here will tell you she's a great boss. I'm Donna by the way. Can I get your name?"

"Yes, sorry. It's Zale. Zale Ekon. My daughter's name is Mia Ardolf. Her husband is Arty Ardolf. He's the problem I need help with."

"What we need to do now, Mister Ekon. is for you to decide whether you want to talk to Lisa now, a different person tomorrow, or go to another agency. The choice is entirely up to you."

"I guess I don't know for sure what I should do. This agency has such a good reputation, I hate the idea of going somewhere else. At the same time, I hate to drive anymore, so I'd rather not have to go home and come back again tomorrow. I guess that means I'm going to talk to your Lisa. If I decide not to use her, can I come back and meet with someone else?"

"That can be arranged. I doubt we will need to do that through. If Lisa doesn't impress you, I will be surprised."

Donna contacted Lisa to learn how long it would be before she'd be free. "The man waiting is in luck," Lisa answered. "I'll be finished up in about five minutes."

Lisa was right on target with her time, but for Zale it was a long wait anyway. He was full of doubts by the time he joined her in her office. When she stood to greet him, he took sudden deep breath. She was as far from what he was expecting to see as was possible. She was dressed in a simple blue cotton blouse and kaki slacks. Her clothes weren't form fitting, but didn't hang exactly loose either. She also wore minimal makeup, and when she combed her hair that morning, she let it hang down over her shoulders. All put together, she stood out as the beautiful woman that she was. She held out her hand to shake Zale's. It took him a moment to become aware of something, anything, other than the woman in front of him. He quickly took her hand when he did.

"You are Lisa?" he asked, a slight shiver in his voice. "You can't be a detective."

"Why not?" Lisa asked, a slight smile forming on her lips.

"You are way too beautiful. You should be a movie star, or at least a model. I don't think I can talk to you."

Lisa let the start of a smile turn into a frown. "Of course you can talk to me. There's no reason for you not to. Whatever your problem is or your needs are, we can deal with them here. There isn't much you can tell me that I haven't already heard at one time or another."

"What I have to say, what I need help with, is my daughter. She's in a very bad marriage that she doesn't seem to be able to get out of."

"Why not? Nowadays there are places and people who can and will protect her if she leaves him."

"We know that. She's tried to leave. The trouble is, he always comes up with a way to force her to go back with him. He's a vicious man. He hurts people. If she leaves, he always hurts someone close to her. It might be family, a friend, or even someone she works for. The cops are never able to trace it back to him. So there's damn little we can do. I came here, because this agency, this Refuge Rescuers as you call it, has a reputation for solving problems that to others seem impossible."

"I don't know what anyone's told you about us, but we never promise anyone that we will for sure solve their problem. All we can do is our best. There's never a guaranty it will be enough."

For the first time since he got there, Zale let a small smile move his lips. "That's all I would ever expect. People who say they can do more than that can rarely be trusted. I think I can trust you, Lisa. I want to hire you, if you'll let me after I tell you the problems my daughter and I are facing. And who the cause of those problems is."

"We won't know that until you tell me what they are," Lisa answered. "So you probably should start talking. And just so you know, I will be recording the rest of our conversation. It's the only way I can be sure I don't miss anything you say. Also, since there's always a chance that there will be more than one detective working on your case, they'll be much quicker picking up on the problem by listening to the recording than they will from only hearing what I tell them."

"Okay, I'll go along with the recording. If it's okay with you, before I get too deep into what needs fixing, I want to tell you about her husband."

"That's fine. Tell me what I need to know in any way you feel comfortable with."

"To start with, he's a respected member of our community. He's a member of the church board that serves Trinity Lutheran. It's the largest church in our county. He owns a lot of the retail stores in the town where they live. The super market, hardware store, and drug store, to name just three of them. He coaches the girl's basketball team and the track team. I can't prove it, but I'm sure that he's involved in any and all the drug trade going on in our area. Especially the stuff being sold to the kids. I'm also pretty sure that he's running some kind of prostitution ring. What bothers me most of all is the fact that he can't control his temper and frequently beats my daughter."

"Why don't you go to the police?"

"She has, but he's always got a story to cover what he did. I think he bribes them too. Either way, he's been getting away with it. When he does, he beats her some more."

Lisa wasn't exactly pleased with Zale's explanation. He didn't come across as someone who had tried very hard to help his daughter all that much. Which made her wonder if he'd done much of anything to help her prior to his visit with them.

"What is it," she asked him, "that you want us to do? One thing we don't do is get involved with domestic problems. If you're looking for someone to follow him around and take revealing pictures, along with gathering information to be used during a divorce, we don't do that kind of work. There are a lot of agencies who do though, and we can help you contact one of them."

"No," Zale protested. "That's not what I'm here for. What I'm hoping you can do is help me get her away from him, and do it in such a way that he believes she was kidnapped or something. I want to make her safe, but neither her nor I want her escape to cause harm to someone else. I've tried to find a way to do that on my own, but I just can't come up with anything. I guess I'm just too damn old to be good for much anymore."

"Now comes the part that's difficult for me to to tell you. Doing something like that will take a lot of planning and will involve more people. It will get expensive. Can you afford to hire us?"

Zale hesitated before answering. He knew this was coming, but it was a difficult thing for him to deal with anyway. "The money doesn't matter near so much to me as Mia does. I can't think of anything that does. Since I lost my wife two years ago, nothing much does matter. I can either sell or remortgage my home. It's paid for, so with the ridiculous price of housing now, I should be able to come up with about two hundred thousand dollars. Will that be enough to hire you?"

"It will. But don't you have any savings or something. I hate to see you have to give up your house."

"No, Lisa, I don't. Even with insurance, the hospital bills took a lot of what we'd saved over the years. Even worse than those bills, was the cost of drugs my wife needed. I didn't care so much then. I still don't. The doctor said they gave her a couple more years than she would have had without them. I would have been glad to give up anything to have more time with her. We had fifty-nine years together. I know that sounds like a lot to you, but it really wasn't enough. Only forever would have been enough. The longer we were together, the more I loved her. All I have left is my daughter, and she needs my help. The money, the house, nothing else matters. Do I have enough to hire you?"

Lisa could now feel the man's anguish. "You have more than enough money. So the answer is yes, we'll do what we can to help you. My question for you is this. Are you prepared to go over every detail of your daughter's husband's activities? It won't be once. You'll probably will have to answer questions from several people, and they will often be difficult and/or unpleasant to answer. So will some of the things we will expect you to do. That will be even more true of many of the things we'll be doing."

"What ever it takes. All that really matters is that Mia is made safe. What happens to me, what I might need to do, doesn't matter compared to that."

"Okay then. We have an agreement. You can go home tonight knowing we'll be doing our best for you. When you come back tomorrow we will have a contract ready for you to sign, and a preliminary report that covers our initial plans on how to accomplish our goals."

"Okay, that sounds good. I do have a question though. Will you be needing me to come here real often? It's a fairly long drive from home to here, and at my age, I'm not all that big on driving."

"I can understand that. Let me see what I can do to alleviate most, if not all, the driving."

As soon as Lisa finished with Zale and he was on his way back home, she contacted Mack. "I know this is probably too soon for me to be wanting your help, but I just took on a case that I need your advice on. I'd like it if you'd bring Shanty with you when you come. There's something I want to ask her about too."

"Do you need us right now, or is the end of the day soon enough?"

"The end of the day will do fine, Mack. It's not any kind of emergency. It's just something I think is important enough to put some extra effort into."

"Okay. Do you want to meet at home or the office?"

"I think the office will be best. To start anyway. After we talk, we'll decide what else to do tonight."

Lisa contacted Sue next. "I know you've probably got about ten other things to do," Lisa explained, "but this one is somewhat more urgent than normal." She told Sue about the problem. Sue didn't need to be told what to do. She was experienced enough to know.

Sue went to work online, investigating Arty Ardolf. She used all her online resources along with her own expertise to do an in-depth search of his history and background. The more she learned about him, the more dislike she had for him. By the time she finished putting together his profile, she knew he was a man she could easily hate.

While Sue was doing her job, Lisa called Larry and asked him to meet her in her office at the end of his day. He was finishing up with the case he'd been working, so he met with her about an hour after she called him. Lisa played the recording she made of her conversation with Zale right away. By the time Larry had heard all of it and they had a short discussion about it, Mack and Shanty arrived.

Lisa gave them a brief description of the case to start. She then asked them if they thought it would be okay to take on the case using the trust fund instead of charging Zale for it. She especially wanted to know what Shanty thought about it, since she was the one who set up the trust fund so Refuge Rescuers could take on cases for worthy people who couldn't afford their normal fees.

"I don't have any problem with you doing that at all, Lisa. That's what I set up the fund for."

"How about you, Mack? Do you think it's the right kind of case to use the trust fund on."

"I do, Lisa. But I also don't think you needed to ask for our permission to do it. You're the manager now, so I think you should always go ahead with whatever it is you think is right. As far as the case itself goes, from what you've told us so far, I think it's the kind that having any extra help you might need available would be a good idea. So if you get to the point where you want some help, Shanty and I will be there."

"I really appreciate that. And as long as you're going to be available, do you want to hear the recording I made when I interviewed him?"

"No. You did a good job of explaining the problem. We don't need to hear every word the two of you said."

Sue joined them then, with her report on Arty Ardolf. She'd learned enough about him to believe he was involved in drugs. As bad as that, he was an unlicensed gun dealer. His main business was in assault type weapons. She was sure too, that he was running a prostitution ring. In that, his primary product was teenage girls. That did it for Lisa. Given the fact that she was kidnapped and treated as a prostitute when she was a young girl, she had less than zero time or patience for anyone involved in that activity. Arty Ardolf was now doomed as far as she was concerned. She especially knew she needed to do something about his coaching girl's teams at the high school. That could easily be where he was getting some of his girls from.

Sue had also found a lot of information about Arty's involvement with the church. He was apparently doing everything he could to convert the Lutherans into evangelicals. He was having a hard time with that one though. A large portion of the congregation was made up of older Swedes, Norwegians, and Germans, all people too stubborn to easily change their minds.

They were, however, going along with one of his low-life community efforts. There were few complaints when he started to remove books banned in other states. He hit the school libraries first, but quickly followed with the local library. A book store, that had been part of the community for nearly fifty years, refused to go along with the book banning. Arty tried to buy them out, but they refused to sell. He then tried to buy the building their store was in. The book store people owned it, so he lost that battle too. It was less than a month later though, that a mysterious fire one night got out of control.

The entire building burned to the ground. That was bad news for the book store. It was every bit as bad for the pet shop in the same building. During the fire, the screams of the burning animals could be heard throughout the entire town.

Long before Sue completed her findings, they all knew that this case was no longer just about making Mia Ardolf safe. While that task was still very important, even more important was taking Arty completely out of the game. If the end result wasn't a life term in prison for him, then something else would have to be done. Whether it would be something legal or not, remained to be seen.

They called it a day then and everyone got ready to go home. After supper that night, Lisa and Shanty spent a couple of hours working on Shanty's defense training. They both went after it harder than normal. It didn't take long for them to realize they'd better back off some before someone got hurt.

"This probably isn't a good time for this kind of training," Lisa said. "We're both too pissed off right now to hold it down to a reasonable level."

""I think so too," Shanty agreed. "Learning about that asshole you guys will be going after has sure got me riled up good. It all reminded me of my father, and what he did to me all those years. It made me upset with myself too. I should have stopped him long before he died."

"Maybe. If you could have."

"I could have said no."

"That's easy to say now, Shanty. It wouldn't have been so easy then. So stop putting the blame on yourself. Instead of that, start thinking about that Arty Ardolf and how the hell we are going to stop him. Dying isn't the answer. It's too good for him."

"Castration would be a good start, Lisa. Then maybe some other kind of mutilation. I think about anything we could do to him is justified."

"You are definitely right about that. His little empire that he's built for himself should go first. Take away his money, and he'll lose his power."

"I can help with that. I still have a fair amount of influence in the financial world. Maybe we can come with some things that will take him down."

"I have no doubt about your ability to do that. The thing is though, whatever it is we do, we need to do it fast. If we don't, god only knows who he'll hurt next."

"Give me a little time, Lisa, and I'll come up with something."

"Good. And I will tell Sue to see what she can do to his finances. With people like him, she's always been able to give them at least some trouble.

CHAPTER 31

The following morning Lisa and Larry drove to the town of Belden. It was located about fifty miles southeast of Kingsburg, so they were able to drive there without going through the twin cities of either Minneapolis or St. Paul.

It was what most people would call a cute town, with an old-time main street and a lot of old fashioned store fronts. There was something about it though, that bothered Lisa. It almost seemed too perfect. Even the setting for it was just right for taking photographs, which a lot of tourists were doing. The slow moving river flowing by was a perfect background for it. A closer look told them otherwise.

Inside most of the old-time store fronts, they found that they were nothing more than a cover for souvenir shops, filled with trinkets from China, Mexico, and Florida. The Hardware store was a group of store fronts covering a single store. Along with hardware, there was a large kitchenware section, a complete hobby shop, the equivalent of an auto parts store, and an area called the Children's Palace. Inside it were hundreds of different candies. Books with no depth or meaning to them. Children's versions of the bible. And last but not least, for the boys, every kind of toy gun imaginable.

The town's super market was outside the town, on the highway. Along with groceries it sold clothes of all types for women, men and children. It also contained a cafeteria of sorts, with food representing about fifteen countries. Foods which, on close examination, all tasted much the same. Relatively bland. The town's only drug store was also located inside the supermarket. For every health related item it carried, there were many hundreds of beauty aids, even more types of candies and other snacks, and closest to the largest tobacco shop in the state of Minnesota. The liquor store carried what seemed like and endless supply of alcoholic drinks of all types. The specialty of that department was cheap whisky and even cheaper wine. Its book and magazine sections were extremely limited. It was easy to see that any kind of serious reading material wasn't popular in that store. The only magazines with much variety were the ones on hunting and guns. Even the selection of woman's magazines was sparse.

Overall, neither Lisa nor Larry were much impressed with the town. Even so, they decided to eat lunch there. They quickly ruled out the food at the supermarket. When they looked around for the usual collection of fast food places, they discovered that there weren't any. They finally settled on a local bar with a sign claiming they made the greatest hamburgers in the state.

The sign lied. The burgers were overcooked and the bacon on them was only slightly past raw. The cheese was added as an afterthought, so it wasn't melted. The tomato on it was sliced paper thin and the lettuce was wilted. The fries had come from a frozen bag. They were over salted and dry and otherwise lacking in flavor. Over all, it was an overpriced meal barely fit to eat. So they left the food and their nearly full glasses of beer on the table. Larry asked for the bill.

When he paid it, he told the gruff older man at the register, "That was close to the worst burger and fries I've ever been served anywhere in my entire life. I haven't been ripped off this much for a very long time."

The man's answer was just a glare. He didn't say anything.

Lisa shook her head at him, and like him, she didn't say anything. She waited until they were outside the place before she spoke to Larry. "Given what we already knew about Arty Ardolf, and that he basically runs this town, I guess what we've seen so far shouldn't be any surprise. It kind of is anyway. This sure is a shitty little place."

"It is," Larry agreed. "And they even serve it between buns in their local bars."

"Yes, that was as bad a burger as I've tasted anywhere. The only good thing is the fact that we can stop somewhere on the way home. I noticed that there were several bars along the highway on the drive down here."

"Yeah, there were. And no matter what, the food has to be better than what they serve here."

They weren't out of town very long before Larry began to wonder about the large SUV behind them. It was staying close, and even when Larry slowed his speed below the limit, it made no attempt to pass them.

"We're being tailed," he said when he decided that's what was going on.

"Are you sure?"

"As sure as I can be, Lisa. So I'm not going to stop for a while. Probably not until we're in Clayborne County. If we have trouble with whoever it is behind us then, we'll at least have a friendly sheriff's department to deal with. Out of our county, lord knows how anyone will react if there's trouble."

"Good idea. But I do want to stop somewhere. I am getting hungry."

The SUV stayed with them until they finally stopped about five miles into their county. It was a smaller truck stop that had the usual store and a locally run cafe.

Four men got out of the SUV that parked at the closest to them gas pumps. Lisa went inside to get a table as Larry filled his pickup with gas. Two of the men followed her inside. They sat down at her table when she did.

She was far less than pleased with their arrogance, so she told them, "You assholes weren't invited to sit here, so I strongly suggest that you remove your ugly selves and get as fucking far from me as you possibly can."

"We sit where we want to sit, Darlin," one of the men said, "and there ain't gonna be a damn thing you can do about."

The second man told her, "We don't want the likes of you snoopin' around our town. Mister Ardolf said for us to let you and your boyfriend, or whatever he is, that you are to stay far away from our town. We know who you are, and we aren't about to put up with your liberal bullshit. You try to mess with us the way you did with them good folks from Wisconsin, you ain't gonna like the result."

"That's for damn sure right," the first man said. "And for now, since we got you about where we want you, Lisa Thomas, I think I for one will have some fun out of this." He reached over and wrapped his big hand over her breast.

Her reaction was instant. Before the man realized what she was doing, she had his finger and was holding it on the breaking point. He was strong though, and a trained fighter, so he managed to pull his hand away from her. She pushed her chair back, letting it tumble to the floor, and stood facing him.

Larry joined her then. The other two men were right behind him. Before they could do anything, Lisa managed to land a punishing blow to the gut of the man who put his hand on her.

Larry was soon in the middle of three of the men. Only the one was going after Lisa. For a few moments she acted as if she was now afraid. Her man took what he considered was full advantage over her. His moves were what she expected. He left his head unguarded and at the last moment, she jammed the palm of her hand into his face. Her blow landed perfectly and with such force that she knew she'd done some serious damage. Damage that went far beyond a broken nose. He went down and stayed there.

While she was fighting her fight, Larry had his hands full. He was landing his share of blows, but so were the men he was fighting. All three were better than most hired goons, so he was being punished.

Lisa didn't hesitate. She was behind one of the men. He bent low like a boxer. His legs were spread for better balance, leaving Lisa the perfect target. She put everything she had into her kick. It landed hard on his testicles, and her pointed, western style boots added to the blow. The man's eyes rolled up high in his head and he went down. The pain was severe enough to render him harmless.

Again without hesitation, Lisa moved in front of one of the men Larry was fighting. He wasn't quite as good as the other two she'd already taken out, so she toyed with him for a couple of minutes. When she decided he had enough blood flowing from various parts of his face and head, she took him out.

When she turned to Larry she found him standing there, his arms hanging down his sides and blood running from a couple of cuts on his face. For some season the way he looked made her heart go out for him. She took him in her arms and pulled him to her, kissing him with all the enthusiasm she had in her. She pulled away and their eyes met. They kissed again, followed by several more. They didn't release each other until the police arrived.

Lisa and Larry lucked out. The police were from the Clayborne County Sheriff's department. Since Lisa had worked with all four deputies when she was a deputy sheriff, dealing with them went well. In less than two hours the four men were on their way to jail and Lisa and Larry were on their way home.

They got to Kingsburg before they decided to try again to stop and eat. There were only a few tight spots to park in the lot at the Mystic Curve, so Larry drove around to the back of the bar. He parked in a spot that was out of sight of the street. He shut his truck off, then took off his seat belt. Instead of getting out, he sat back, taking a few deep breaths. When he turned to Lisa, she was staring at him. He reached over and took her hand.

"It has been quite a day," he said.

"It has," she agreed. She squeezed his hand. He returned it. She slid over closer to him. "What we did after the fight," she asked, "did it bother you?"

"It did. A lot."

"I'm sorry. I was just being impulsive. The adrenaline was flowing pretty strong. Besides, you looked like you needed something."

"There's nothing for you to be sorry about. I loved it. You're a beautiful woman, Lisa. How could I ever not want to kiss you?"

She moved closer to him. "How about now?" She put her hand on his cheek, turning his face directly toward her.

He kissed her. She returned it. Quickly they were locked in a deep embrace. She made no move to stop him when his hand moved over her breast. She did nothing to stop him either, when he unbuttoned her blouse. She then let him unhook her bra and put his hand on her bare breast. All this time they continued to kiss each other.

He moved his hand to her skirt slid it under and up between her legs. He moved a finger inside her panties and was about to push it inside her when she suddenly realized just how far they'd already gone.

Remembering now who she was and who she belonged to, she pushed his hand away. "I'm really sorry. I can't do this. I never should have done any of this. I love Mack. For me, doing this is wrong." She slid over to the far side of the truck and started to cry. "What have I done?" she asked herself out loud. "Just what the hell have I done?"

Larry was now in shock. He was asking himself the same question. He then thought about facing Sue if she ever learned what they'd just been doing. It terrified him. Losing her would be the worst thing that ever happened him.

Lisa was thinking much the same thing. "We can't ever tell anyone we did this," she told him. "Not ever."

"Don't worry. I won't. I don't want Sue to know about it anymore than you want Mack to know. So we'll keep it to ourselves."

"That's not just the best thing to do. It's the only thing to do."

The fear and trauma they were now feeling killed their appetites, so they skipped eating. It was a quiet drive home. Larry went directly in his house. Lisa stopped at the office first. She returned a few phone calls and answered some emails, cleaned off her desk, and finally went home.

By the time Mack got there, she was showered and dressed in some comfortable sweats. She greeted him with a kiss. It made her feel guilty about what she'd done with Larry, so she kissed him a second time. It had a lot more urgency in it than the first one did.

Mack enjoyed what she did, but it did leave him a bit curious as to why. She was always glad to see him when he came home, but her kiss this time seemed to carry something different in it. She then kissed him again, with so much emotion that he was really filled with curiosity about what she was thinking or wanting.

He finally asked her. "Is there something special going on, or is something wrong? Don't get me wrong. Kissing you is close to the greatest thing I've ever been able to do. But you seem so different tonight. I don't know what it is. I just know that there's something different about you."

Lisa's face carried a stricken look when their eyes met. "You know, don't you, Mack. I was so scared you would, and now you do. I'm so sorry. I didn't mean for it to happen. I'll leave now if you want me to. I don't blame you if you do."

"What are you talking about, Lisa? why would I ever want you to leave. I love you. Just tell me what it is that's bothering you. I'm sure it'll be okay."

"I have to tell you all of it then." she choked back some tears. "Everything we did today, so at least you kind of know why. It was wrong. I was wrong. But there is a why."

"Okay, Lisa, tell me all about it. Tell me the why." Mack thought he knew now, what her concern was. It was likely that she and Larry had gone beyond the boundaries they'd agreed on. But whatever it was, he had no doubts that he would forgive her. Her own guilt was already punishing her enough. He didn't have to add to it.

Lisa told him about their day from the beginning. When she described the town of Belden, she even made him laugh a couple of times. Her description of the fight was far more detailed than she normally would have given him. Tears began in a heavy flow when she told him about the kisses that followed. Her descriptions after that were brief until she got to the part where they parked behind the bar.

She choked then, and began sobbing. "I'm sorry, Mack. I shouldn't have started it. I shouldn't have let it go so far. I was so wrong. I never should have done it." Her crying continued.

Mack held her then, his hand moving up and down her back as he tried to ease her tension. "It's okay, Lisa. It'll all be okay. As I've told you before, it's your body, so if you decided to give it to Larry that one time, I can live with it."

Lisa's crying eased up as Mack's words registered in her guilty mind. "Do you mean you think I did it with him?"

"Well, yes. As upset as you are, what else would you expect me to think."

Lisa's heart skipped a beat. She almost smiled at what Mack just said. He thought she'd actually done it with Larry and he'd forgiven her anyway. She looked into his eyes. "Thank you, Mack," she said, then kissed him with the feelings he was familiar with. "I have to tell you though, I know what I did was wrong. I never should have done it. I didn't do that with him though. We kissed a lot and I let him touch me. In both places where he shouldn't have. That's all we did. I didn't touch him at all."

"Then why were you so upset about it? I'd rather you didn't do things like that with anyone, but I sure won't ever want to lose you because of it. I think that having me all the time and Dale now and then should be enough. I also think it'll be best if you avoid getting into anymore mischief with Larry."

"I don't think you need to worry about Larry ever again, Mack. He's so scared Sue might find out what we did today, that he might not want to partner up with me again. I was so upset because I just shouldn't have done it. I just didn't have any excuse for my behavior. I stepped out of our agreed boundaries. That's why it was so wrong."

"Tomorrow tell him that his secret is safe with me. As far as partnering up with you, I'd prefer that you spend less time in the field anyway. You should be able to stay plenty busy in the office."

"I've been thinking the same thing. Even so it'll have to wait until after we complete this new case. But now that I know you still love me even after I did another very stupid thing, I would like to go to bed for a while. We can always eat supper later."

Mack very much agreed with her idea. He took her hand and led her to the bedroom. Once there, Lisa did everything she possibly could to make up for the way she thought she'd wronged him earlier in the day. When it was done, part of Mack felt as if it was almost worth it for her to somewhat screw up now and then. Either way, he was as much in love with his wife as ever. She loved him even more.

CHAPTER 32

Sue and Emma arrived at Ben and Theresa's for breakfast at their normal time. Larry used a couple of feeble excuses to cover his not getting ready the way he usually did. The truth was, he wanted to be the last to get there to ensure that he could sit away from Lisa. After what they'd done the previous day, he was sure people would wonder about them if they sat next to, or even near, each other. What he didn't realize was the fact that what he was trying to do made them more curious than almost anything he could have done. As much as he didn't want her to be, Sue was the one who was most suspicious of his actions.

It worried him some when Mack started talking about what he and Lisa had spent the previous day doing. He felt his face color slightly as Mack talked, even though he didn't say anything about what he and Lisa did that they shouldn't have. Sue was by then paying more attention to him and Lisa than she was to anything Mack was talking about, so she did notice that something was bothering Larry. Lisa though, didn't seem to be affected in anyway by what Mack was talking about. Instead, she seemed to cling to Mack's every word.

Sue became ever more suspicious as she watched Larry. He was slowly moving his lowered head back and forth as if he was trying to tell himself no about something, and seemed to be somehow unable to so much as look in Mack and Lisa's direction.

Since Larry was normally the kind of person who faced everything head on, his behavior was something Mack picked up on. At first he had trouble making sense of it. He then remembered the scene he had with Lisa the previous evening. He quickly realized that Larry was going through the same guilt feelings she did.

He understood why, but didn't think it was necessary. He decided to talk to him later to ease his mind. Sue joined Mack, Larry, and Lisa when they talked, and the episode was ended peacefully all the way around. Only Sue was left somewhat irritated, and she settled that by cutting him off for a few days. They still slept in the same bed, but they didn't keep each other warm for a while.

The rest of the breakfast went well, and was reasonably productive. They didn't come to any final decisions on how to deal with Arty Ardolf and his crew, but did decide to go after his book banning right away. The best way to do it they decided, would be to go into the town of Beldon with three of the book mobiles. The libraries who now had them were happy to let them borrow them for as long as they needed them. They knew from experience that it would shakeup all those people responsible for banning books. An activity they all hated.

Since there was good chance that the local law enforcement, under Arty Ardolf's direction, would try to intimidate or possibly arrest whoever was in the book mobiles, Shanty suggested that they have a half dozen lawyers on standby. She also had another six prepared to go to Beldon if necessary. It would be enough legal things going on to totally disrupt the town. They could even have the needed legal documents prepared if the town police did what was expected they might do.

Mack didn't put the teams together in the mobiles until after he had the talk with the other three about Lisa and Larry's escapade. After that, he decided to shake all of them up a little. It was time to remind them that they were all human and susceptible to mistakes. He decided first that he needed to show Lisa and Larry that he still trusted them, and that it was important that they trust each other, so he put them together. The other four who were going also had some history, so Mack put Roy and Sue in the same book mobile.

That left him and Wanda in the last one. Their history went back several years, It was something rarely even thought of by either one of them, but Mack thought it was a good idea for them to work together in close quarters one more time. Of all of them, Wanda was the one who smiled when he told her about the arrangement. Even after all the years that had past, and as much as she truly loved Roy, she still had a special place in her heart for Mack. So she welcomed the chance for a little time to spend more or less alone with him.

Sue had fallen in love with Roy after a few years of a close friendship, and for one night circumstances had left them together. It was recent enough to sometimes leave them uncomfortable. At the same time, their friendship was still meaningful enough for them to appreciate some time alone together.

Lisa and Larry found the arrangement uncomfortable. They still considered themselves to be friends, but after what they came so close to doing, they felt unsure as how to deal with each other. Especially since they both felt that they should never again allow themselves to get too emotionally close to each other. Any kind of physical contact was totally out of the question for both of them.

When they drove to Beldon, they did it like a like a convoy. They didn't split up until they were inside the town. Mack and Wanda parked in front of the high school, which had just opened for the school year. Roy and Sue were in front of the middle school, and Larry and Lisa distributed books outside the town's library.

To their surprise, there was soon a crowd around all of the book mobiles. Most of the books they brought with them were given away by shortly after noon. By two that afternoon, they decided to pack it up and head for home. They didn't get far before a half dozen squad cars pulled all of them over.

Mack was driving the lead mobil van. As they had planned, he was the only one to get out of the three mobiles. He stood quietly next to his mobile. All of the cops exited their vehicles. They immediately drew their weapons, pointing them at him as if he were the most dangerous criminal they'd ever been up against.

One of the cops started searching him for weapons. "It's in a shoulder holster on my left side," Mack told him. "I also have a backup attached to my right ankle, inside my boot. My permit to carry is in my wallet, which is in my back pocket."

The cop searching Mack decided to prove how macho he was. Rather than just take Mack's gun out of its holster, he first jabbed him hard in the ribs. Mack let him have his fun on that one, but when he tried to kick Mack's legs apart before he reached into Mack's boot to get the backup gun, Mack out maneuvered him. The cop landed on his ass.

"I think," Mack told him, "that you'll be better off not trying to pull anymore of that kind of shit on me or anyone else in our group. As it is, even without that shit you, your department, and your town will be tied up in court for a long time. It will be from the lawsuits we will be serving you with because of the what you're doing now. Someone in one of these bookmobiles has already notified a team of lawyers. They are on their way here now to serve you all with the appropriate legal documents. The more you push us, the more we will hang your sorry asses in court."

"The hell," the cop whined. "There ain't nothing you can do to me. Not to any of us. You are the one who broke the law, and who's breaking it now. You are going to end up in jail for attacking a police officer."

Mack couldn't help himself. He laughed at the cop. "Not hardly. I was defending myself. And I can guaranty you, that what you did to me and tried to do to me, has been recorded on video and is safely tucked away someplace where you will never be able to get at it. The same thing is happening to everything you or any of you cops do or say. So if you think you are going to do anything to any of us, because we gave away some books, you'd best think again."

"When you came into our town and spread all that filth around, you broke a few ordinances. You are all guilty of several crimes."

Mack shook his head, letting the cop know how disgusting Mack found him. "You try to arrest us for giving some books away, and you will be violating the first amendment to the constitution. Freedom of speech. You will violating our civil rights too. And as bad as all that. you will be pissing off all of us. You do too much of that, and you will regret it for the rest of your life."

"I don't hardly think so. Ain't none of you got the guts. If you was ever in a place where you needed to face any one of us down, you'd be dead meat. I could kick your ass without no effort at all." His cell phone went off then. His face went red after he listened to the caller for a couple of minutes. Just as fast then, he turned pale. He gave Mack a furtive look, then turned and walked to his squad car. The rest of the cops did the same.

That was the end of the incident. The lawyers, who were waiting just outside of Belden had moved in on city hall and raised so much hell that the police were called off the mobiles. By the time Mack and everyone else reached home, the lawyers had filed enough lawsuits against the city to keep them busy for the next several months.

One of the things that had gone unnoticed by everyone in Belden was the escape of Mia Ardolf from her husband. While all the chaos and confusion of the book distribution was going on, she loaded many of her belongings inside her car and drove away. She had spent the previous two days preparing to leave. She managed to keep her packed suitcases hidden for that short time. When the book distribution started, her husband was so busy watching the crowds around the mobiles, along with telling the police what he expected them to do, that he forgot to watch Mia.

For temporary housing, she stayed in one of Mack's RVs, which was hooked up to sewer and water near Mack and Lisa's house. It was also close to Shanty's RV, which she was living in while her new home was being built.

The next couple of days were filled with a guarded anticipation by everyone who was in any way connected with the Refuge Rescuers's detective agency. Everyone knew that Arty Ardolf would, in one way or the other, come after his wife, Mia.

She knew it too, but had resolved to not let him intimidate her ever again. So she was determined to make the best of her situation. The RV she was in was smaller by far than anything she'd ever lived or stayed in, so it did feel cramped to her. At the same time, she was living there without her abusive and domineering husband, so she found herself enjoying it.

Because of that she never complained about her situation. She spent much of her time working with the lawyers Shanty found for her, getting ready for her divorce proceedings. Because of her attitude and the way she dealt with what was happening to her, she helped everyone relax some. It seemed as though they might, at least for a while, have some real peace.

That was what Lisa and Larry felt like the day that peace came to an end. She was driving them home early. They'd finished up with a case that they'd been working on, part of the time, for months. So they were in a good mood and anxious to get home, just so they could spend the rest of the afternoon kicking back and relaxing with a cold beer.

Lisa was driving and they were within a few miles of their destination when a shot rang out. Larry doubled over against his seat belt as blood slowly darkened his shirt. It was a bad chest wound and Lisa knew that she had to get him to the hospital immediately.

The quickest was was too continue straight ahead and pick up the next county road, which she knew was paved. She slammed her foot down on the accelerator and her pickup jumped ahead. Two more shots hit her windshield, but they missed both of them.

In a very short distance she drove passed a car parked at the side of the road. Next to it on the driver's side, Arty Ardolf stood with a high powered rifle in his hands. He was grinning widely, sure that he'd hit both of them. From his look, she could tell that he was expecting her to crash any second.

In other circumstances, Lisa would have stopped and dealt with him. She didn't this time. Larry's life was at stake so she continued on, her speed taking them to the edge of disaster. The reached the hospital several long minutes later.

She drove next to the emergency entrance, with her siren, left over from her days as a deputy sheriff, blasting away. The instant she was stopped, she slid over and put pressure of Larry's wounded chest. Some ran out of the hospital to see what was going on. He called for backup, then helped Lisa stop the flow of blood.

Larry was still alive and breathing without too much struggle, so they knew that the bullet missed his heart. Within just minutes of arriving at the hospital, Larry was in an emergency operating room with a team of doctors and nurses working on him.

Lisa called Mack first, and asked him to let everyone else at Refuge Rescuers what happened and where Larry was. She then called Roy. He and Wanda lived closest to Sue, so Lisa told him what happened and asked him to tell Sue and to give her a ride to the hospital. The last thing she wanted was to have Sue panic and then have an accident on her rush to get to the hospital. Roy did as Lisa asked him to do, and arrived safely with Sue and Emma.

Mack was so busy notifying everyone what had happened that he was one of the last to arrive there. Shanty was with him. She'd waited for him to be sure he didn't push too hard and end up in an accident himself.

The afternoon was gone and they were into early evening by the time Larry was out of surgery. The doctors said that everything considered, things looked okay. It was a serious wound, but that with some luck, he would recover. He told everyone that it would be sometime tomorrow before Larry would wake up, so they could all go home. Only Sue decided to stay the night at the hospital. Emma went home with Roy and Wanda.

When Lisa and Mack got home, she wrapped her arms around him and kissed him passionately before they got more than a few feet inside the door. "I feel terrible," she told him. "He could still die. I didn't see it coming. I don't remember even seeing the car on the side of the road. All I can remember about it was seeing Arty Ardolf standing next to the car as I drove by."

"Well, he will be arrested. The state police will see to that."

"They better. Because he damn sure isn't going to walk away without paying for what he did."

"He won't. No matter what, he won't."

Lisa looked at Mack then, wondering if she should tell him what was running through her mind since Larry was shot. No matter what she did, she knew there would be negative repercussions either way. She knew too, that the only way anything positive could come out of what she was thinking would be to tell Mack what it was. He was the only one who could tell her what to do about what she was thinking. So she talked.

"Can I tell you something, Mack?" she asked. "Even if it sounds terrible and like want to do something I don't really want to do?"

Mack looked at her and knew right away that whatever was on her mind was serious. At least to her. So as much as it bothered him to think he was about to hear her tell him something he didn't want to know, he told her to go ahead.

Lisa sat down on their couch and pulled him down next to her. She kissed him again, then whispered in his ear, "I love you, Mack. More than I will ever be able to tell you or show you, I love you. So don't judge me too harshly for what I'm going to tell you."

"You know I won't, Lisa. I love you too. So tell me what's wrong, and we will try to talk it out. Or otherwise do whatever it is you think you need to do."

"Okay. What I want to say isn't about something I think I need to do now. It's more about something I kind of wonder if I should have done."

"That doesn't sound so bad. We all have things we think we should have done but didn't do. Just like we've done things we wish we wouldn't have."

"I know, Mack. It's just that I'm kind of wishing I'd done something that I'm really glad that I didn't do. With Larry being shot and in the hospital, my feelings about this are really mixed up."

"So what you are thinking about is what happened between you two. You stopped it before it went too far, and I haven't judged you for what happened. So what is the problem with it?

"That is the problem. And I feel so damn guilty even thinking this way at all. But, Mack, even though I'm really glad we never really did it, I've been thinking now if not doing it was the best thing. He could still die. If he does, I will always wonder if it wouldn't have been better for him, to come to the end of his life, if I'd have gone ahead and let it happen. I could have given him a special moment before he died."

"From the way he's acted since you two had your close call, I'd say you did the right thing. I think that the guilt you'd both have been forced to live with would have far outweighed any special feelings you might have gotten out of it."

"You are right, Mack. I know you're right. And I'm glad I decided to tell you. You are such a good man. You always seem to understand all the goofy shit that sometimes fills my head. It's no wonder I love you to the end of forever." She smiled then and there was a twinkle in her eye. "One more terrible thing I need to confess. I do kind of wonder what it would have been like to have done it with him."

"Well, Lisa," he told her with a smile of his own, "if you are too curious, I'll let you do something about it. All you have to try it out for real is to convince Sue that it'll be okay. Then, of course, you'll have to convince Larry. And last, but not least, you'll have to let me and Sue watch you do it. From start to finish, we'll both have to watch to see if it was a good thing for you and Larry. Okay?"

Lisa couldn't help herself. She laughed. "Okay, Mack. I get your point. I will one more time try to get rid of the shit that's currently screwing up my thinking. I'll need one more bit of help from you to do it though. We need to take a shower and then we need to go to bed. You are the only man alive who can fill the need I have now. Anyone else for any reason would be a poor substitute."

More than once that night, Mack proved that her last words were correct.

CHAPTER 33

Arty Ardolf was disappointed that he hadn't shot Lisa, even though at the time he was sure he had. He couldn't admit to anyone, not even himself, that he'd made a colossal mistake. Mistakes were something he was never able to admit too. He did, however, know he needed to do what he could to correct the mistake he swore he didn't make.

He had already faced a local judge after he was arrested for attempted murder, and was now free. The judge, who was an ardent Trump supporter and a hundred percent in favor of banning books, ruled that there was insufficient evidence to hold him or to take him to trial. So now he was free to do whatever he wanted to do. And what he wanted to do more than anything else was to get his wife back.

To do that, he first had someone watch around the Refuge Rescuers office until l they learned exactly where she was staying. When they did, he was just smart enough to know how dangerous it would be to try to take her away from there. He would have to wait for her to make some kind of move to another place before he made his move on her.

It didn't matter to him at all that she wouldn't, under any circumstances, willingly return to him. From his point of view she was his property. Virtually his personal slave, so she had no choice in the matter. She would, no matter how she felt about it, return to him. Once there, he would teach her what it meant to run away from him, then be returned to him.

The one thing he was right about, was the fact that it would have been extremely dangerous for him to go after Mia where she was staying. Without being obvious about it, everyone around her was in one way or the other guarding her. They all considered her a friend now. She was outgoing yet never pushy about anything, and had a knack for getting along with everyone she met. She met everyone who was part of Refuge Rescuers, and was liked by all as soon as she met them.

It was only a matter of days until Lisa put her to work in the office, mostly to alleviate Mia's boredom. The tasks she was assigned were basic office work. Filing, data entry on the computer, and other more or less menial tasks. She approached them all with as much enthusiasm as could ever be expected for the work she was doing, and that endeared her to everyone.

In spite of her willingness to do any work she was assigned, the boredom of it did start to overtake her. It wasn't near so bad as it would have been with nothing at all to do, but it was there none the less. Lisa could see it, so she requested that Mack and Shanty put her to work with them in the refuge.

As were most people who faced the seemingly strange world that was the refuge, Mia was very much unsure about the whole idea. But with the friendship she got right away from Shanty, and the constant encouragement from Mack, she quickly picked up on what a special place the refuge actually was.

There was one thing that bothered her about it all. Lisa. She was there all the time Mia was. There was a big difference in what she and Lisa were doing. Mia was busy the whole time, doing productive work that was part of improving the refuge. Especially the newly acquired land. Water control structures were being installed and a lot of existing roads were being torn up and the land they occupied returned to the natural world. She even spent a day helping to load a truck with the residue from a torn down house that was on a recently added plot of land. The time she liked the best was that spent helloing to construct a new hiking trail.

Lisa, on the other hand, didn't get the chance to assist with any of the work. She instead kept a constant vigil around them, always looking to be sure that nothing or no-one was around that could harm Mia in any way. That left Mia feeling guilty that someone was forced to doing a job that looked to her to be totally tedious and boring.

For Lisa though, it was proving to be a rather pleasant task. Given the life she lived with Mack, she was wise enough about the refuge to know how much pleasure there was in just being there. It was especially true when it was her job to do nothing but keep watch on her surroundings.

All the time she was watching for any sign of trouble, she was also watching the comings and goings of hundreds of different living critters. Anything from the smallest of bugs and ants, to lizards, snakes, frogs and toads and turtles. Those alone could have filled enough of her time to keep her from boredom. Again, the large amount of time she spent with Mack had given her an insight into all of the rest there was to watch and learn from.

The birds alone could have filled all of her time for many days. All of the nearby ponds and lakes were crowded with many species of shorebirds, and out on the water there were several species of ducks and geese, in all there were thousands of birds. Over the land an uncounted number of birds flitting and flying in every direction. Often, they could command her attention by simply landing close enough to her so that she could study them without the aid of her binoculars.

Last but definitely not least were the mammals. Along with the deer, coyotes, fox, and many other delightful to watch critters, twice she was able to catch a glimpse of Mack's special friend. She, in turn, seemed too Lisa to be keeping a careful eye on Mack. It was almost as if she was somehow determined to keep him safe. And while she was doing that, she was protecting all of them.

She didn't get the chance this time. The trouble came at the end of the day. They were on their way home when Lisa, who was riding shotgun in Mack's pickup, caught a glimpse of a car parked in a cluster of poplar trees about a half mile ahead of him.

"Stop, Mack," she literally screamed at him.

He slammed on the brakes. "What the hell is is, Lisa?" he asked her, a confused look on his face.

"There's car up ahead. It looks like the one Arty Ardolf was driving when he shot Larry. I think we have a good chance of surprising him this time."

"What about Shanty and Mia? Is it a good idea to try to do anything with them here?"

"I think it's better to go after those assholes, Mack, when we have the chance, than it is to wait until they shoot another one of us."

Shanty spoke up then. "I agree with Lisa," she said. "Not to mention, you two have given me enough training on self defense and gun handling, that I can at least be a good backup for you."

It was Mia's turn to state an opinion. "I lived with that no good bastard for years. I took all the abuse from him I ever intend to take again. So I agree with Lisa and Shanty. Go after him and his cronies. I'd rather die than give so much as another inch to him."

"I think that says it , Mack," Lisa told him. "We are going after him. I have to warn you though. When we get the drop on him and he's disarmed, I will be teaching him a lesson. And when I am done, he won't ever again be able to hurt anyone. Not by himself anyway."

Mack watched her face change as she talked. He knew then, that if they pulled this off, Lisa would give him a fair fight. Even so, it would be a fight he had no chance of winning. He considered trying to talk her out of it, but knew it was a waste of time. The only way he would stop it would be on the slim chance she was going to be hurt.

Part of the lessons everyone got that spent any amount of time with Mack in the refuge was the art of moving quietly through the natural world. Mia had only a little of that training, but the amount of noise she made had no affect on Arty and his hired guns. They were all so confident that they were going to take Mack and the women with him by surprise, that they were being totally careless about their own noise.

That proved to make it easy to surprise them, and before they knew it they were under gunpoint and forced to drop their weapons. As soon as they did, Lisa moved in close to Arty.

"You've got two choices, you useless bastard. You can fight me. One on one. With no interference from Mack or anyone. Or you can die where you stand. Because if you don't fight me, I will put a bullet in your forehead and watch you die."

"Why do you want to fight with me? You don't stand a chance to win. Is it so one of you has an excuse to shoot me?"

"We don't need any excuse to shoot each and everyone of you. The only reason I want to fight you is so I can hurt you really bad with my own hands. I have so many reasons for wanting to do it to you that I've lost count of all of them. But the tipping point was when you shot my friend, Larry."

"I'll fight you," he finally agreed, "but I again have to warn you. You don't stand a chance with me. And because of your mouth, I will be the one doing the hurting."

Lisa didn't wait for anymore dialogue. Just to irritate him, she slapped him hard across his face. The she raked deep gouges into his left cheek with her fingernails. She followed that with the palm of her hand slamming his nose. She could feel it break just before his blood poured from it. She made a quick step back, knowing he would be confused by her quick action. His legs were slightly spread apart, leaving him open to the most vulnerable part of a man there is. It was what she was looking for and she took full advantage. Her kick was right on the mark, and he grabbed for his manhood and the pain vibrated throughout every part of his body. As he doubled over, she took hold of his hair and slammed his head down on her rapidly rising knee. She let his unconscious body drop to the ground, then moved her foot back before applying a kick to his teeth. At the last second she stopped. She knew that the kick was overkill.

She looked up then, to see that everyone there was watching her. She caught Mack's eye. "Did you call Dale yet?" she asked.

"I did. The sheriff and some of his deputies are on the way."

"Good." She looked at the goons that had come along with Arty. "While we wait," she asked, "would any of you like a little go around with me?"

All four of the men shook their heads no. It was just as well, because Dale arrived a short time later. Arty was still out cold so he called for an ambulance. The other four were arrested and charged with assault.

Mack and Lisa showered when they got home, then settled down on their deck for what they hoped would be a relaxing evening together. It was not to be. Shanty was the first to join them, with Mia not too far behind. Dale and Kathy were out on their deck too, so when they heard voices coming from Lisa and Mack's they decided to walk over to see what was going on.

Kathy was a little jealous when she found Mack in the company of three good looking women, but quickly made the best of it by immediately sitting in his lap. Not to be outdone, Lisa did the same thing with Dale. Mia was mildly surprised by the arrangement, but not offended. Shanty quietly watched, all the time wishing she could do exactly what Kathy was doing.

They spent a quiet evening then, and somehow managed to keep their conversation away from the happenings of the day. When it was time for them to end the pleasant visit they all had, Kathy gave Mack a long, lingering kiss goodnight. Lisa kissed Dale too, but not with anywhere near the power Kathy had put into her's.

Later, in bed, Mack asked her why she had held back when she kissed Dale. "Because," she explained, "I wanted you to know that despite whatever silly ideas I get in my head, or stupid things I might do, you are the one and only person for me. I can't help it, Mack. I honestly do love you as much as I love life itself. More even maybe. I've done enough things wrong and said and thought enough things with and about Larry lately, so that you shouldn't have to watch me giving Dale a passionate kiss."

"I love you too, Lisa. And no matter what ever happens between Kathy and I, you will always be the one person for me."

"Good. And does that mean that you're going to make love to me tonight?"

"Of course it does. Why would I ever not?"

"I can't think of a reason, but the thought that there ever might be one, does terrify me."

Mack did his best then, to keep the terror away.

EPILOGUE

The swat team, Fahrenheit-now, was investigated by the FBI. About half of those who were still part of the group were arrested for various crimes, including the school they burned and the children they murdered. When they were brought to trial, they drew a Trump appointed judge, so the sentences they were given were minimal. Even for the murders. It was the end of them anyway. Wisconsin did a rare thing for them, and elected a Democrat for governor after the man who took over for Dasadist was impeached.

The book banning came to an end too, thanks to the new governor. At least for the most part. There was still a majority of Christians on the Wisconsin school boards, so censoring or outright banning of books continued on a local basis in the state's school system. It was all done on a, 'God forbid' the children might actually learn something, basis. There was little more that could strike terror in the hearts of conservative parents than the idea their children might gain some real knowledge beyond the ability to make money.

*****

After the death of Rod Dasadist, both Ted Crustiest and Maggie Taylor Blue planned to run for president. Neither one of them managed to do so. They both landed in the hospital on a long term basis.

Maggie Taylor Blue gave Ted Crustiest an antibiotic resistant strain of syphilis. One so serious that he was near death for months. He, in turn, gave her a nearly as serious a case of gonorrhea. She too required a long hospital stay. Since they infected each other, it meant that they both had both diseases.

It didn't really matter that much in the political arena anyway. It didn't matter who the Republicans nominated for president or any office. There wasn't any of them that reached beyond a state of uselessness, unless the harm they did was counted.

*****

Larry was in the hospital for nearly three weeks. While he was there he endured three surgeries and constant pain. Sue spent some time with him every day, and she was by is side when he came home.

He was forced to ride a wheel chair when he left the hospital, but when he got home he walked from the car into his house under his own power. He was still in the healing process, so when he got inside he was exhausted and quickly sat down.

Mack and Lisa were the first to visit him. They were concerned and curious about how he felt about the future, and especially wanted to know if he planned to return to work when he was healed enough to do so.

"Damn right I do," he told them without the slightest hesitation. "If getting shot the way I did taught me anything, it taught me that what we do is important. If we hadn't have taken Mia's case, then she'd still be his prisoner. Now, because of us, she is free."

Lisa gave him a happy smile, letting him know she was pleased that he would continue working with and for Refuge Rescuers. Larry loved the way she smiled at him, but it made him realize there was something he had to tell her. He wanted Mack to know what it was too.

"I have to tell you, Lisa," he said, "that your smile is about as beautiful as anything I've ever seen. In fact, you are beautiful. Both what I see on the outside and what we all know is there on the inside." He paused, took a deep breath, then continued. "I've found it a pleasure as well as an honor to work with you. So I have to tell you, what I did with you, what I did to you, was wrong. It was my fault and I wish I could do more than say I'm sorry. I can't though, so I'll say it again. I'm sorry for what happened."

"There were two of us there, Larry," Lisa answered, "so you should stop blaming yourself. I'm responsible for what happened between as every bit as much as you are. Maybe even more."

"Something else, Larry," Mack added, "you both ended up doing the right thing before there was any real hurt done. I think you can forgive yourself for any wrong you might think you did, and that we should all put it behind us. After all there is a lot more life, probably both good and bad, ahead of us."

Without saying a word, Sue let everyone there know how she felt about what happened and how it was dealt with. She put her arms around Mack's neck and pulled him down to her. Their lips met and she kissed him with all the passion she could put in it. Even Larry nodded his in acceptance of what she did.

*****

When Arty Ardolf went to trial this time, he faced a real judge who wasn't a book banning conservative. The District Attorney rebuilt the attempted murder case from his shooting Larry, and he was found guilty. His cronies and goons were also tried for various offenses and crimes. Only two of them were found not guilty. All the rest were convicted of the crimes they were guilty of and sentenced to prison terms.

Mia was then able to return to her home. She easily obtained a divorce from Arty. She didn't need the money, but in order to stay busy, she got a job at the local library. She became a specialist on books that had been banned. Both recently and through the ages. She tended to promote them when she was asked about books.

With Arty and his gang out of the picture, the Lutheran church in the town of Belden slowly reverted back to a Lutheran church. Mia never went back to it anyway. After her time with Refuge Rescuers and many long conversations with the people there, her view of religion was changed. A walk in the refuge on a Sunday morning now had more value than sitting through church service did.

*****

After several long negotiations, Shanty purchased the entire Lands Magnificent Resort. She did what was required to officially make it a part of the refuge. It was given a simple new name. The Refuge Resort. When she was asked how much it cost her, her answer was simple, "Not enough to matter. It was only money."

They didn't have to put any effort into finding someone to manage the resort. Rodney Twilabee, the CEO of Lands Magnificent, resigned from his job there and happily took over as manager of the resort. He had been involved with the resort from the first dealings with the government to buy half of the original refuge and turn it into the resort that was there now.

At the beginning, he was just another typical CEO. He was a different man now. The years dealing with and sometimes working with the Thomas family had seriously changed him. Especially his dealings with Mack. Now he was an avid organic gardener and one of the biggest supporters of the wildlife refuge and everything they were trying to do.

He was also in favor of changing the resort from a playground for the rich to a place the average wage earner could afford to visit. He was even more in favor, in addition to that change, to making it a place to learn about the environment. It proved to be a great teaching tool, even though many of the people who stayed at the resort never realized how much more they knew about it when they left than they did when they got there. For Mack, it was the next best thing to tearing it down and returning all the land back to nature.

*****

It was Saturday and on this day Kathy would not settle for anything less than what she wanted. And that was a day walking the refuge with Mack. And only Mack.

"If anyone else wants to walk with you, you can take them tomorrow. Today it's going to be only you and me. No one else. Three months is too long for me to have to wait for my walk with you. I'm not waiting any longer."

Mack agreed, and when he and Lisa talked about it, so did she. The only thing she had to say about it was, "I think though, given all that's happened lately, it will be best if all you do is walk together. Your holding hands and occasional kissing is okay. So try to keep it at that."

"I will," Mack agreed. "But what are your plans with Dale?"

"To be very careful that nothing happens between us. He and Kathy might be disappointed by that, but for now it's best if we all behave."

She proved to be right about Kathy and Dale. They were disappointed. At the same time they were good friends and understood the need to keep things at a platonic level for the foreseeable future.

Even so, Kathy's idea of a platonic relationship was somewhat tilted. As soon as they got out of Mack's pickup at the trailhead they'd picked to walk that day, she kissed Mack with all the passion she could possibly put into it. She then held him for several minutes before letting him go. When she did, she took his hand and was reluctant to let it go for the rest of the day. Unless of course, she had her hands wrapped around his neck while kissing him.

It proved to be a good walk anyway, with the highlight of it being Mack's special friend. She never approached too close to them, but she never lost sight of them either. It still seemed somewhat strange that a bear would take such an interest in Mack, while at the same time Mack would have wondered, and even worried, about her if she wasn't around.

They enjoyed too, the play of a pair of otters along one stretch of the trail running alongside the river. Nearly everywhere they walked, they saw deer. So many that Mack knew they had no choice but to open the refuge for hunting in the fall. If the deer herd wasn't thinned the overcrowding would cause an enormous amount of environmental damage. That would mean that too many deer would end up starving. A fate worse than a quick end from a bullet.

Thinking about that made him wish again for the days when large predators kept things in a balance. Something that could never again happen. Not, at least, as long as so many humans lived where they did. Even with Shanty's billions of dollars, it would be impossible to purchase enough land to create an environment with a completely natural balance. All they would ever have now was something close, but always something that needed to be managed by humans.

Mack had a backpack on, and along with the drinking water in it, he carried a lunch for them. Shortly afternoon they found a lush patch of grass under a sweeping maple tree. It was on a high bank above the river and gave them a nice view of it for nearly two miles. Something they enjoyed while they ate their lunch.

"I wonder, Mack," Kathy asked after a while, "if our relationship has changed? In some ways. like today, we seem to be able to do things the way we have since what we have between us started. Then, at the same time, I kind of get the feeling that we are losing something. Maybe we've already lost it. Have we?"

"No, I don't think we have. I think that what it is that is making you feel that way is the fact that I've been so careful for a while not to do anything that would upset Lisa. She's kind of confused right now, but I think she's getting better. I'm as sure as I can be about things like this, that she'll get beyond her wondering about who and what she is pretty soon."

"I can understand all that. Her little episode with Larry really threw her off. Given her history, especially the rape when she was still a kid, has had one hell of an effect on her. But I still worry about us. No matter what, Mack, I don't ever want to lose what we've had. I don't want to ever hurt anyone because of it, but I damn well want to keep it."

"So do I. All I ask for now is for you to be patient for a little while longer."

"I will. I want you to remember too, Mack, that I'm not trying to steal you away from Lisa. I just want to get back to the point that we can share again. As much as that doesn't seem to fit in the world we live in, it is the best part of the small place the four of us live."

"It is that. So, are you ready to do some more walking yet?"

"Not quite, Mack. I know that what we can do today is limited, but right now I want to push those limits just a little bit. Let's start with you kissing me. Then I'll return the favor. We can take it from there."

*****

Mack, Lisa, and Shanty were relaxing with a beer. It was Saturday, late afternoon, and Mack and Shanty were especially enjoying the free time. They'd been pushing it hard, trying to get immense amount of work done in the refuge that needed doing. They'd settled the acquisition of several properties, and even with the crew they had to work with, they still felt like they were running behind.

They didn't get the chance to totally relax for long. Larry, Sue, and Emma were out for a walk in the meadow, and when they saw them sitting on the deck, they joined them. Mack got up and brought Sue and Larry a beer and Emma an orange soda.

They were no more that settled in when Dale and Kathy decided to stop by. They took up the last of the chairs, so when Roy and Wanda got there, Mack and Dale needed to fish a couple more of them out of the garage. Ben and Theresa were the next to come. They brought their own chairs, which they knew to bring because Mack asked them to when he called to invite them over. Donna and Julie did the same thing when they came.

They probably could have gotten by without two of the chairs, because before long Kathy was in Mack's lap. Lisa only smiled when she sat there, then whispered something to Shanty. She then got up and sat in Dale's lap, which surprised him. He was expecting Lisa.

Shanty proved to be more than just pleasant company so Dale wasn't too upset by Lisa's unexpected move. He knew as well as anyone that she had some serious issues she needed to work through before she could go back to what was normal for them.

Kathy watched Dale and Shanty for a while, then said, "I think that you two look good together. You, Shanty, could probably be one of his deputies if you wanted to. Your match is that good."

Shanty laughed. "No, for me just sitting in the sheriff's lap is pushing it. I don't know that I'd ever fit in with real law enforcement. Besides, for the first time in my life, I really like what I'm doing. No. I love what I'm doing. Working with Mack every day out in the refuge is great. Watching it come alive and grow the way it is, is awesome too. Just being around all of you is something better than I've ever had before. Watching what you do, what you can do. You did so much to stop a lot of the book banning. And with you letting me work with Mack, we've managed to keep something incredibly important from becoming a refuge banned. Because if we let them, that's what they'd do."

"I can only agree with that," Kathy answered, "Last week, when Mack and I had our monthly walk, I really noticed how much you guys have improved and expanded it. How much farther are you going to go?"

Shanty shocked them with her answer. "To about another billion dollars worth of land. After that, I'll need to invest a lot more to do everything we need to do before the refuge is where we want it to be."

Roy had a question for Shanty then. "Doesn't it scare you sometimes," he asked her, "to spend that kind of money on something you are just giving away?"

"No. What scares me is having all that money and not spending it on something that has some real value. This refuge has a lot of real value. Maybe not as much as all of you have, but a hell of a lot anyway."

That's when they all realized that it didn't matter what kind of life Shanty came from. She was one of them now.

www.ingramcontent.com/pod-product-compliance
Lightning Source LLC
Chambersburg PA
CBHW030136010826
48973CB00002B/589